THE LOST AND
THE FOUND

CAT CLARKE

THE LOST AND THE FOUND

CROWN
New York

Text copyright © 2016 by Cat Clarke
Jacket photographs:
Woman © 2016 by J. A. Bracchi/Getty Images
Girl © 2016 by Cristinairanzo/Getty Images

All rights reserved. Published in the United States by Crown Books for Young Readers, an imprint of Random House Children's Books, a division of Penguin Random House LLC, New York.

Crown and the colophon are registered trademarks of Penguin Random House LLC.

Visit us on the Web! randomhouseteens.com

Educators and librarians, for a variety of teaching tools, visit us at RHTeachersLibrarians.com

Library of Congress Cataloging-in-Publication Data is available upon request.
ISBN 978-1-101-93204-9 (trade) — ISBN 978-1-101-93206-3 (ebook)

Printed in the United States of America
10 9 8 7 6 5 4 3 2 1
First Edition

For Julia Churchill

THE LOST AND THE FOUND

CHAPTER 1

She knows. She definitely knows.

I'm not sure *how* she knows. I'm not stupid enough to keep a diary, and I'm not one of those weirdos who's all Mom's-my-best-friend-and-we-tell-each-other-everything. Maybe it's some kind of sixth sense unique to mothers?

It's there in her eyes every time she looks at me. The problem is, I can't tell how she feels about it. Why can't that show up in her eyes, too? Is she angry? Disappointed? Disapproving? Resigned? A little bit proud?

"How's Martha's mom doing at work? Have they announced the layoffs yet?"

It's a trap. Classic. Of course there's no way I'm falling for it. I shrug. "Dunno. She came in pretty late last night. I think she went out for drinks after her evening class." I sip my tea, cool as you like. "Martha says she's been pretty stressed about it."

Mom nods. She knows when she's beaten. "It must be tough."

"They're loaded, though, aren't they? Martha's dad earns enough for both of them. I don't know why she bothers working in the first place."

This was the wrong thing to say. I wouldn't normally be so careless, but I'm exhausted. Mom's big-time into feminism and equal opportunities and not relying on men. Funny thing is, I agree with her, but I'd never tell *her* that. Arguing is much more fun. But Mom's not biting today; she's obviously got other things on her mind.

"Are you okay, Mom?" I try not to ask more than three times a day, but it's a habit. One that I learned at a very early age. When she retreated into herself, into that hellish world inside her head, sometimes it was the only way I could get her to talk to me. I never believed the answer, which was always the same, no matter what sort of day it was: *I'm fine, love.*

There's no deviation from the script today, which is oddly reassuring. I was half expecting her to come out with something like, *No, I'm not okay, thanks for asking. My daughter lied to me about where she was last night so that she could go and lose her virginity to Thomas Bolt in the back of a van.*

There's a newspaper lying facedown on the kitchen table. I hadn't noticed it before, because I was too busy trying to work out how I feel about losing my virginity to Thomas Bolt in the back of a van.

All I can see is the sports page: some team beat some other team, and some guy scored more points than he'd ever scored before. But I know the kind of thing I'll see if I flip over the newspaper. That's why Mom is giving me all these weird looks. That's why she put the newspaper down as soon as I came into the kitchen; she doesn't want me to see it.

In a normal house—in Martha's house and Thomas's house and houses all over the country—a newspaper is just that: some paper with news in it. Wars and politics and celebrities doing inane celebrity things. In our house—our anything-but-normal house—a newspaper is often an unexploded bomb.

I don't let on that I've noticed the paper. Mom gets up to wash the dishes, her shoulders slumped with the unbearable weight she carries with her every day. While her back is turned, I slide the paper over and onto my lap. Unexploded bomb or not, I need to know.

It's always bad. Even when it looks like it's good, it turns out to be bad. That's actually worse: getting your hopes up only to have them dropped from a great height and splattered on the pavement. It's hardest for Mom; that's what everyone always says. And I suppose they're right, but it's hard for Dad, too. And it's not exactly a walk in the park for me, either. But Dad's got Michel and I've got Thomas; Mom has no one.

I pray that this won't send her into full-on tortoise mode. Last time she didn't leave her bedroom for a week. I brought her meals on a tray, but she barely ate a thing. She wouldn't talk to me and she wouldn't answer the phone. When Dad came over to see her, I listened at the door. "You have to snap out of this, Olivia. For Faith's sake. She needs you." He was wrong about that. I was coping perfectly well, even though the timing was hardly ideal—right in the middle of my exams. I don't *need* her, not like when I was little. It'd

3

just be nice if she talked to me about it once in a while. I wish she knew that there are other options besides "complete and utter breakdown" and "plastic smile, everything's fine." There's a middle ground, waiting to be found.

I turn the paper over. It's bad.

I KILLED LAUREL LOGAN!

An involuntary noise escapes my mouth and Mom turns around. She whips the paper out of my hands and crumples it up. She stuffs it into the trash even though the can needs emptying. Some of the headline's huge black letters are still visible because the lid won't shut. Mom sees me staring at it and swears and stuffs the paper as deep as it will go. The lid swings back and forth.

She sits down and takes my hand. Her hand is cold—her hands are always cold. I often wonder if they used to be warm. *Before.* "I was going to talk to you about that." Lie. "I've already talked to the police, and it's nothing. The man's a lunatic. They would lock him up for this if he weren't already serving two life sentences." She sighs. "It's just more irresponsible journalism—it even says inside that there's no way he could have done it. But that wouldn't sell papers, would it?"

There are tears in my eyes, and I'm not even sure why. This happens on a regular basis—these stories in the papers or on TV or online. It's been happening almost my whole life, so you'd think I would be immune to it by now. And I usually *am* immune, but for some reason today I've decided to be pathetic.

Mom doesn't like it when I cry. I'm sure that's true of all mothers about their daughters, but there's something about Mom saying, *Oh, darling,* please *don't cry,* that always makes me think it's more about her than me. As if it just makes things harder for her. So I try not to cry when she's around, because there's nothing worse than being upset and then being made to feel guilty for being upset.

When she's sure I've got the tears under control, Mom tells me all about this guy who claims to have killed my sister. He killed his whole family ten years ago and is safely locked up in a high-security prison. Recently he's decided his favorite thing to do is to make up lies about murdering people, as if the ones he *actually* killed aren't quite enough for him. Mom does a good job of pretending it doesn't bother her, but I can see through her.

Even if I didn't know from experience, I'd know from that interview she did last year. I think she forgets that I read it, or maybe she forgets that she talked all about how awful and heartbreaking it is for her when these news stories appear.

Dad claims he never reads the interviews Mom gives. It's difficult for him, having stuff about their marriage splashed across the newspapers he despises. But he can't say anything, because he knows we need the money. Plus, there's always the chance someone who knows something about Laurel will see one of these stories and call the police. Whenever anyone asks Dad's opinion about Mom's "media activities," he always says the same thing: *Let's hope the ends justify the means.*

"What time is Michel picking you up?" There's always

something slightly off about the way she says *Michel*—a slight wrinkling of the nostrils. Or that could just be my imagination.

I check the time on my phone. "He's coming at ten."

"But you've only been home for an hour!" There's silence for a moment or two, and then Mom coughs, and I know she's about to say something awkward. "I've been thinking . . ." It's never good when parents *think,* is it? "It might be nice for the two of us to spend a whole weekend together sometimes. We could do whatever you like—we could even go away somewhere. A long weekend trip to Prague or Paris?"

"Um . . ." A text from Martha flashes up on my phone, and I angle the screen away from Mom to read it. It just reads: Well? SPILL. x

I have no idea what to say to Mom. She knows full well what the deal is: I spend Saturdays and Sundays with Dad and Michel. It's been that way for six years. It wasn't decided by a court or anything; Mom and Dad arranged everything between them. It was a remarkably amicable divorce—that's what they always tell people.

I don't want to argue with her this morning. I don't want to tell her that I can't imagine anything worse than wandering around Prague or Paris or any other city beginning with *P* with her. Because we both know full well how it would turn out. She would pretend to be enthusiastic, dragging me around, doing all the boring touristy stuff. She would smile and make me pose for pictures in front of the Eiffel Tower or whatever, but she'd never let me take a photo of her. And the reason she wouldn't let me is that then there would be

6

photographic evidence of her unhappiness. She would smile and you'd see her teeth, which might make someone else think that it was a real, proper smile. But I would look at her eyes and see that there was something dead there.

There are photos of Mom in the newspapers all the time, and none of them ever show her smiling; she's careful never to smile when there are photographers around. She says they'll criticize her for it, and she's probably right. (*What's she got to smile about? How can a mother smile when her daughter's still missing?*) So she doesn't smile . . . and they criticize her anyway, calling her "cold" and "hard." It's lose-lose.

So I tell Mom I'll think about it—spending the weekend with her—and say maybe we could talk to Dad and Michel about it in a month or two. She nods, but I can tell she's disappointed by my reaction. I feel guilty. Guilt is never far away in this house. It lurks under the floorboards and behind the walls. You can hear it whispering late at night if you listen closely. I'd hoped that we'd left it behind in the old house when we moved, but Mom must have packed it up carefully, safeguarding it in Bubble Wrap and putting it in a box, labeling it in fat black marker pen, and putting it in the moving truck along with everything else. The guilt will follow us wherever we go.

I get up and give Mom a hug. She's tense for a second, then she relaxes and hugs me back. She's so very thin. So sharp and pinched and angular. She used to be slightly overweight; she looked much better like that. I wish I could remember that version of my mother, but all I've got are photos. My favorite is one of the three of us baking a cake together—Mom, Laurel, and me. Mom's wearing a pink apron and her cheeks are rosy and she's laughing—*really* laughing. I'm standing on a chair so that I can reach the counter. I have a streak of flour across my nose, and I'm sticking out my tongue at the person taking the photo. (Dad? I can't remember.) Laurel is stirring the mixture in the bowl, her brow furrowed in concentration. For some reason, she's wearing a feather boa and I'm wearing a tiara—obviously appropriate baking attire for a six-year-old and a four-year-old.

The phone rings and Mom gives me a kiss on the cheek before she goes to answer it. Her lips are dry and chapped.

"Hello? Speaking." She tucks the phone between her shoulder and her ear and starts to wipe the crumbs from the kitchen counter.

I run upstairs to pack my bag for going to Dad's. I don't need much—I keep some clothes and toiletries there. It can be annoying sometimes; I'm always leaving my favorite jacket at Mom's when I go to Dad's and vice versa. Still, it's worth the inconvenience just to escape for a couple of days a week. I feel different when I'm at Dad and Michel's apartment—it's easier to breathe somehow. But maybe that's just the air-conditioning.

Mom's standing with her back to me when I return to the kitchen. She's still holding the phone in one hand even though she must have ended the call. "Mom?"

She ignores me.

"Mom? Are you okay?"

The *I'm fine, love* that I'm expecting doesn't come. She's deviated from the script.

She still won't turn to look at me, so I have to shuffle around the side of the kitchen table and position myself right in front of her. She's paler than she was when I left her. A single tear is trickling down her left cheek, and she does nothing to halt its progress. I watch as it negotiates the contour of her jaw and continues down her neck.

She finally looks at me, and there's something different in her eyes. I have no idea what it is, but it scares me.

Mom clears her throat. She starts to speak and then stops herself. I can't decide if I want to hear what she has to say, but it looks like I don't have a choice in the matter.

"That was the police."

No. Please, God, no. Not today. The call she's been dreading every single day for thirteen years. It can't be today.

Mom sways a little as if she's about to faint, so I help her over to the table. She slumps into a chair, and the phone clatters onto the tabletop. She takes my hands in hers, and I crouch down in front of her.

"Tell me, Mom. *Please.*"

She clears her throat again. "A girl has been found. At Stanley Street." Stanley Street is where we were living when it happened. "They think it's . . . Laurel." She squeezes my hands so hard it hurts. "They want me to go down to the police station right away to . . . identify her."

My legs buckle beneath me, and it's a good thing I'm so close to the floor already. "Oh, Mom, I'm so sorry. I can't . . . Oh God."

And that's when Mom smiles. "Oh no, Faith! I didn't mean . . . Goodness, I should have thought!" She lets go of my hands and reaches out to touch my cheek. "They think it's her. . . . They're almost certain. . . . Faith? She's alive. Laurel's alive!"

9

CHAPTER

2

I don't believe it. I won't allow myself to believe it. Mom's trying to stay calm, too, but I can see it in her face—something I haven't seen for years: hope. She thinks it's different this time, which means the police must think it's different this time. They wouldn't have called her otherwise. They think this is *it*. After hundreds, maybe even thousands, of crank calls and false sightings and psychics claiming Laurel was living with goatherds in the mountains of Uzbekistan.

But it makes no sense. Her turning up in the front yard of our old house after *thirteen* years? I picture a six-year-old girl, shiny blond hair. She's wearing a brand-new dress for the first time. The dress is white with multicolored polka dots on it. There's a tiny grape-juice stain on the front, but you'd never know because it just looks like another polka dot. The girl is smiling, and she's missing one of her front teeth. She's cradling a teddy bear in her arms like it's a baby. The only thing slightly spoiling this perfect photo is a nasty scab on the girl's right cheek. Perhaps it looks like the sort of scab that a child might end up with if she'd been chased around the living room by her little sister and she'd tripped and fallen and hit her cheek on the corner of the coffee table.

If you saw that little girl, you'd probably think she was the cutest little girl you'd ever seen. Chances are, you *have* seen her. The photo of blond-haired, gap-toothed, polka-dot-dressed, teddy bear–cradling Laurel Logan has surely been printed in almost every newspaper in the world (probably even the *Uzbekistan Times,* now that I think about it). You must have seen the polka-dot ribbons that people used to wear, or the ones they tied to trees all along Stanley Street. I think it was Mom's idea, that polka-dot campaign. Anyway, two hours after Mom took that photo, Laurel was gone.

I was also in the original photo: four years old, cute in the way that all four-year-olds are, but nothing special. Not like her. Frizzy brown hair, beady little eyes, hand-me-down clothes. I was playing in a sandbox in the background, slightly out of focus. That's how it's been my whole life: in the background, slightly out of focus. You hardly ever see that version of the photo—the one where I haven't been cropped out.

Laurel would be nineteen years old now. An adult. My brain struggles with that concept. Of course we've all seen the age-progressed photos. The last one was four years ago: Laurel Logan at fifteen. None of the images ever look quite right, though. You can see that they've taken that photo—*the* photo—and done some computer wizardry, but the results are always weird in some way. They never end up looking quite like a real person.

I'm looking at Mom, and she's looking at me and she's still holding back. There's some small part of her that doesn't believe it can be Laurel. That won't allow her to fully believe that the nightmare could finally be over. She's had her hopes raised and dashed so many times before.

I realize she's shaking and I take hold of her hand to steady it. "Are they sure? How do they *know*?"

"I have to phone your father. Natalie said she'd call him, but I thought it would be best if I did it. Do you think he'll be at home, or should I try his cell first?" She looked at her watch, too big for her wrist. "Michel's probably on his way over here by now anyway. You should still go. . . . I'm not leaving you here by yourself. . . . I'll call as soon as I know more. . . ."

"Mom! Stop! Just stop talking for a second. How do they know it's . . . her?" For some reason I can't seem to say her name.

"Remember she hurt herself the day she was . . . Natalie says she has a scar on her cheek! After all these years . . ." She shakes her head in disbelief as she squeezes my hand tightly. "And there's something else. She's got Barnaby!"

It's her. My sister has come home.

There were lots of photos of Barnaby in the newspapers, too, at first. I don't remember, of course, but I've done enough research that I could probably write a book about what happened. Mom and Dad gave Laurel a teddy bear for

Christmas—six months before she was taken. I got a bear, too. I lost mine years ago.

Mom and Dad took us to one of those shops where you can customize your cuddly toys. Apparently, Laurel took ages, making sure her bear was just the way she wanted it. You can record a voice message that will play every time you squeeze the toy's tummy. Laurel was too shy to do it herself, so Mom and Dad did it for her. Her bear said: *Merry Christmas, Laurel! Lots of love from Mommy and Daddy!* I recorded my own message, babbling some nonsense about a teddy bear's picnic.

Laurel's bear was brown and extra fluffy. He was dressed in blue dungarees with a red-and-white-striped T-shirt and a blue hat with his name embroidered on it. Laurel didn't have to think long about the name—she said "Barnaby" as soon as they asked her.

Barnaby the Bear is unique. Even if there happened to be another bear with the same dungarees and T-shirt and hat and embroidery, there is only one bear in the whole wide world that has a message from my parents recorded on it. And when Laurel was taken, Barnaby was, too.

It was a tiny crumb of comfort to my parents, I think. Knowing that wherever she was, Laurel wasn't alone. She loved that bear. She carried him everywhere and told him all her secrets. Depending on her mood, she would sometimes insist that he had his own chair at the dinner table. I can picture that, if I close my eyes and really try. But I'm sure the details are wrong. Like all my memories of Laurel, this one is secondhand. It doesn't even count as a memory, does it?

Sometimes I lie in bed at night and try to clear my head of everything. I empty my brain bit by bit—Mom and Dad and Michel and school and Thomas and Martha and what I had for dinner. I let all of it leak out of my ears and onto the pillow, leaving nothing but blankness. Then I wait for her. For a real memory—one that's mine and only mine and not something I've read in the newspaper or on the Internet or something that my grandparents told me.

Sometimes it works. I can see her laughing, and I know it's really her—it's not from one of the three home-video clips that the whole world has seen, or from any of the other videos I used to watch over and over again until I mouthed the words coming out of Laurel's mouth when she had her first pony ride and was scared she was going to fall off. This laugh is different—it's just for me. Secret laughter between sisters. And she has two clips in her hair—they're shaped like stars, and they shimmer in the sunlight.

That's it. That's all I have: a laugh and a couple of hair clips. That's all I was left with for thirteen years. But now she's back.

CHAPTER

3

Mom comes back into the kitchen after phoning Dad. She's been crying a lot—her face is red and blotchy. Clearly she didn't want me to hear that conversation. I'm not sure why.

Then it hits me. "Is she hurt?" I can't believe I didn't think to ask before.

"What?" Mom's distracted, trying to find her car keys. They're on the shelf in the hall, exactly the same place they always are.

"Is she hurt? Is there something . . . wrong with her?" It's a perfectly reasonable question.

"No! The police said she's in remarkably good health, considering . . ."

I wait, but Mom doesn't finish her sentence. She's too busy trying to fix her makeup in the hall mirror.

"Mom? I'm . . . I'm scared."

She turns to me, and I can tell right away that she doesn't get it. "Scared? Whatever for? There's nothing to be *scared* of, Faith. This is . . . well, it's a miracle, isn't it?" She makes

15

a face at the mirror and adds a slick of lipstick to her chapped lips. "There." I stare at her as she stares at her reflection. "Do you think she'll recognize me?" she asks in the smallest voice imaginable.

The doorbell rings. There are a few possible answers to Mom's question, but only one that's honest. I go and stand behind her, and our eyes meet in the mirror. I tuck a few strands of hair behind her ear. "Of course she will, Mom." Honesty isn't always the best policy.

Her face lights up and she turns to hug me tightly. "My baby's coming home," she whispers. The mean, twisted little voice in my head—the one I have to silence every single day—whispers something so pathetic and selfish that it makes me want to hug Mom extra hard and never let her go: *What about me? I'm your baby, too.*

Michel already knows; Dad must have called him in the car. He says "I can't believe it" at least three times in as many minutes. While Mom's filling him in on the rest of the details, he keeps on glancing over at me.

Mom seems to have forgotten her feelings about Michel. She hugs him, the first time I've ever seen her do that. Michel's as surprised as I am when she launches herself at him. She babbles away, barely pausing for breath. She's usually painfully polite—but distant—toward Michel, and I hate her for it. Especially because he never has a bad word to say about her. He just shrugs it off like he doesn't mind one little bit. Sometimes I wish I could be more like him ("be a little more *French*," he says).

Michel tells Mom that we'll wait at the apartment for news. We were supposed to be going to a new exhibition at the art gallery, but he says we can go next week or the week after.

"Maybe the three of you can go, when Laurel's back with us?" Mom says this as if it's a normal thing to say.

Michel moves his head, and you can tell Mom interprets it as a nod, but it wasn't one. "You'd better get going, Olivia. John will be there soon." That was exactly the right thing to say to get Mom out of the house—she won't want Dad to get there first.

The good-byes are awkward. Mom seems to have re-membered that hugging Michel is not the kind of thing she does, and she doesn't seem to know what to say to me. The moment is too big, so she settles for kissing me on the cheek and telling me she loves me.

"I love you, too, Mom. I hope . . ." Now it's my turn to leave a sentence hanging in the air. Mom just nods as if she knows exactly what I wanted to say. But she doesn't.

I hope it's really, truly, definitely her. I hope she recognizes you after thirteen years even though I have my doubts. I hope you don't die in a terrible car crash on the way to the police station. I hope things are going to change around here but not too much. I hope you don't forget all about me once you've got your perfect daughter back.

Maybe the sentence *was* finished after all: I hope.

Michel drives carefully—both hands on the steering wheel, checking his mirrors all the time. I always feel safer in his car than I do in Dad's. "How are you doing, *ma chérie?*"

Michel knows that I like it when he speaks French, so he indulges me once in a while.

I close my eyes and listen to the traffic. How *am* I doing? An hour and a half ago, I had a pretty good idea how this weekend was going to play out: the exhibition with Michel; meeting up with Dad for a café lunch; baking in the afternoon; takeout and film tonight; an early start on Sunday morning and off to the food market with Michel, where he miraculously transforms into the most French person you could ever imagine (wearing a beret, for crying out loud), ramping up the accent and charming all the women into buying our (admittedly amazing) macarons; back home on Sunday evening to slump in front of the TV with Mom.

The routine of the weekend is comforting to me. Michel and Dad's place feels like *home*. I'd have asked to move in there full-time if I hadn't known it would break Mom's heart. Plus I'm pretty sure Dad wouldn't be all that keen on having me around all the time. Being a weekend dad suits him perfectly, I think.

I was eleven years old when my parents got divorced. Apparently, most kids are upset when their parents split up, but I wasn't. I don't remember crying at all. Not even when Dad drove away with his car packed full of his belongings. Mom still finds it strange that I didn't react how a normal kid would (should) react. You'd think she'd be relieved that I wasn't upset. Surely it showed that I was remarkably well adjusted for my age, understanding and accepting that my parents could never be happy together after what had happened to Laurel.

Dad's bisexual—always has been, as far as I know. Mom

knew that he was bi when they met in college and fell "head over heels in love with each other." The only reason I know this is because she talked about it in an interview a few years ago. Dad was *not* happy about that. She was on a mission, though—a mission to set the record straight. So many awful things had been written about them both—and about Dad in particular (LAUREL'S DAD IN GAY ROMP!)—that she wanted to tell the truth. The papers always say he's gay—they never bother to get it right. And back then they said that he pretended to be straight and lured my mother into marrying him because he was desperate to have children. For a while the media was obsessed with the fact that Laurel was adopted. They wanted to know WHY.

I was a miracle baby. Something to do with a very low sperm count (gross) on Dad's side and something wrong with Mom's ovaries. The chances of them conceiving naturally were minuscule. Technically I shouldn't even exist. I often wondered how they *really* felt about that. Mom usually sticks to the whole "miracle baby" spiel, saying how blessed she and Dad felt to have two beautiful daughters. I've never asked her for the real story because I know she'd never tell me the truth.

So for a few years the papers liked to make my father out to be some kind of depraved sex fiend. The GAY ROMP headline came after he was photographed coming out the front door of Michel's apartment building three months after they started dating. Not exactly the news story of the century.

It was hard on Michel, but he doesn't like to talk about it. I have no idea why he got involved with my dad in the first place. Surely any sane person would run a mile from someone with that much baggage. But Michel is a Good Person. The best person I know, probably. He's a veterinarian; I think it's probably a prerequisite that you have to be nice to be a vet. You have to be caring and sympathetic and not mind being puked on by a parrot.

Dad's okay, too, but I'll never understand what Michel sees in him. Michel is very, very good-looking. He has good skin and messy black hair and permanent stubble. If he were a couple of inches taller and a lot more vain, he could have probably been a model. Dad's not ugly or anything; he looks like you'd expect a man called John to look. Boring hair, regular enough features, pale skin, slightly too thin, shoulders permanently hunched.

"Faith? Are you okay?" Michel asks again.

I still don't have an answer, so I decide to go down a different route. "I had sex with Thomas last night."

CHAPTER

4

I have my very own spot on the sofa at Michel and Dad's apartment. They've got one of those huge corner sofas, and my spot is right in the corner, where I can look out the window and see the canal. I always try to sit in corners when I can. I didn't even realize it until Michel pointed it out to me one day. Then Dad laughed and said it was true, and that I'd been doing it since I was a little girl. He stopped laughing when I said that maybe I didn't like having my back to the room because photographers have a nasty habit of popping up from nowhere and snapping away. I like to see them coming, at least.

Michel's made us both a cup of tea, and I'm sitting in my usual spot; the sun is streaming through the windows and Tonks, the cat, is curled up on my lap. (Michel is a massive Harry Potter fan; Dad barely even knows who Harry Potter is.)

"So . . . you and Thomas . . . ?"

"Yeah, me and Thomas."

"That's big news! How are you feeling about it all?"

I shrug. "I don't know. Good, I think. It was . . . nice."

"Wow. That bad? You mean the earth didn't move and angels didn't sing and there were no fireworks?" I shake my head. "Well, that's exactly how your first time is supposed to be—average at best. God, I remember my first—"

I stick my fingers in my ears. "La-la-la, I'm not listening!" I only take my fingers out when I'm sure that he's stopped talking. "I don't want to hear about you having sex, because that makes me think about Dad having sex, and that's just . . ." I shudder and make a gagging sound.

Michel smiles at me. "Oh, right, so I have to sit here and listen to you, but you don't want to hear about the time when Jean-Luc waited for me in the changing rooms after soccer practice and—"

I throw a pillow at Michel's head and laugh so hard that Tonks leaps from my lap and stalks off without a backward glance. It feels so good to laugh with Michel, even though I know he's only trying to distract me from thinking about what's happening at the police station.

"Seriously, though, are you okay about all this?"

"Okay about what? Losing my virginity or Laurel?"

Michel shrugs and smiles. "Both, I guess."

"I'm okay." I nod as if to reassure myself. "Yeah, I'm okay. I think I love Thomas and I think he loves me, and we've been together *forever,* so there really wasn't any reason *not* to have sex. And I think I'm going to like it. We just need to practice a bit more . . . and find somewhere a bit better than the back of his van."

"Romantic," Michel deadpans.

"As for Laurel . . . well, I'm happy, of course."

22

Michel shuffles over to sit right next to me. "You don't have to pretend with me. You know that, don't you?"

I *do* know that. I've always been honest with him. I don't know what it is about Michel, but I've trusted him almost since the day we met. I can tell him *anything,* and he would never even dream of telling Dad. I close my eyes and take a deep breath. "I'm scared, Michel."

"What are you afraid of?"

"You know that thing they say—be careful what you wish for? I've wished for this my whole life, it seems. I've dreamed of this day, but I suppose I never really thought it would happen. I mean, at the time I *thought* I believed it would happen. . . . It's only now that I realize I was so sure she was gone forever. Does that make sense?"

Michel nods.

"I've been in her shadow ever since she was taken. You know how much I've hated that everything is *always* about Laurel. And that I couldn't have a normal childhood like everyone else. But now that she's back, it's all going to be different, isn't it? And maybe . . . I don't know . . . maybe I'll realize I was sort of okay with being in her shadow after all."

Michel puts his arm around my shoulders, and I lean my head against his. "It's okay, you know? Whatever you're feeling is okay. There's no right way to feel about this. It's hardly a normal situation, is it?"

Normal. I've always been jealous of normal. Boring too. I'd have been perfectly happy with the most boring, normal childhood you can imagine—like Martha's. Nothing remotely interesting has ever happened to anyone in Martha's family, and she doesn't even realize how lucky she is.

Michel's phone rings, and it's Dad calling from the police

station. Michel looks at me guiltily, and I can tell we're both thinking the same thing: he really should have called me first. Michel's end of the conversation mostly consists of "yes," "okay," and "I see"; it's not particularly enlightening. I leave the room to look for Tonks and find her under the duvet in my room. I scratch her head until she forgives me for spooking her.

Eventually Michel comes in and hands me the phone. He leaves the room to give me some privacy, and I immediately wish he'd stayed.

"Faith? It's her. . . . It's really her." Dad's crying over the phone—I've never heard him cry like this, huge, gulping sobs. "The teddy bear . . . you remember that bear of hers?" He doesn't wait for me to answer. "Well, somehow they got the sound chip to work! They played us the recording! Can you believe it?" Again he doesn't wait for me to speak. "She's . . . Oh my god, Faith . . . it's really *her*! Laurel's come home!"

I say, "That's great, Dad," and it sounds like he's just told me his soccer team has won the league. My reaction is *all* wrong, so I try again. "It's amazing." A little better, but not much.

Dad clears his throat. "She's been asking for you. She *remembers*. Isn't that wonderful? Just wait till you see her, Faith. She's a beautiful young woman . . . just like you." It couldn't be more obvious that the "just like you" is an afterthought.

"She's really asking for me?"

"Yes! She wanted to know if you're still obsessed with building sand castles!" Dad chuckles.

24

I was building a sand castle in the sandbox when she was taken.

"We showed her a picture of you, Faith. She couldn't believe how grown up you are!"

This is all very nice, but there's something he's not telling me. "Where has she been? What happened to her?"

I hear muffled voices. Dad must have put his hand over the phone. I wonder if Mom's been listening in this whole time. "We'll talk about that when I get home, love. All that matters is that Laurel's back—safe and sound."

Dad tells me that Laurel will be staying in a hotel for the next few days. Mom will stay with her, but he'll come home. The police need to talk to Laurel, and she needs to get checked out by a doctor and a psychologist and various other people. There's a specialist counselor on her way up from London.

I'm not allowed to tell anyone yet—not even Thomas and Martha. (*Of course* I'm going to tell Thomas and Martha.) Apparently there's going to be a press conference tomorrow afternoon. I wonder how they can possibly have all this planned out already.

"You can meet her tomorrow, love. How does that sound? Seeing your big sister?" Dad's using his coaxing voice—the one that makes me feel like a child.

How does that sound? Utterly terrifying.

"I can't wait," I say.

CHAPTER 5

Michel manages to convince me that making macarons will make me feel better about everything. For the past couple of years, the two of us have spent every Saturday afternoon in the kitchen together. Dad's usually watching soccer or out on one of his bike rides.

It started off as a bit of a laugh. My pathetic efforts would often end up in the garbage, and Michel would take his perfect macarons into the veterinary practice and share them with his colleagues (after we'd eaten our fill, of course). It was Dad who suggested we start selling them at the local farmers' market. At first we weren't sure that people would go for them, but on the first day, we sold out within an hour. That was when we discovered that the French accent was definitely an asset. It was my idea that Michel should play up the whole French thing. Who wouldn't want to buy authentic French macarons made by an authentic Frenchman who just happens to be very, very handsome?

Thomas texts when Michel and I are having our customary pre-macaron-making cup of tea. He wants to know why I haven't been in touch all day. He's worried I might be upset about what happened yesterday. I text back: Upset after all the sex, you mean? Thomas doesn't like to talk about sex. I don't have to worry about him bragging in the boys' changing rooms. Not that he'd ever be in the boys' changing rooms—he's not exactly the sporty type. Thomas likes to think of himself as a tortured artist. He sketches and writes poetry and drinks far more coffee than can possibly be good for him.

I reply to Martha while I'm at it. I bet she's been waiting patiently all day, trying not to check her phone every two minutes: Last night was good! Thanks again for covering for me. Speak later? I have news (not sex-related).

Martha texts back first: WHAT NEWS?

Thomas: I miss you. I roll my eyes at that; I can't help it. Thomas does not do text banter, no matter how hard I try to lure him into it.

I'll tell them both about Laurel tonight. They deserve to know.

Today's macarons are a spectacular failure on my part. Michel's are fine, though, so he makes another couple of batches (one batch of raspberry and one of salted caramel— my favorite). He realizes that I'm missing my macaron mojo and tells me we don't have to go to the market tomorrow, that it's totally up to me. He can go on his own or stay home—whichever I'd prefer. I don't think it's possible for me to love him any more than I do at this exact moment. I tell him I want to go to the market. I don't tell him the reason why: this might be the last time that we get to do this—

just the two of us. Maybe Laurel will want to come next week, and maybe she'll be miraculously brilliant at baking, and her macarons will have perfect, shiny tops every time.

Dad arrives home early evening; he looks worn-out. He quickly hugs Michel, then he hugs me for the longest time. They say a few words to each other in French—speaking quickly so that I can't even try to understand.

We sit down on the sofa and Dad talks. Laurel is slightly malnourished, with a serious vitamin D deficiency from lack of sunlight, but she's physically okay otherwise. First impressions are that she's in better psychological shape than anyone could have expected. But at the same time, she's clearly traumatized; she lashed out at a police officer trying to take a cheek swab for DNA testing. It took an hour for Mom to calm her down, but she wouldn't let anyone else near her. Apparently everyone was very understanding about it. After all, says Dad, Laurel has been through a terrible ordeal.

Dad doesn't go into much detail, other than to say that she was taken by a very sick man who kept her locked up in a basement. A lot of people had suspected that was the case. Mom always maintained that maybe she was taken by a couple who were desperate to have a little girl—and maybe they were raising her as if she were their own and taking the best care of her. Nobody dared to disagree with her whenever she mentioned this theory of hers. They tended to nod and smile awkwardly.

"Did she escape?" I like the idea of Laurel escaping, being daring and brave. Fighting back.

Dad shakes his head. "He let her go."

"*Why?*"

"We don't know."

"Why would you go to the trouble of keeping someone locked up for all that time only to let them go all of a sudden?"

"I'm just glad he did."

I am, too. Of course I am. "Did the police catch him?"

Another shake of the head. "No. We don't even know where she was being held. The guy blindfolded her, drove her to Stanley Street, and left her in the front yard. By all accounts, the couple living there got a bit of a shock when she knocked on the door. The police are doing everything they can to find the man, obviously. And Laurel's trying her best, but it's hard for her. She can't really remember how long they drove for. And she can't tell us much about where she's been kept all these years—the bastard was clever about it." Dad *never* swears in front of me.

"So this psycho's still out there? What if he comes back?"

"The police think he'll lie low—go into hiding. But they're not taking any chances. They'll be watching us, okay? There's no need for you to worry about that."

I sit back and try to process this information. The police have *no* idea who this man is. How is that even possible? I try to picture the sort of man who would do something like this. A man who would keep a girl locked in a basement for all those years. "He abused her, didn't he?"

Dad looks at Michel, and Michel nods, and it makes me so angry that my father can't make a decision by himself for once. "Yes. He beat her, too." Dad's jaw is tight. "The abuse was . . . systematic."

I close my eyes to blink away the tears.

"I'm not saying this to upset you, Faith. But you need to be prepared. What she's been through . . ." He shakes his head and breathes out slowly. Then he sits up straighter and pats me on the leg. "But the most important thing is that she's safe now. We can be a family again." I think he's forgetting that we can't exactly go back to being the sort of family we were thirteen years ago.

Dad says we need to give Laurel time to heal, and that she'll be getting the best help available—therapy and counseling and whatever she needs.

Mom and Dad have arranged for me to go see her tomorrow morning. It looks like I won't be going to the market with Michel after all. There's no point in arguing—they wouldn't understand.

It doesn't seem to have occurred to my parents that I might have slightly conflicted feelings about seeing my sister for the first time in thirteen years. That I might be nervous—even scared.

CHAPTER

6

Michel tells Dad he should go lie down for a bit, and Dad gives me another hug. "I can't believe it's over. I didn't think . . ." He shakes his head and murmurs something about a miracle before he trudges off to his bedroom.

Michel's going to pick up the takeout. He asks me to go with him, but I say I'd rather be alone for a few minutes.

"It's a lot to take in, isn't it?" His brown eyes are full of warmth and understanding.

I nod. "Are you not . . . worried?"

"Worried about what?"

"I don't know . . . That Mom and Dad might get back together?" I'm not saying it to be mean, I'm really not.

Michel smiles. "What are you trying to do? Make me paranoid? I'm not worried at all. Why? You think I should be?"

"I don't know! Dad's acting all weird."

"Of course he's acting weird! It's been a pretty weird sort of day, don't you think?"

"Did they tell her that they're not together? Does she know about you?" I can't believe I didn't think to ask earlier.

Michel picks up his leather jacket—I think it must be older than I am. "She knows. Your mom wanted to wait for a few days before telling her, but John insisted."

"And?"

"And . . . nothing! She was totally fine with it. So you don't need to worry your pretty little head about it!" He moves to ruffle my hair, which he only ever does to annoy me.

I try to put myself in her shoes. Coming back to your family after all that time. You'd want things to be the same as when you left, wouldn't you? But a lot can change in thirteen years. Your mother can wither away to nothingness, and your dad can get together with a lovely Frenchman, and your little sister can stop building sand castles and start building a wall around herself instead.

I go to my room as soon as Michel leaves, closing the door so Dad can't hear. I call Thomas first. He's annoyed that I've hardly been in touch all day, so I tell him immediately.

"Are you serious? This is a joke, isn't it?" He's never really understood my sense of humor. The fact that he thinks there's even the remotest possibility that I would joke about something like this is baffling to me.

I say nothing.

"Oh shit. You *are* serious. Oh my god. What happened? Where has she . . . ? Is she . . . ?"

I tell him everything I know, finding it vaguely reassuring that he asks a lot of the same questions as I did. It makes me feel like less of a freak. And when he asks how I'm feeling about it all, I feel a surge of love for him.

Now I know I did the right thing, having sex with him last night. Because I hadn't been sure about it at all. I was scared. I'd never have admitted that to him or to Martha. Luckily, losing my virginity turned out to be very unscary. It was mostly sweet and awkward and a little bit hilarious (for me, anyway) when Thomas got a cramp in his leg. I don't know why people make such a big deal about it.

Thomas is a good listener. He never interrupts and hardly ever disagrees. He is, to all intents and purposes, a good boyfriend. Even if I will never understand any of his poems. And he writes *a lot* of poems.

I tell Thomas that I might not be able to see him after school for the next few days. I have no idea how things are going to go with Laurel. Is she just going to come home and move into her room right away? Because she *does* have a room in our house—Mom insisted when we moved. At least she didn't insist on decorating it like Laurel's old room—all pink and sparkly. It just looks like a nice guest room, with a few of Laurel's possessions dotted around. Mom felt so guilty about moving. She hated the idea that everything wouldn't be exactly the same when Laurel came home. (It was always "when," never "if.") The only reason she eventually agreed to the move was to release more money for the fund to find Laurel.

Thomas tells me to take as much time as I need and says that I should call him any time I need to talk. He tells me he loves me, and I tell him I love him too, and I hang up, feeling sane for the first time in hours.

Martha says, "I can't believe it." Over and over again. I give her a quick rundown of everything I know, which isn't all that much now that I think about it, and she says "I can't believe it" a few more times. She asks when I'm going to meet Laurel, and it makes me realize that I won't be *meeting* her, because you can only meet a total stranger, can't you? But *meeting* feels like exactly the right word in this case.

I hang up after promising to call Martha tomorrow. She didn't ask how I'm feeling. Why would she? Laurel's abduction has dominated (and ruined) my whole life, and now she's back. Problem solved.

We eat our takeout (sushi) and Dad doesn't stop talking about Laurel. We have coffee and I eat six macarons and Dad doesn't stop talking about Laurel. We try to watch a movie, but Dad keeps mentioning Laurel, so we give up after half an hour. He apologizes, but that doesn't stop him from talking about Laurel. He spends the rest of the night phoning family and friends—presumably the ones Mom hasn't already called—to tell them the good news, and to swear them to secrecy about it. Not one of them asks about me.

I say I'm going to get an early night, and Dad nods enthusiastically. "Good idea, love. Big day tomorrow." He hugs me and says he can't wait to see "my two girls together, side by side." Michel hugs me and tells me he loves me. I wonder when he'll get to meet Laurel—there's been no mention of him coming with us tomorrow.

When I go to close the blinds in my bedroom I realize that I can see where she's staying. The neon blue *H* of *Hilton* peeks out from behind a high-rise office building. Laurel is in there somewhere, with my mother. *Our* mother.

CHAPTER 7

A persistent buzzing rouses me from sleep. The intercom to the doorman. By the sound of it, someone really, really wants to come in. I stumble from the bedroom to find Dad taking the receiver off the hook and Michel hovering nearby, looking worried. Before I can ask what's going on, the phone starts ringing. Then Dad's cell phone, which is charging on the kitchen counter.

"Journalists," Dad says. "Didn't take them long, did it? Not much point having a press conference now." He looks more resigned than upset.

I look at the clock on the kitchen wall. It's not even eight. Michel yawns as he fills up the coffee machine with water. I hear my phone ringing from the bedroom and go to get it. I'm vaguely aware of Dad trailing behind me, saying, "They wouldn't dare. . . ."

I don't recognize the number. Dad says, "Faith, don't." But I do.

"Hello?"

"Am I speaking to Faith Logan?"

"Who's this?"

"This is Jeanette Hayes. Can I ask how you're feeling this morning?"

Jeanette Hayes. Only *slightly* more popular than Satan in our family. Mom and Dad got along okay with some of the reporters over the years—one or two have even become friends—but Jeanette Hayes is most definitely not one of them. It started a couple of months after Laurel went missing. The campaign to find her was in full swing, and the story was still mentioned in one paper or another almost every day. Jeanette Hayes decided that the amount of attention Laurel's case was getting was unfair. She wrote this big article about all the other children who had gone missing at the time—and there were more than you might expect. The headline was: THE FORGOTTEN CHILDREN. Hayes had this theory that Laurel's case was getting all the attention because she was pretty and blond and middle class, and that my parents had "connections" to the media. She even went so far as to say that vital police resources were being taken up by the hunt for Laurel when they could have been put to better use elsewhere.

All that would have been bad enough, but she wrote another story a week later saying Laurel was probably dead and it was high time the whole country "got real" about it. Neither of these stories made her very popular. Other journalists were falling over themselves to disagree with her, to call her "unfeeling" and "heartless," and to say that the reason she didn't understand was that she wasn't a mother herself. She even got death threats. It didn't seem to bother

her, though, because she went right ahead and wrote a book all about it. I used to look at it in the library when Mom's attention was elsewhere.

The book was full of photos and stories of other missing children. In some cases, Hayes had interviewed their families, asking how they felt about their child's plight being sidelined to a tiny column on page 12, while Laurel Logan's was still splashed all across the front page. ("What's so special about *her*?" said one father.) The rest of the book was a bit of a hatchet job on my family. She hadn't even tried to talk to Mom or Dad to find out the truth.

There was a black-and-white photo of Jeanette Hayes on the back cover of the book. She was staring at the camera in a challenging sort of way. She looked like a serious journalist, I thought. But that was probably just the glasses perched on the end of her nose. I used to stare at that photo, wondering why she hated us so much. Wondering why she didn't want Laurel to come home to us.

I clear my throat, and Hayes repeats the question. How am I feeling this morning?

"I'm more interested in how *you're* feeling this morning."

"I'm sorry, I don't quite understand. I'm looking for a quote—something short and snappy but heartfelt; you know the sort of thing."

"And I'm looking for a quote from *you*. Something about how you were wrong about Laurel and wrong to write all that stuff about my family. . . . You know the sort of thing."

Dad's gesturing for me to hang up the phone. Reporters have never been allowed to talk to me, or even print a picture with me in it without blurring out my face. The one or two times they tried, they found themselves on the receiv-

38

ing end of a hefty lawsuit. That was another thing Hayes criticized my parents about—their "litigious nature."

"Okay, I see what you're saying." She doesn't sound angry. "I was wrong about Laurel. And I'm obviously *delighted* I was wrong. . . ." I smile, triumphant. "But I stand by everything I wrote about the police and your parents."

Bitch. I want to say something clever—something that will cut her deeply. I want her to know how much pain she's caused my family—as if the pain of losing Laurel wasn't enough—and I want her to feel bad about it. But Dad saves me the trouble by grabbing the phone from my hand and shouting expletives before hanging up and throwing it on the bed in disgust. "There. See if they'll print *that.*"

I've never heard my father say some of those words. It's kind of cool.

"It was her, wasn't it?" he asks softly.

I nod.

He puts his arm around me. "We're not going to let them ruin today, okay? This is *our* day."

I nod again. "I'm going to take a shower."

What do you wear to meet the sister you thought was dead? My closet here only has a few things in it, so my options are limited. I settle for gray jeans, Converse, and a black T-shirt; I want to look like me.

Michel tells me I look great, which can't be true because I've hardly slept. He manages to keep a cheerful sort of chatter going all through breakfast, ignoring Dad's phone buzzing every few minutes. I wish he were coming with us.

In the elevator, Dad tells me to keep my head down in the

car. When the car pulls out of the garage, the flashes go off and photographers crowd around, shouting and jostling one another and risking getting run over just to get a picture of us. I stare at the dashboard, where the plastic nodding dog I gave Dad for Christmas a few years ago is nodding away as if he approves of this madness.

Dad manages not to run over anyone's toes—he must be feeling charitable. And then we've left them behind and we're on our way to the hotel. I keep checking in the mirrors in case any photographers are following us on motorcycles, but it looks like we're in the clear.

Dad drums his fingers on the steering wheel until I ask him to stop. He apologizes and I apologize and he asks why I'm apologizing. Then we both laugh nervously.

"Are you okay, love? You look a bit green around the gills."

I look up at the sky, gray and heavy; I wouldn't be surprised if it started snowing. "I hope she likes me."

Dad barks out a laugh. "*Like* you? She's going to *love* you! She's your sister!" And weirdly enough, this does make me feel better.

There are no photographers waiting outside the hotel or hanging around the lobby, which is something to be grateful for. A red-haired woman in a too-tight black suit hurries over to us as soon as we enter. Her gold badge identifies her as GILLIAN CROOK, ASSISTANT MANAGER. She is very keen for us to know how very, very happy she is for us and how honored she is to have "Little Laurel" staying here. She shakes Dad's hand for far too long, then she hugs me, which is awkward because I make no effort to hug her back. I don't tend to go around hugging random hotel assistant managers.

Gillian Crook starts crying because it's all too much for her, thinking about Little Laurel being reunited with her family here in her hotel (of all places!). She just knows it's a story she'll tell her grandchildren one day (not that she's even married yet!), and I feel sorry for those hypothetical grandchildren. Dad and I nod as politely as we can and try to leave her behind, but she says there's someone we have to talk to before heading upstairs.

Gillian leads us over to the bar, empty except for a woman tapping away on a laptop. She stands when she hears us approach. She's around thirty years old, with shoulder-length, curly brown hair and the type of face you forget as soon as you turn away. Her name is Maggie Dimmock. She's the counselor who flew up from London last night. Maggie is a specialist in "family reunification," which is a real thing and not something someone made up yesterday because no one has a clue how to deal with a situation like this.

We sit down with her, and Gillian Crook hovers nearby until Maggie gives her an even more pointed look than she did the first three times. Maggie tells us her qualifications as if she's trying to prove something. Apparently she flew over to Switzerland last year to deal with a case "remarkably similar to this one." Except it wasn't all that similar at all, really, because the Swiss girl had only been gone for two years. You know your perspective is pretty messed up when you think two years is hardly any time at all for a girl to be away from her family.

Maggie Dimmock has already spent a couple of hours

41

with Laurel, which doesn't seem fair when I haven't even seen her yet. Maggie says she's a remarkable young woman, and Dad nods along with everything she says. She'll be having sessions with Laurel every day for the next week or so, as well as with the four of us together. It's all about creating a "smooth transition." She says that we can't expect everything to be hunky-dory straightaway. She sounds like a kids' TV host, full of enthusiasm and good intentions. I feel sorry for her.

Maggie talks some more, but I've stopped listening. I just want to see my sister. I want to get this over with. The nerves are too much to bear.

Dad and I take the elevator to the top floor. Apparently the hotel insisted that Laurel stay in the presidential suite. No doubt they're hoping for some good publicity out of this.

There's one more obstacle between us and Laurel—Sergeant Dawkins, our family liaison officer, is waiting outside the room. I've known Sergeant Dawkins—Natalie—for years. I like her, but I just want to get inside that room. Still, I let her hug me, because she's been through this whole thing with us from the start. This is a big day for her, too.

"She's so looking forward to seeing you, Faith." I wish people would stop saying that.

Sergeant Dawkins takes Dad to one side and they whisper. There's always something they don't want me to know or don't think I can handle. I'm so used to it happening that it barely even registers anymore.

And then Dad's knocking on the door, and Mom answers

it so fast I'm sure she must have been standing right there all along, and Dad's hand is on my shoulder, almost but not quite pushing me into the room. And I'm standing in front of my sister.

I have a sister again.

CHAPTER
8

She hesitates for a second, this new sister of mine. Then she runs over from the window, and she hugs me tightly, and I stagger backward a couple of steps, but she doesn't let go. Mom and Dad hang back for a second or two; they have the biggest smiles on their faces. I've never seen them smile like that before. They can't resist for long, and they soon pile in so that I'm right in the middle of this big, laughing, crying, disbelieving family hug. There's a wholeness, a completeness, a certain symmetry to it. It amazes me.

After a while, we disentangle ourselves and step back and just look. Mom and Dad are looking from Laurel to me and back again. Laurel is staring at me as if she can't quite believe I'm real, and I'm staring at her because I can't believe how beautiful she is even though I always knew she'd be beautiful. I had a picture in my head of what she would look like, and it never quite matched the age-progressed pictures the police came up with, but it was actually pretty close to the girl standing in front of me.

She's a couple of inches taller than me—about five foot seven. Her hair is a little longer than shoulder-length; it looks like she cut it herself. Her eyes are very blue. She's not wearing any makeup and her skin is slightly greasy and sallow, but her beauty still astounds me. The scar looks a little like a silvery white teardrop on her cheekbone.

She's skinny—the hoodie and jeans she's wearing are hanging off her. That's when I realize that the clothes she's wearing are mine. There's nothing I can say about that without it sounding petty and wrong. I want to make a joke about it—because it's such a classic sisterly sort of thing (*Moooooom, she borrowed my jeans without asking again!*)—but this probably isn't the right time. I don't mind that she's wearing my clothes, but it would have been nice if Mom had bothered to ask me. Knowing her, she's already got some big shopping spree planned for Laurel. She's always wanted a daughter to go shopping with, and I have never been that daughter.

"You're so grown up!" Laurel smiles through her tears.

Dad's got his phone out of his pocket. He wants to take a photo. Laurel and I stand in front of the sofa, and she puts her arm around my shoulder, and we smile for the camera. We have to keep smiling a little too long while Dad presses the wrong button and accidentally starts recording a video of us, but he manages to get it right eventually.

"Right," Mom says. "We're going to go out and get some coffee and leave you girls to it."

I'm panicking slightly at the thought of being left alone with Laurel, but at the same time I know it will be easier without Mom and Dad here, watching everything, trying to record it for posterity. They dispense more hugs before they leave. It looks like we're going to be a huggy sort of family from now on.

Laurel curls up in one corner of the sofa, tucking her bare feet beneath her. I sit on the armchair next to the sofa. I haven't had a chance to look around the presidential suite, but it's obviously bigger than my house.

Laurel notices me looking around. "It's too big."

"What?"

She fiddles with the cuffs of her (my) hoodie. "I wish it were smaller. I'm used to . . ."

Oh god. She's been locked up in a basement for thirteen years. It stands to reason that big spaces would freak her out. "You should say something. Tell Mom. They'll get a smaller room for you, no problem."

Laurel shakes her head. "Mom really likes it."

It is unbelievably odd to hear someone else calling my mother "Mom." And I can't get my head around the fact that I am sitting in this ridiculously opulent hotel room, talking to my sister.

"This is weird, isn't it?" Sometimes it's just best to get these things out in the open and acknowledge the awkward-ness before someone else does.

Laurel smiles. "It's definitely weird."

We sit in silence for a moment or two. Laurel stares at the door, and I wonder if she's trying to work out when Mom and Dad will be back. Maybe she'd have preferred it if they'd stayed. They seem to know the right things to say and do; clearly I do not.

"I'm glad you're back." It's a banal thing to say, but it's important that I say it out loud. It's important that she hears it. Laurel smiles again. Her teeth are perfect. "Your teeth are perfect."

"Um . . . thanks?" She's looking at me as if that was a weird thing to say, probably because it *was* a weird thing to say.

"Sorry . . . I was just . . . It's just that I was thinking that you haven't been to the dentist, and here's me going every six months or something and having fillings and braces and . . . Okay, I'm going to stop talking now. Sorry." What is *wrong* with me?

Laurel doesn't look at me like I'm crazy. She doesn't look at me at all. "I brushed my teeth for five minutes, three times a day. Mouthwash and flossing, too. It was one of his rules."

Oh god. "I'm sorry. I didn't mean to . . ."

"It's okay. I'm going to have to get used to talking about it, aren't I? I only brushed my teeth for a couple of minutes last night. Same this morning. And I haven't flossed." Finally a ghost of a smile appears on her face, and I breathe again. "You don't need to worry, you know. I can talk about it. About . . . him."

If the things that had happened to her had happened to me, I don't think I'd ever talk about them again. "I can't even begin to imagine what you've been through." Yet more banality.

"Good. You shouldn't have to." She goes to bite her nails and then stops herself, tucking her hands inside the sleeves of the hoodie. I wonder if that was another one of his rules. "Anyway, I want to hear about you. I've got some catching up to do, haven't I? How about you tell me every single thing you've done in the last thirteen years?" She laughs at the alarmed look on my face. "I'm kidding! Sort of."

"Um . . . where do you want me to start?"

"I'm sorry. I didn't mean to put you on the spot." She stares off into space again, and I'm not sure where she's gone, but I'm almost certain I should be glad that I can't follow her there. "You know . . . no matter how bad things got, I was always glad he took me and not you. Whenever I was scared or couldn't sleep, I thought about you."

I've read articles asking that question: why her and not me? Most people seem to think it came down to age or hair color. I was four years old with brown hair; Laurel was six years old with blond hair.

I used to have recurring nightmares of a man standing over the two of us. The sun was always behind him, so his face was in shadow. He would lead Laurel away by the hand, and I would go back to playing in the sand. Sometimes I would run after them and ask for an ice cream, and the man would take my hand, and the three of us would walk down the road together.

"Have you still got that night-light?"

I have no idea what she's talking about, and she can tell from the look on my face.

"The penguin one? With the red hat and scarf? You had this weird name for it, but I can't seem to . . ."

All of a sudden, I can picture it, crystal clear. "Egg!" Laurel nods vigorously, eyes bright, and we both laugh at the miracle of a shared memory.

How could I have forgotten about Egg? For years I

couldn't get to sleep without that penguin's tummy glowing from the corner of the room. Egg was the only thing protecting me from the monster under the bed and the monster in the closet. And then he was the only thing protecting me from the monster in the front yard—the one who led little girls away by the hand and made their families sad.

Laurel tells me that she used to think about Egg when she couldn't sleep, when she felt suffocated by the darkness around her. She would try to picture him in her mind, focusing on every little detail. "Sometimes it felt like I could actually *see* him—but only if I concentrated really, really hard. Those were the best times. I was able to go to sleep then. But sometimes I couldn't quite remember the exact shade of red of his hat, or the shape of his beak didn't feel right."

I nod as if I understand. And I do understand, in a theoretical sort of way. But I'll never truly understand what she's been through, will I? Even if she was to tell me every single thing that happened to her, I will never really *know*. I'll never know what it's like to be locked in a pitch-black basement, scared and alone—or even worse: scared and *not* alone.

CHAPTER
9

Laurel is disappointed that I have no idea what happened to the night-light, so I tell her we'll look for it when she comes home. "Home," she says. "I like the sound of that."

She asks me about school, and it all sounds amazing and interesting to her because she can barely even remember going. I ask her if she can read, then I apologize because it seems like an insensitive question. Laurel doesn't mind, though. She learned to read and write. She learned pretty much all the same subjects I did. I ask how that's possible, not bothering to hide my skepticism.

"He taught me."

"Like . . . proper lessons?"

She nods. "He hated ignorance. He said there was no excuse for it."

"So you had textbooks and everything?"

"Some. Mostly he had his own handwritten notes. A colored folder for each subject."

It's too bizarre to get my head around. The idea of this

monster—this *psychopath*—teaching her math and grammar and science. He brought her novels to read, too—but only if she was good. She didn't go into detail about what being "good" entailed. A couple of years ago, he taught her how to use a computer, saying everyone needed to be able to use computers in the modern world. He wired up an old desktop one for her. It wasn't connected to the Internet—obviously.

We talk and talk, and gradually I begin to build up a picture of her life for the past thirteen years, and she begins to build up a picture of mine. We swap information, filling in the gaps, asking questions and answering them. I steer clear of anything that I think might upset her, though, which means a lot of my questions aren't the ones I really want to ask.

Laurel finds it fascinating that I have a boyfriend. She asks lots of questions about Thomas, and I try my best to answer them. She even asks if Thomas and I have had sex. There's an awkward silence before I tell her the truth. She asks me if I liked it, and I say I sort of did. Then she goes quiet, and I say maybe we should talk about something else.

She shakes her head fiercely and says, "I *hate* it. I never want to do it again. It's disgusting." She looks so intense and angry, and I want to kill the man who made her feel like this. No—I want to hurt him, inflict the worst sort of pain, and *then* kill him. What he did to her doesn't count as sex. He attacked and violated a little girl in the most horrifying way possible. She *must* see the difference.

"What was he like? The . . . man. It's okay if you don't want to talk about it."

51

Laurel leans forward and grabs a sheet of paper that was facedown on the coffee table. She hands it to me without comment.

It's a drawing of a man's face. It's hard to tell how old he is—somewhere between forty and fifty, perhaps. His eyes are slightly too far apart, which is supposed to make a person look more trustworthy. His face is utterly nondescript, apart from the nose, which is big and hooked, with weirdly distracting nostrils. His hair is short and spiky. "This is him?" Laurel nods. I am looking at the man who took my sister.

"It's not quite finished. The police artist is coming back later to work on it before the press conference. The nose isn't quite right yet." She stares at the picture, and I have the strongest urge to scrunch up the paper, to set fire to it and watch his face blacken and burn.

"What's his name?"

A faint smile appears on Laurel's face. "At first I called him Smith. He was hardly going to tell me his real name, was he?"

Smith. Probably the most common name in the country. "At first?"

Laurel tilts her head questioningly.

"You said at first you called him Smith. What did you call him after that?"

She looks away and keeps her eyes averted from mine as she tells me the name she called him—the name he made her use even though she knew it was wrong.

"Daddy."

• • •

My parents choose that exact moment to come back. They've brought drinks and food. When I look at the clock, I see that Laurel and I have been talking for more than two hours. Glancing out the window, I see that it's snowing, thick and fast.

I manage to get rid of the appalled look on my face while Mom and Dad take their wet coats and scarves off. They both try to hide it, but they're looking at us closely to see how things are going. Laurel and I smile to show them that things are going just fine, thank you very much. I bet Mom wanted to come back ages ago, but Dad made her wait, to give us more time.

Daddy. The thought of her saying it to that man sickens me. I hope she hasn't told my parents. *Our* parents.

Dad starts pulling sandwiches out of a plastic bag. "Shrimp salad?" Laurel says, adding, "Eurgh!" And I make a gagging noise, and then we both laugh. Dad rolls his eyes and says, "I suppose I'll be having that one, then," but you can tell he's delighted that we're *bonding.*

Laurel and I both reach for the BLT baguette, and she insists that I have it, and I insist that *she* has it. In the end it all comes down to who's more stubborn, so of course I win. I end up with ham and cheese; it's dry and hard to swallow. I want to ask Laurel what kind of food she ate, because whatever it was, she clearly didn't eat enough of it. She makes short work of the baguette and devours a bag of chips, too. I realize that all three of us—me, Mom, and Dad—are watching her eat. Laurel doesn't seem to notice, or if she does, she doesn't seem to care.

There's a slightly awkward moment at lunch when Mom

says something about this being our first family meal together in thirteen years. She apologizes that it's not something more special and says she'll cook something soon—a roast dinner, perhaps?—so that we can sit down as a family at long last.

Laurel says that would be really nice, and Dad requests roast beef. Mom blushes (I have no idea why).

"Will Michel be invited, too?" I can't help myself. Someone needs to remind them that things are different now.

For a second, the only sound is that of Laurel tearing into a second bag of chips. She says, "I hope so. I can't wait to meet him." And Dad smiles gratefully because he knows as well as I do that Laurel has just averted an argument.

Mom says, "Of course Michel will be there," as if that was the plan all along. As if she hadn't completely forgotten his existence for a minute there. She's a bit quieter after that, which makes me feel guilty, but I won't allow Michel to be sidelined. He's as much a part of this screwed-up family as the rest of us. And unlike the rest of us, he actually *chose* to join it.

A bunch of people turn up after lunch, and it's chaos. They're trying to organize this press conference, even though everyone's fully aware that the press already has the story. It's on the Internet, of course. #LaurelLogan is trending on Twitter. When I check my phone, I see that lots of people have messaged me. Only a few of these people are actually my friends. Martha and Thomas have both texted, and I text back to say everything's fine. Martha texts again immediately: What's it like having a brand-new big sister? A stranger might think she's being insensitive, but this is just Martha being Martha. I think for a second, looking over to where Laurel and Mom are talking to a high-ranking police officer. I wonder why he has to wear a uniform if he's so senior. Perhaps he thinks the uniform adds gravitas. There's another, much younger police officer standing behind the first one. He has the beginnings of a black eye, which makes me wonder if he's the one Laurel supposedly lashed out at yesterday. I must remember to ask Dad later.

Whatever it is they're talking about, Laurel doesn't look happy. She shakes her head a number of times during the conversation. Eventually, Mom puts her arm around Laurel and leads her off to the bathroom. What was all that about?

When they finally come out of the bathroom, Laurel sees me watching and aims a shy little wave in my direction. She even manages a smile.

Everyone told her that it would be better if she stayed away from the press conference. They said it would be overwhelming for her, but she was adamant that she wants to be part of it. She wants to read a statement, too. "I won't let him win," she whispered to me. I felt something suspiciously close to pride.

I text Martha back: I think I'm going to like it.

CHAPTER
10

I watch the press conference—alone—on the massive TV in Laurel's suite. They didn't want me down there any more than I wanted to be there.

It's surreal, watching my family (*now new and improved, with added Laurel!*) walk into the ballroom fifteen floors below. Laurel's flanked by Mom and Dad; Mom's crying already. I can't help comparing it to the press conference they held when she went missing; I must have watched it a hundred times on YouTube. Dad spoke straight into the camera, talking to whoever had taken Laurel. *She belongs with us. Faith keeps asking where her big sister has gone. Please, if you're listening, do the right thing. Bring our daughter back to us. Bring Laurel home.* That was the moment when Dad really broke down. He'd managed to keep it together up until then, but you could tell it was there, bubbling under the surface. He slumped back into his chair, and Mom took his hand and squeezed it tightly, as if she was trying to force some of her strength into him. But by that point she was sobbing, too.

This press conference is very different. It's rowdier, for

56

one thing. Journalists start shouting questions the minute my family walks in. The camera flashes go crazy. The high-ranking police officer reads a statement, after pausing to take a pair of glasses from his breast pocket. Another police officer reads another statement and shows the cameras a new picture of "Smith." This one's been done on a computer, I think. It's a bit different from the one I saw—the face is narrower, the nostrils larger. Both police officers say that while they're delighted that Laurel is home, they will not rest until the "perpetrator of this sickening crime" is brought to justice. They used that line at the press conference when Laurel was taken—not these police officers, but ones just like them.

Police Officer Number Two says investigators are knocking on doors and asking questions *as we speak.* Laurel was able to give them some very useful information about her captor. (Really? That's news to me.) It's only a matter of time, apparently.

The police ask if there are any questions, and of course there are. Most of them are aimed at Laurel and Mom and Dad, so they ignore those. But they do answer a couple.

"How can you be sure that Laurel is safe now? Why would he just let her go?"

"We are as sure as we can be that Laurel's ordeal is over, and we will be doing everything in our power to keep her safe. As to why she was released after all this time? I think, today of all days, we should just be grateful that she's back home with her family. There will be plenty of time for those questions in the coming days and weeks."

"Were there any sightings of the suspect leaving Laurel in the yard yesterday? Any CCTV?"

"We're not aware of any sightings at the moment, but

officers will be going door-to-door on Stanley Street, speaking to every resident. We will, of course, be reviewing CCTV footage for anything that might be relevant."

"Did the police fail Laurel?"

An almost inaudible sigh from Police Officer Number One. "We did everything we could to find Laurel Logan, mounting the biggest search the county has ever seen. But sadly, tragically, it wasn't enough. . . . Now Bernard Ness would like to say a few words before I hand this over to the Logans." He doesn't quite manage to hide the disdain in his voice.

Bernard Ness is the mayor. God knows what he's doing there. Bernard Ness is not a fat man, but he walks as if he is. He huffs and puffs his way up to the microphone, and I become transfixed by his nose. It's bulbous and red, much like the rest of his face. His sideburns are damp with sweat.

He was also present at the press conference thirteen years ago. Deputy mayor back then, slightly less red, less bulbous, milling around in the background. This time he's right there up onstage with my family. It quickly becomes clear that Bernard Ness is here for two reasons: he likes the sound of his own voice, and he's desperate to associate himself with a good-news story (and let's face it—this is the best good-news story there's been in a long, long time). Maybe he thinks it will help people forget the financial scandal he was involved in last month.

Ness says that thirteen years ago "our community" was shocked and devastated and a few more words that all amount to the same thing. The crime against "Little Laurel Logan" threatened to tear "our community" apart, but in the end it brought us closer together. "We" never gave up hope. Apparently.

He talks for far too long, but no one tries to shut him up. Laurel and Mom and Dad listen politely in the background. Laurel's face is perfectly expressionless. Finally, Ness starts winding down. He ends his pointless speech by turning toward Laurel, pausing for effect, then saying, "Welcome home, Laurel." Laurel nods; she doesn't smile.

Dad's up next. The first thing he says is, "I'm going to keep this short," and I love him for it. In the background, Bernard Ness nods as though this isn't a dig at him. Dad talks about how happy we all are to have Laurel home, and thanks everyone who never gave up searching and hoping and believing she would come back. He thanks the police and says (emphatically) that they should not be held responsible for what "that man" did to his daughter. Then he does something weird. He addresses Laurel's captor directly. "Whoever you are, wherever you are, I want you to know that we *will* find you, and you will be held accountable for your crimes." He lets that hang for a beat or two before taking a steadying breath. His hands grip the sides of the lectern. "But for now, today, I want to thank you." There are no gasps from the crowd or anything, but you can tell people are shocked. I certainly am. "Thank you for giving our daughter back to us."

Dad sits down, and no one seems to know what should happen next. The police officers exchange glances, and Mom looks at Dad, and Dad looks at Laurel, and Bernard Ness looks at the photographers (of course). Laurel stands and walks over to the lectern.

Laurel looks out at the crowd in front of her, and it seems like she's looking at each and every face and camera. She doesn't flinch under the constant flashing. "My name is Laurel Logan." She clears her throat and takes a shaky breath. I can't believe how brave she is, doing this. "My name is Laurel Logan, and I'd like to take this opportunity to thank some people." She echoes what Dad said—thanking the police and the public—but she also mentions the press. "Thank you for keeping my story alive—thank you for never forgetting." It's a little odd, but I bet the journalists down there are lapping it up. I'm sure Dad doesn't approve, after everything he's been through with the press, but I think Laurel's earned the right to say whatever she wants.

Laurel stares into the camera, and it feels like she's looking at me. It must feel the same way to everyone who's watching—our friends and family, Thomas and Martha, people up and down the country and all over the world. The camera moves in closer on Laurel's face so that you can't see anyone else. They didn't do anything about her hair before the press conference, and it still doesn't look like she's wearing makeup—maybe just a bit of powder. She looks like a girl who has been through some seriously bad stuff.

"Yesterday my nightmare came to an end. I don't think I ever believed it would happen. I hoped for it and prayed for it every single night, and when things got really bad"—she pauses and blinks hard to stop herself from crying—"well, I hoped and prayed even harder. Yesterday my prayers were answered." She bows her head for a moment before looking at the camera again. "I don't have the words to express what I'm feeling right now. To know that my family never stopped looking for me. Never stopped caring. And they've told me that *you* never stopped caring, either. They told me that total strangers from all over the world have sent cards and letters—even money. They told me that the police worked tirelessly to try to find me and that my story has hardly been out of the newspapers—all this time. I can't tell you how much this means to me. To know that I wasn't forgotten." Another bow of her head. I bet half the people in that room have tears in their eyes.

Laurel finishes by thanking everyone. She doesn't mention Smith. She says she's looking forward to getting to know her family again—especially her little sister, Faith. She smiles when she says my name, and the camera flashes start up again. I realize I'm smiling, too.

As soon as she stops talking and moves away from the lectern, the journalists start shouting questions. You might think they'd have a little bit more respect—and sensitivity—today, but you would be wrong. It's hard to distinguish individual questions, but most of them seem to start with some variation of "How do you feel . . . ?"

A man takes Laurel's place. He was one of the people milling around the suite earlier. He makes calming motions with his hands; he looks like he's directing traffic. It takes a long time for the shouting to die down, and when it does, you can hear a woman's voice shouting out one final question: "Laurel! Laurel! Have you been shopping yet?" I swear at the TV while laughter ripples around the room downstairs. Even Mom and Dad smile; Laurel does not.

The press conference is over, and a man and a woman with perfect hair sit in a futuristic-looking TV studio and talk about how brave Laurel is. They use the word *remarkable* a lot, and they say that they hope the media will leave our family to heal in peace, which is ironic because one of their correspondents has been known to shout questions through our mail slot.

The shiny hosts decide that the moral of the story is that we should never give up hope, no matter how bad things look. They seem very pleased with themselves for having found a greater meaning in Laurel's story.

Martha texts: That was surreal.

Yes, it was.

CHAPTER
11

Mom stands back to admire her handiwork. "There. What do you think?"

The room looks much better than it did a week ago. It looks cozy and comfortable and welcoming. Mom asked Laurel what colors she liked and whether there was anything special she wanted in her room. Laurel said she didn't feel strongly about the decor as long as the bed faced the door; Mom didn't need to ask why.

It took hours of rummaging through boxes in the attic (not to mention a traumatic spider-in-hair incident), but eventually I found what I was looking for. I plug it into the socket next to the door and switch it on. Egg the Penguin is the finishing touch. Laurel's room is ready for her. My sister is coming home.

Someone (Maggie the counselor, perhaps?) had decided that Laurel shouldn't come home right away. She needed some time to adjust to life in the outside world. Mom wasn't too happy about that, but Dad persuaded her to go along with it. "It's only one more week, love." He was right: one week was nothing compared to thirteen years. The two of them took turns staying in the extra bedroom in Laurel's suite.

Laurel's been talking to the police almost every day, repeating her story over and over again to different officers. Mom told me that Dad lost his temper with them on Wednesday because they kept on asking the same questions, and Laurel freaked out when they tried to do the cheek swab again. They got a female officer to try this time; the reaction was less violent, but the result was the same. Laurel locked herself in the bathroom until the woman went away. Laurel refused to tell my (our) parents what the problem was, but I guess it must have triggered some bad memories or something. Dad thinks they really need to leave her alone now. (*"She's got enough to deal with without the police hounding her all the time. And what do they need a DNA test for, anyway?"*)

Laurel's been talking to a psychologist, too. About the abuse, I think, but I haven't asked. We've had two family sessions with Maggie Dimmock—one in the hotel and one in what used to be our favorite Italian restaurant. That second one was a big deal; Laurel isn't used to going outside. She has *been* outside. Once a week the man would blindfold her and put her in his van and drive her to a forest. The police were obviously keen to learn as much as they could about that forest, even showing Laurel pictures of different kinds of trees in case they could narrow it down that way. But Laurel thought the trees were probably pines, which are just about as common as you can get. She wasn't even sure how far the forest was from where she was being held. She tried to count the seconds and minutes she spent in the van, but Smith wasn't stupid—the journey would take anywhere between one hour and three hours, but they would always end up at the same place. He would let Laurel out and tell her to exercise—jumping jacks and push-ups and crunches. She only tried to run away once; he made sure she didn't try ever again.

So that was Laurel's only experience of the outside world—for thirteen years. Just walking down the street was a huge achievement for her. We took it slowly and tried to ignore the journalists and photographers shadowing our every move. The police made sure the press kept their distance.

I walked with Laurel, a little way behind Mom and Dad. Maggie was behind us, not really dressed for the weather, her shoulders hunched against the cold wind. Laurel couldn't stop staring at everything—the cars, the shops, the people. She grabbed my hand when an ambulance screamed past, siren blaring. I murmured words of reassurance and squeezed her hand. I tried to imagine what this must be like for her, but of course I could never know. She didn't let go of my hand until we were safely inside the restaurant, which was empty. Maggie must have called ahead to make sure.

Laurel was baffled by the menu—confused by being able to choose what to eat. "Can I have *anything* I want?"

"Anything," Mom and Dad said in unison.

Mom suggested spaghetti. "It used to be your favorite."

Laurel loved it. She made a complete mess of eating it, and I did the same with mine so she wouldn't feel self-conscious.

It didn't really feel like a counseling session, but maybe Maggie is just really good at her job. Sometimes she'd throw out a question and we'd remember why we were there. She asked if we were worried about anything. I shook my head, even though there were lots of things I was worried about.

We talked about how things would work when Laurel came home. Mom and Dad had obviously talked about this beforehand. They'd decided that Laurel and I would stay at his place on the weekends. I wondered if Mom had put up a fight about that. Laurel and I would have to share a room.

"You don't mind, do you, love?" asked Dad as he snapped a breadstick in half.

I shook my head.

Laurel cleared her throat. "I don't mind sleeping on the sofa." She looked down at her empty plate.

"No, really, it's fine. It'll be fun." I smiled at Laurel; I wanted her to believe me.

Maggie seemed pleased with how things were going, but she warned us that there might be "bumps in the road ahead," and we shouldn't put pressure on ourselves for things to be normal right away. "The important thing is that you keep talking—and listening—to each other. Communication is the key." She said that any one of us could call her if we had anything we needed to talk through, and that we would keep going for sessions with one of her colleagues who lives locally.

Laurel tried Dad's wine and grimaced at the taste of it; she's never tried alcohol before. Then she asked if she could order a glass of her own. Mom had to explain that you're not officially allowed to drink alcohol until you're twenty-one.

At first I thought Laurel was going to argue, but she just nodded and took another sip of water. She didn't talk much for the rest of the meal.

I had to go back to school on Thursday, even though Dad was taking the whole week off work. It wasn't fair. Mom and Laurel were going shopping for clothes, then on to the hairdresser. It seemed like something the three of us might have done together—if you ignore the fact that I hate shopping.

Thomas and Martha had been keeping me up to speed about how things were going at school. I'd talked to Thomas most days and texted Martha whenever I had the chance, but I hadn't actually seen either of them since the day Laurel was found. I hadn't wanted to leave the house, and I didn't feel quite ready to invite them over yet. I felt like I needed time to myself—to get used to how life was going to be from now on. Martha was a little more understanding about it than Thomas, or at least she *pretended* to be more understanding.

School was just as insane as Thomas and Martha had warned me it would be. Thomas was already in the cafeteria when I arrived half an hour before homeroom. He was sitting on the floor with his back against a radiator dappled with peeling paint. He was reading a book and eating an apple. Thomas always eats the whole apple—seeds, core, everything except the stem. The first time he did it in front of me, I told him it was disgusting; he lectured me about the "frankly appalling" levels of food wastage in the world.

I sat down next to him, sliding my back down the radiator, probably peeling off some more paint in the process. I started to speak, but he held up a finger to silence me. I was used to this: Thomas never stops reading until he's reached the end of a paragraph. Still, I thought that today might warrant some kind of exemption from the rule. I was about to say as much when he finally put his book down and kissed me. Unsurprisingly, he tasted like apples.

He put his arm around me, and I leaned my head against his. "Crazy week, huh?" he whispered.

"The craziest." I closed my eyes. For the first time in days, I felt like myself again.

"I'm here if you want to talk about things, okay? But it's fine if you don't. Whatever you need." He kissed my forehead, and I remembered why I liked him so much.

The door opened and a group of girls piled in. They spotted me immediately. I knew what was going to happen, and I wanted to avoid it at all costs. I stood up and turned my back to them, pretending to look for something in my bag. "Thomas, let's go," I whispered.

Thomas was too slow getting his stuff together.

"Faith! Oh my god, Faith! Oh. My. God!"

I could stay facing the wall, but it wouldn't do any good. Laney Finch would wait all day if she had to. I turned around slowly, as if facing a firing squad.

Before I knew what was happening, Laney Finch had flung herself at me. I stumbled back against the radiator, hitting my elbow on the corner. Her arms were around me, and it felt like she had too many of them—I was being hugged by a Laney squid. My arms stayed rigidly by my sides.

The hug went on far too long. Over Laney's shoulder, I could see her friends hanging back, whispering and staring. At least two of them looked like they might want to hug me, too. There were tears in their eyes, and they held their hands to their chests as if the emotion was just too much for them.

Laney pulled back but still had my arms firmly in her grip. She was crying, of course. "I can't believe it, Faith. It's just *too* amazing for words. It's a miracle, isn't it? I totally think this qualifies as a miracle, don't you? I prayed, you know. Every night. I told you that, didn't I?"

Laney had indeed told me that she prayed every night for my sister. It was her opening line the day she decided we should be best friends. That was five years ago. Laney Finch likes to think that she feels things more deeply than the average person. Of course, this is total bullshit. She has no more empathy than anyone else—it's all talk. She's the type of person who sees a natural disaster in some faraway country on the news and cries about it. (*Oh, those poor people . . . Imagine what they must be going through. . . . It breaks my heart.*) Five minutes later she's on the phone to one of her pathetic friends, moaning about how unfair it is that her parents won't buy her a new MacBook Air for her birthday.

From the day she arrived at school, Laney Finch tried to latch on to me; I was determined to be unlatchable. She never seemed to get the message, though. Every time there was a story about Laurel in the papers, Laney Finch popped up, shooting sympathetic looks across the room or asking intrusive questions. I only lost my temper with her once: when she said she knew exactly how I felt because her cat had gone missing and hadn't been seen for a week. I didn't

69

punch her in the face, which was what she deserved. I *did* tell her to fuck off, which seemed to shock her just as much.

I was determined to at least *try* to be nice this time, so I mumbled, "Thanks," and tried to extricate myself from her grip. Thomas was no help at all—he was busy putting his book back in his bag oh so carefully so that he didn't damage the cover.

Laney let go of my arms and daintily dabbed at her eyes. I wondered if she wore waterproof mascara every day so that she was fully prepared for her regular crying stints. "It's such wonderful news, Faith. I haven't stopped smiling since I heard, so I can't even begin to imagine how you must be feeling." She shook her head and smiled, as if that proved that she had *literally* not stopped smiling for the past five days. I waited. She smiled some more. I said I'd better get going, even though there was nowhere I had to be for at least twenty minutes. I turned to take Thomas's hand, but Laney somehow managed to maneuver herself between us. "So . . . what's Laurel like? I bet she's really . . . God, I don't even know . . ."

Laney likes to *know* things—especially things that other people *don't* know. Gossip is oxygen to her—without it, she'll, like, literally, you know, die or something.

"She's fine. Thank you." I gave Thomas a look that very obviously said, *Get me out of here!* but for some reason he didn't seem to understand it.

Laney leaned close to me, and I could smell toothpaste on her breath. "Why do you think he let her go? It's weird, isn't it?" she whispered, eyes wide.

"Fuck off, Laney." Martha's timing was impeccable.

Laney flinched and turned to face Martha. "Excuse me, but this is a *private conversation*."

Martha stood next to me and smiled sweetly. "I don't think so. In fact, I don't think it counts as a conversation at all when you just talk *at* someone. So why don't you leave Faith alone and go and cry over some Cambodian orphans or endangered pygmy elephants? Or endangered Cambodian pygmy elephants who also happen to be orphans."

Laney was too shocked to speak. Her mouth opened and closed again.

Martha crossed her arms, looking like a burly bouncer. Martha is tall. Sturdy. Intimidating if you look at her in the right light. "Go. Away."

Laney looked to me for help, eyes pleading. "I was just trying to . . . I really do care, you know."

I nodded.

Laney fled, her gaggle of friends enveloping her, sweeping her away, and shooting us dirty looks at the same time.

Martha waved at them before turning to me. "You're welcome."

"Thank you."

We hugged. It's quite nice having your own personal bodyguard.

Martha and Thomas stuck to me like superglue for the rest of the week. If one of them wasn't with me, the other one was. Laney wasn't the only one who wanted to talk to me; the teachers were at it, too. At least I'd missed the special assembly they held on Monday.

It should have been nice, and I shouldn't have minded the attention. But it wasn't nice, and I did mind. I just want to be left alone. It's bad enough having photographers and camera crews stationed outside our house night and day— and a police car down the street—without being scrutinized at school, too. Hopefully things will get back to normal soon. Whatever normal is.

CHAPTER 12

"Laurel! Laurel! How does it feel to be coming home? Laurel! Can you tell us . . . ?"

The front door closes, muffling the shouts from the yard. The curtains are already closed, but you can still see the flashes from the cameras. I wonder why they're still snapping away—there's nothing to see now that she's safely inside.

Dad locks the door and leans against it. "So much for them giving us some privacy," he says. He was interviewed on the news last night—*on the eve of Laurel's homecoming*—and he'd asked for exactly that: privacy. Unfortunately, it seems that's the one thing the media is unable (unwilling) to give.

Mom's clasping her hands together and looking anxiously at Laurel, who is standing rooted to the spot, looking around the room, taking it all in. A teddy bear is nestled in the crook of her arm. It's battered and worn, and I can smell it from here. It also seems to be missing one arm. Barnaby has been through more than your average bear.

I bet the photographers got a shot of Laurel clutching the bear. That will be *the* photo—the one that will be on the Internet in a matter of minutes, on the news in a few hours, on the front page of the papers tomorrow morning. Maybe they'll print the old photo of Barnaby the Bear next to the new one. Maybe they'll use the word *poignant* a lot and draw ridiculous parallels between the bear and Laurel.

The noise from outside dies down. Laurel (and Barnaby) and I sit on the sofa and Dad takes the chair next to the fire. Mom makes tea. I notice Laurel staring at the mantelpiece—there's a picture of her, aged five, right in the middle. There's a picture of me around the same age, just off to one side. There are no pictures of my parents. In the old house, we used to have a photo of the two of them on their wedding day on the mantelpiece. They looked young and kind of drunk, both of them raising glasses of champagne to the camera. I wonder what happened to that picture.

Mom wanted to put up a "welcome home" banner, but I managed to convince her it would be tacky. It's the kind of thing you do when your daughter's come back from her gap year in Nicaragua or from a stay in the hospital, not when she's been kidnapped and repeatedly raped by a psychopath.

Laurel likes tea. Smith brought her tea when she was feeling sad. He said, *The world always looks brighter when you've got a mug of tea in your hand.* Mom was horrified when she heard that; she says almost exactly the same thing. When she was with him, Laurel always drank out of the same bright yellow mug with a smiley face on it, until she dropped it one day. It smashed on the concrete floor. Smith slapped her so hard she fell and cut her hand on one of the broken shards of mug. He stitched up the wound himself, doing such a good job that you can barely even see the scar on her palm. The police wondered if that meant that Smith might have been medically trained, but Laurel said she didn't think so. He had several huge medical books that he used to refer to whenever she was ill.

Mom comes back in with the tray and hands around the mugs. Laurel's is red, with her name on it. Her face lights up when she sees it, then she looks to Mom for an explanation. Mom nods in my direction.

"I . . . I thought you should have your own mug. It's the same as mine." I hold mine up as proof. My mug has a chip on it, and the *i* in my name is starting to wear off.

Laurel looks at her mug as if it's something precious and miraculous. Then she looks at me in pretty much the same way. "Thank you, Faith. That's"—her voice catches—"really kind of you."

I shrug. "It's no big deal." But I'm really pleased she likes it. Everyone should have their own mug; it makes tea taste so much better.

After tea, we all head upstairs to show Laurel her room. Mom clears her throat as she steps back to let Laurel go first. "I'm so sorry we moved, Laurel. . . . I always wanted you to come home to your own bedroom. . . . That's how it was supposed to be." She doesn't look at Dad, and he doesn't look at her.

Laurel doesn't seem to notice the awkwardness, though. "I don't mind at all. *This* is home. Wherever you are." She couldn't have said anything more perfect. Mom's eyes glisten with tears.

"Well, what do you think?" I wish Mom didn't sound so needy. The room is nothing compared to the presidential suite—for one thing it has a single bed instead of a king-size one—but it's a whole lot better than where she was before. With *him*. A camp bed and a dirty sleeping bag. A bare lightbulb. Mice. Cockroaches.

Laurel spots him immediately. "You found him!"

I shrug again. I seem to be doing a lot of shrugging these days. "I thought you might like to have him."

"I can't believe it! He looks exactly like . . . He looks the same!" She shakes her head and kneels down to inspect the night-light; she touches his head with a certain reverence. She looks up at me, eyes shining with unshed tears. "Is it really okay if I keep him? I don't like the dark."

I nod. "Of course it's okay!"

Mom crouches down next to Laurel. "You can leave your door open at night, if you like. That way you'll get the light from the landing, too."

Dad says, "Why don't we leave the girls to it? Faith can show Laurel everything she needs. I'll bring up the bags in a bit."

Laurel sits on the bed, moving her hand back and forth across the duvet cover. Her other hand still clutches Barnaby. "It's nice. This room, I mean."

I sit down next to her. "Mom was worried you'd hate it. She says we can redecorate anytime you want."

"Why would I hate it? It's perfect. . . . A room of my own."

She sets Barnaby the Bear down on the chair in the corner. I want to tell her that he could really use a bath, but it doesn't seem like the right thing to say.

Mom's thought of everything. Toiletries and pajamas and a hairbrush. There's even some brand-new makeup on the dressing table. Laurel touches everything, as if to make sure it's all solid and real and isn't going to be taken away from her at any second. She spends a long time looking at a tube of foundation, and it hits me: she won't know how to use makeup. I explain what everything is and tell her I'll show her how to use it all. "Not that you need makeup. You're beautiful without it." I feel my cheeks flush.

"I'm not beautiful," she says flatly.

"You are."

Laurel shakes her head and moves from the dressing table to the bedside table. There's a cell phone—an old one of mine, with a new SIM card. "Is this for me?" I nod, and she picks it up. I show her how it works and scroll through the numbers I've already added to her contacts: me, Mom, Dad. I probably should have added Maggie Dimmock, too.

"See? You can call me anytime."

Laurel presses a button, and my phone buzzes in my jeans pocket. I take out my phone and say hello. She says hello into her phone, and we both laugh.

"Where's your bedroom?" she asks.

"Right next door. Want to see?"

My room has a lot of stuff in it. More stuff than a room this size should probably have. Mom's always trying to get me to throw things out or give them to charity, but I like it this way. There's something comforting about it. I don't like getting rid of stuff; I don't like throwing memories away.

"Wow," says Laurel.

"Sorry it's such a mess."

She shakes her head and turns around, trying to take

everything in. There are pictures all over the walls—photos I've taken, pictures cut out from magazines. You can barely see the walls underneath. I realize there are no photos of Laurel, and I wish I'd thought to put one up before she came home.

On the desk there are three rows of little toys from Happy Meals and cereal boxes. They're lined up like little soldiers. There's a stack of shoe boxes on the floor next to the desk. Laurel doesn't investigate, but I wonder what she'd make of a box full of sugar packets and cubes. For a while it was a bit of an obsession of mine. I only stopped collecting them last year.

Laurel asks me about some of the pictures on the walls, which means I end up talking about my favorite films and bands. It's easy to forget that she has no frame of reference for most of the things I talk about. She doesn't seem to mind that I keep having to go off on tangents, that I keep having to explain more and more things before I go back to telling her what I wanted to tell her in the first place. She just takes it all in. She seems to concentrate hard on what I'm saying. She really listens; I like that.

Laurel has seen *some* films. Occasionally, Smith would bring an old TV and video player and hook them up in the basement. (Who has *videos* in this day and age?) Laurel says it only happened once a month, or even less often than that. There was no rhyme or reason to it—it didn't seem to be a reward for good behavior. The films she watched were all really old—*Mary Poppins* and *The Sound of Music* and one called *One of Our Dinosaurs Is Missing,* which she particularly liked.

"Is this your boyfriend?" Laurel points to a photo next to my bed. It's the last thing I see before I turn off the light at night.

"Yeah, that's Thomas."

"He's very good-looking." Thomas *is* good-looking, but not in an obvious way. He *looks* like he writes poetry. His hair is too long, and he's pale and interesting rather than tanned and chiseled. There's something gentle about his features—a softness that I like. When he first turned up at school, you could tell none of the boys were threatened; there's nothing remotely alpha male about Thomas. But something strange happened within days: girls were drawn to him. Some of the most popular girls in my grade started trailing after him, offering to show him around the school and help him "settle in." He saw straight through them, politely declining their advances, preferring to spend time alone. Then he started following me around.

I didn't even notice at first; Thomas is very good at skulking. But then I realized that I was seeing him *all* the time—in the corridors, in the library, in the courtyard. I mentioned it to Martha one day, and she rolled her eyes at me. "*Finally.* I was wondering when you were going to notice." She was the one who encouraged me to talk to him, although "Why the hell are you stalking me?" probably wasn't quite what she had in mind.

Thomas was startled when I confronted him in the library, but he didn't try to deny it. He said, "I think you're interesting."

"Look, if there's something you want to ask about my sister, just do it." It happened all the time—people staring and

79

whispering. It got to a point where I almost preferred the ones who were brazen enough to actually talk to me about it—like Laney Finch.

Thomas just stared at me.

"Well? I have better things to do than stand here being gawked at, so if you don't mind, I'm just going to go." I wasn't usually quite so rude, but something about his face riled me.

"Why would I want to ask about your sister?"

I crossed my arms and waited.

He closed his notebook and waited, too. Eventually, he broke the stalemate by asking a question I'd never been asked before: "Who's your sister?"

I think it was those three words that did it for me. I'm not saying I fell head over heels in love with him as soon as he said them, but they unlocked something inside me. They made it possible for me to not hate him, to start sort of liking him, to start really liking him, and finally, after a few months, to maybe sort of almost love him. None of that would have been possible if he hadn't asked me that question.

Thomas has lived in more countries than most people have been to on vacation—he's an army brat. He moved here when his parents retired a couple of years ago. He doesn't like to talk about the army thing—it doesn't exactly mesh with his strictly pacifist views.

When I realized Thomas wasn't joking, I told him who my sister was. He nodded vaguely. "Oh yeah, I think I've heard of her." He said this in exactly the same way I do when I tell him I've heard of this poem or that book, when the truth is I have no idea what he's talking about.

I stayed and talked to him until the bell rang. Two weeks later, he asked me out. I kissed him for the first time one week after that. I've never told him that I wouldn't even have considered going out with him if he'd asked me about Laurel.

Laurel sits down on my bed and asks me more questions about Thomas. She asks why I like him. (She doesn't say *love*.) Why, out of all the boys at school, Thomas is the one I chose to be my boyfriend. It makes me smile, her saying that. As if all the boys in school are clamoring to go out with me. I don't tell Laurel the truth: that the reason I chose him to be my boyfriend was because he was the one person who never—not even once—asked about her.

CHAPTER
13

Mom didn't ask Laurel if this was okay—she went right ahead and organized it, only telling her this morning. I wonder what Laurel would have said if she *had* been consulted. It's overwhelming even for me, so god knows what it must be like for her.

I have never seen so many members of my family in the same room before. Laurel sits in the middle of the sofa, and everyone else forms a ring around her. There have been lots of tears; there has been quite a bit of champagne. (These two facts may or may not be linked.)

The only person missing is my grandmother. Dad's mother lives in the South of France; she's very frail. My grandfather died when I was five years old, almost exactly a year after Laurel was taken. I don't remember him. Mom's parents are here, though; Gran keeps fussing over Laurel, brushing imaginary bits of fluff from her T-shirt just for an excuse to touch her.

The party is strictly a family affair. Mom had suggested

inviting a couple of other people—she'd even asked if I wanted to invite Thomas and Martha—but Dad had said we should try to keep the numbers down. I was relieved; I didn't want Thomas and Martha here. I'm not even sure why. Maybe it feels a bit like I need to keep the different parts of my life in separate boxes. For now, at least.

Mom's sister, Eleanor, has had six glasses of champagne. (I've been counting.) Mom and Eleanor look really similar, but when they stand next to each other, it's obvious that one of them has been through some awful shit and the worst thing that's happened to the other one was missing out on a Marc Jacobs coat in the January sales. Maybe that's a little unfair. Mom always says she couldn't have made it through those first weeks and months without her sister. Eleanor dropped everything and moved into our house, spending most of her time looking after me.

At one point in the afternoon, Dad's brother, Hugh, thinks it's appropriate to ask Laurel about the offers she's had. "Might as well get something out of all this, eh?" He nods emphatically and doesn't seem to notice the suddenly uncomfortable atmosphere.

His wife, Sally, elbows him. "Hugh!"

And Hugh says, "What? What did I say?"

Dad glares at Hugh until Hugh turns his concentration to the crudités, taking a long time to decide between a carrot stick and a radish. No one's going to tell him that the offers have been pouring in. TV interviews, newspaper interviews, magazine features, photo shoots (a fashion designer with a ridiculous name that I can never remember saw Laurel at the press conference and is convinced that she's his new muse. He wants to design a whole collection—"Lost & Found"—inspired by her.

Laurel is baffled by it all. "Why do all these people care about me?" I haven't got the heart to tell her that they *don't* care. They're only interested in money, just like everyone else. Everyone wants a piece of Little Laurel Logan.

I think she'll end up accepting some of the offers. Dad's warned her that she needs to be careful, that she needs to get advice and talk to her psychologist before she does anything. He's worried about the repercussions of her doing anything other than hiding out at home. He thinks she's too fragile. But this morning I overheard Mom talking to Dad in the kitchen. "It's hard. . . . The money would come in handy. I mean, what's she going to do now? Get a job? Go to college? She needs some financial security, John." Dad's voice was quieter, so I couldn't hear what he said.

Dad stayed over last night. He wanted to be here for Laurel's first night at home. "What about Michel?" I asked when Dad wheeled in his little case and put it in the corner of the living room yesterday morning.

Dad looked blank. "What *about* Michel?"

"Shouldn't he be here? He's part of this family, too, *remember*."

"I'm perfectly aware of that, thank you very much." I stared at him. "Your mother thought it would be nice if the four of us were here tonight, together."

"I bet she did. She hates him." Mom was at the supermarket, stocking up on supplies for the party she hadn't bothered to tell anyone about.

"She doesn't *hate* him. It's more complicated than that." Parents always say things like this, trying to make out that you couldn't possibly understand the complexities of their relationships.

"He should be here." I wasn't willing to let it go.

"It's not up to me. Her house, her rules." That made it sound like he wanted Michel to be here, at least. That my mother was being unreasonable, trying to re-create a perfect, simple family that hadn't existed in thirteen years.

"I hope he's okay."

"Why wouldn't he be?"

I shrugged. "It can't be easy for him . . . Laurel coming back." Dad looked genuinely confused by this, so I elaborated. "Maybe he's worried you're going to leave him, go back to Mom." There. I'd said it. It had been on my mind all week. Most kids I know would be thrilled at the idea of their parents getting back together. Not me.

Dad laughed. "What? Are you . . . ? You're serious, aren't you? Oh, Faith . . ." He put his arm around me, pulling me close. "That's never going to happen. Your mother knows that. Michel knows that. I *love* him." It made me squirm a bit, Dad saying that. But it reassured me, too.

I texted Michel last night, just to check on him. He texted back to say he was watching the Alien movies back-to-back, making the most of having the apartment to himself. He asked how things were going with Laurel. *Great,* I said.

Mom cooked a roast dinner. She really went overboard—it was like Christmas. We discovered that Laurel loves peas but doesn't like brussels sprouts. She had two helpings of roasted potatoes. She's starting to put on a little weight. You can see the difference already; she looks a tiny bit healthier every day.

No one was quite sure what to do after dinner. We sat in

the living room, drinking tea. Laurel sat in my usual spot on the sofa, but I didn't mind. It was me who suggested watching TV. That's what normal families do on a Saturday night, after all. Dad handed Laurel the remote control, and she flicked through channel after channel. I presume she must have done the same in the hotel room, but she still had this look of amazement on her face at all the choices on offer. She couldn't decide between a film featuring a giant killer shark and a documentary about earthquakes. She looked to me for help, and I mouthed the word *shark* and nodded hard. She nodded back, grinning, and for the first time I felt something. We were *sisters*. We had a bond. It was new and as fragile as a strand of spiderweb blowing in the wind, but it was there, glinting in the sunlight if you saw it from the right angle.

Then we saw Laurel on the TV. She flicked right past the channel before she realized what she was seeing, then flicked right back again. Mom tried to get her to change the channel, but it was no good. I wouldn't change the channel if I saw myself on TV, either. It's human nature, isn't it? If you walk past an open door and hear your name, you're going to stop and listen to what's being said.

It was a studio setting, and there was a huge screen with a picture of Laurel, a photo from the press conference. I'm almost sure it was that moment when she smiled when she mentioned me. The caption under the photo was: LAUREL LOGAN—WHAT'S NEXT? Two men in suits were sitting there, talking about my sister. One of them was supposedly a psychologist, an expert in post-traumatic stress. He wore the kind of geeky glasses a person wears when they're perfectly secure in the knowledge that they're not actually a geek. He kept on using the word *damaged*. When he said it the second time, Mom said, "I think that's enough," but Laurel said she wanted to hear it.

"The hard truth is that it will be difficult for Laurel to live a normal life. The details we're starting to hear about what she's been through . . ." He shook his head in disbelief, trying to convey just how awful those details were without actually mentioning any of them.

The news anchor (shiny black hair, jutting chin) leaned forward in his chair. "But surely this is the result we've all been waiting for?" He made my sister's homecoming sound like a football match. In fact, I think I recognized him from a TV show *about* football. So what the hell was he doing sitting at a serious desk for serious people, asking questions about my sister? "Her return is fairy-tale stuff—happily ever after . . . isn't it?" He sat back in his chair. He was pleased with that line, you could tell.

"Of course, it's wonderful news that Laurel's been re-united with her family. No one's going to argue with that. All I'm trying to say is that things are rarely that simple. A girl who has been through years and years of abuse does not just slide back into the family unit as if nothing happened." Dr. Geeky Glasses touched the corner of his glasses. I bet they were brand-new, bought especially for his appearance on this pointless TV show.

Mr. Shiny-Hair Football Pundit thanked Dr. Geeky Glasses before turning back to the camera. "Well, that was a fascinating perspective on this story, which is, let's face it, the story the whole nation is talking about."

The TV screen went dark; Laurel had switched it off. Mom put her hand on Laurel's knee. "Just ignore it, darling. They don't know what they're talking about. They don't know *you*."

My parents and I are used to that sort of thing happening. You're going about your day, maybe listening to the radio or browsing for a magazine at the newsstand, or looking for something to watch on TV. Then *bam!* You hear her name or see her face, and your day is ruined. Laurel's not used to it, though; she was really upset.

She started to cry. "Everything's going to be okay, isn't it? *I'm* going to be okay? I'm home now. This is *home*."

Dad looked like his heart might break in two. Mom had tears in her eyes. "That's right, love. You're home now. Everything's going to be fine. I promise." And she gathered Laurel up in a hug and rocked her like she was a baby.

I went to make more tea.

CHAPTER
14

The party's been going on for too long now, and I suddenly realize I haven't seen Michel in a while. He was clearly uncomfortable from the second he arrived. He's never met Mom's family before, and he was nervous about meeting Laurel. She was great, though; she gave him the biggest hug and said she was looking forward to getting to know him. She even asked if he could teach her some French.

Aunt Eleanor's been a little bit *too* welcoming, trying to flirt with him whenever Mom and Dad aren't looking.

I find Michel in the kitchen, cracking eggs into a bowl. "What are you doing? Hiding in here?"

"I'm not hiding!" I gave him a skeptical look. "Okay, I'm hiding. But have you tasted that dip your mom bought? *Dégoûtant!* She asked me to whip something up." More like she wanted to keep him out of the way so she can play happy family. I'm almost certain Michel knows this, too, but he's better off in the kitchen anyway.

I check I closed the door behind me. "So . . . what do you think of Laurel?"

Michel starts whisking the eggs. "She's lovely. I don't know why I was so nervous!"

"Because you want her to like you. I was the same."

"Do you think she will? Like me?" He avoids eye contact, concentrating on whisking.

"*Everybody* likes you, Michel."

"Everybody except your grandparents." He's not wrong there. I've caught them staring at him a couple of times. God knows what Mom's told them about him.

I nudge him with my elbow. "But Aunt Eleanor seems to like you . . . *a lot.*"

"She terrifies me," Michel whispers.

"Just make sure she doesn't get you alone. You're lucky I found you first."

We joke around about Eleanor clambering over the kitchen counter to get to him. Michel's pouring a thin stream of olive oil into the bowl when he asks me how I'm doing. "It's a big change, yes? Was everything okay at school?"

Mom and Dad didn't bother to ask. I grimace. "It was fine . . . I suppose. The usual gawkers and fakes. Nothing I can't handle."

"Give it time. They'll have to stop eventually."

I shrug. "Martha's making mincemeat out of them."

Michel laughs. "I *bet* she is. That girl can be pretty scary when she puts her mind to it." He's not wrong about that. "You know, I'm really looking forward to next Saturday."

The plan is for Laurel and me to stay at Michel and Dad's place next weekend. Mom tried to say it was too soon, but Dad said, "Too soon for *what*? Our apartment is their home, too, remember?" I was proud of him for saying that, for standing up to her. Anyway, Laurel's looking forward to it.

Dad comes into the kitchen and slips his arm around Michel's waist. "What are you two up to?" Michel holds out a teaspoon of aioli for Dad to taste. "More salt, I think."

Michel rolls his eyes. "You *always* say more salt. It's not good for you!"

Dad sticks his tongue out. "But it makes everything taste *so* delicious. Faith agrees with me, don't you, Faith?"

I hold up my hands and back away. "Don't look at me! I'm not getting involved in your little domestic drama."

Dad laughs and shakes his head. "Okay, Mich, you win. Serve your bland, tasteless aioli and be done with it." Another eye roll from Michel, but he does reach for the salt.

"Laurel was asking where you'd disappeared to, Faith. I think she could do with some backup. It's probably all a bit much for her—too many people."

I tell Dad that I'd thought it was a terrible idea, having everyone here all at once. Dad shrugs. "I know, love. But once your mom gets an idea in her head, there's no stopping her. And I suppose at least this way Laurel gets it over with all in one go."

Mom sticks her head around the door. "Time for photos!"

Oh god.

Laurel poses for pictures with *everyone*. Almost every single permutation is allowed for—Laurel with Gran, Laurel with Gramps, Laurel with Gran *and* Gramps. No one stands too close to Laurel, though. Mom had already warned them that

91

she (understandably) gets anxious about being touched by people she doesn't know—they just need to give her time. Apparently Gran really didn't get it at first (*"But we're family!"*), but Mom did her best to make her understand without going into too much detail.

The photos take ages. Everyone wants an extra shot taken on *their* camera or phone. Michel watches from the doorway while everyone takes pictures of Mom, Dad, Laurel, and me. At least Mom and Dad aren't standing next to each other; Laurel and I form a buffer zone between them.

Mom insists on having a photo of Laurel and me. We stand in front of the fireplace, a couple of inches apart from each other at first. Mom and Dad both take some pictures; Mom has tears in her eyes. Again.

I hate having my photo taken—always have, always will. But I understand that my parents need this and that their need is more important than my awkwardness. Everyone's watching (apart from Eleanor, pouring the last dregs from the last bottle of champagne into her glass).

I sling my arm over Laurel's shoulder and gently pull her closer to me. She hesitates before putting her arm around my waist. I smile a real, proper, beaming smile, not even caring about the gap in my teeth.

Two sisters, reunited at last.

CHAPTER 15

Laurel turns out to be a natural at making macarons. She really enjoys it, too. I was worried it would spoil things, having someone else there. I've always felt like this time with Michel is sort of sacred somehow, but it's actually nice having her with us. Michel turns up the music on the iPod dock—we always listen to cheesy nineties French pop. I know a lot of the words by heart, even though I don't necessarily know what they mean. We get a little production line going, with Michel at the end, piping the mixture onto the baking trays.

Dad was reluctant to go out, which probably should have offended me. He never minded leaving us when it was just Michel and me. But I can't really blame him, can I? He's missed out on thirteen years of Laurel's life; he's got a lot of catching up to do. It's natural that he'd want to spend every possible moment with her. Mom's been the same, even though you can see she's trying desperately not to smother her. She keeps saying that Laurel needs her space, but it's as if she's saying it to remind herself rather than anyone else.

Laurel's only been home for three weeks. Four weeks since she came back to us. The time has gone so fast.

Things have been a bit more normal since the media circus packed up their cameras and microphones and left. There was no reason for them to stay; there were only so many times they could show footage of Laurel leaving the house. Mom hated having them there, practically camped out in our front yard. It didn't seem to bother Laurel, though. I caught her waving to them from my bedroom window one night. I warned her not to, that it was always best to ignore them. After that, I didn't catch her at it again, but I know she still did it because I saw some footage on TV one day.

The police car is still there, parked a few doors down and across the street. The officers inside must be bored out of their minds. They certainly look that way whenever I walk past.

Laurel is gradually learning how the world works. Sometimes it's easy to forget that she's not a normal nineteen-year-old girl who's had a normal, average, *boring* sort of life. Sometimes she acts exactly like you'd expect a nineteen-year-old girl to act. But then something will happen, or she'll ask a question or do something weird, and you'll remember. Like the time she insisted that Barnaby the Bear had a seat at the table for dinner. Mom acted like that was a perfectly normal request. Luckily, Barnaby was clean by that point; Laurel had given him a bath in the sink.

I've been trying to teach her as much as I can, because I hate the idea of her being out *there*—in the big, wide world—without knowing how to deal with the stuff life throws at you. The counseling sessions are helping her, too. She's still seeing the psychologist twice a week, and she likes her new counselor, Penny. Penny takes her out on trips; Laurel's favorite was the zoo. The trip to the movies wasn't so successful. Laurel had a panic attack ten minutes into the movie. No one knows what triggered it. They weren't watching some torture-filled horror flick or a psychological thriller or anything like that—the latest Pixar movie had seemed like a safe choice. Laurel wouldn't talk about it afterward. When she doesn't want to talk about something, she closes her mouth tight, lips pursed. Her chin dimples up, and she looks like a little girl. Penny told us not to push her. She said there are bound to be lots of things Laurel isn't able to deal with yet. We have to give her time.

I don't think it helps that the police won't leave us alone. There are always more questions they want to ask or something that needs clarifying. It feels like a setback every time they come around. It's hard for us to act like a normal family with the constant reminders that we're not one. Mom completely lost her shit with Sergeant Dawkins and another police officer the other day after they arrived unannounced.

Sergeant Dawkins said they really had to get the DNA swab out of the way. She reassured Laurel that it wasn't going to hurt and it would only take a second, but Laurel was having none of it. She backed away from them as if she thought they were going to pounce on her at any second. Mom asked them whether it was really necessary; Sergeant Dawkins said it *was* necessary. That's when Laurel started freaking out again—crying and clutching at her hair. "No no no no no," she muttered under her breath, shaking her head the whole time. "Don't let them touch me!"

Mom tried to calm her down, to reassure her that everything was okay, but it was no good. Mom told me to take Laurel upstairs. As soon as we got to her room, she crawled under the dressing table. That was the first time I saw the den she'd created. You couldn't tell when the stool was in front of the table, but there were a couple of cushions and a blanket down there. It was a tiny space, barely big enough for a child, let alone a grown woman.

Laurel somehow managed to fold her limbs into the space, then she pulled the blanket up to her chin. The blanket was mine; I hadn't even realized it was missing. I kneeled down in front of Laurel and asked if she was okay. She didn't answer. No matter what I said, she wouldn't answer. She stared into space. I crossed my legs and sat right in front of her. "It's okay, Laurel. There's nothing to be scared of anymore. You're safe now. I'm going to stay right here." I babbled some more, talking about what we were going to have for dinner (baked potatoes), the essay I had to write for English (*Twelfth Night*), anything I could think of to bring her back. Eventually, her hand snaked out from under the blanket, reaching for mine. "I won't leave you, Laurel," I said. She squeezed my hand and looked at me. There were tears in her eyes.

"Thank you," she whispered.

It was the first time Laurel had eaten a baked potato since she was a little kid. I made sure it was perfect—plenty of salt, plenty of butter, far too much cheese. She loved it. Mom was still ranting about the police (*How dare they? Why can't they leave her alone after all she's been through? Why don't they just get on with* catching *that monster?*), but Laurel seemed much better. I'd managed to coax her out from her little den, and she'd folded the blanket and put the stool back in front of the dressing table. She was fine by the time Mom came upstairs to check on her. I haven't told Mom about the den; it would only upset her.

Dad comes home just as we're filling the last couple of macarons. He clearly didn't want to stay away a minute longer than he had to. Laurel gives him a little plate with three macarons. She says she saved the best ones for him. (This is a lie. She tried to give them to Tonks, and Michel had to explain that Tonks should only eat cat food, because she's on a special diet for some weird kidney problem.)

Dad smiles widely and eats the macarons, saying they're excellent. He winks at me. "Look out, Faith, you've got some competition! Macaron mastery must run in the family." We all laugh. No one says that our cooking skills can't possibly run in the family, because Laurel was adopted. And Dad keeps quiet about the fact that he hates macarons. He's never tried any of the ones I've made.

Laurel and I stay up late talking. She gets the bed, I get the inflatable mattress. We tossed a coin to see who sleeps where. There's barely enough floor space for the mattress; it fits snugly between the closet and the bed. It was strange at first, sleeping so close to this person I don't really know that well. When I stay at Martha's, I always sleep in the spare room, and she's never slept over at my house. I'm not really sure why.

Laurel lies on her left side, peeking out from under the

duvet. I lie on my right side, trying to pretend the mattress is as comfortable as the bed (*my* bed). She likes to talk after we've turned out the lights. It's not exactly dark; Dad bought another night-light so Laurel wouldn't have to bring Egg with her every weekend. Laurel likes me to tell her stories—but they have to be *true* stories. She never tires of me talking about my childhood or about school or about Thomas.

She was nervous about meeting him. She didn't say so, but I could tell. She kept on checking her hair in the mirror and fidgeting. I'd arranged for Thomas and Martha to come over for pizza and a movie. That seemed like the best way of getting the introductions over and done with. I just wanted all the most important people in my life to know each other and to get along. I even persuaded Mom to go out for the evening; she arranged to meet a friend in town for cocktails. She's never done that before, as far as I know. Maybe this is part of what's "normal" for her, but if so, it's a normal that hasn't existed for the last thirteen years.

Martha and Thomas arrived at the same time. The introductions were a little awkward, but we all laughed at the strangeness of the situation. Martha was really shy at first, which is not like her at all. Only Thomas seemed to be at ease right away. He was polite and charming and even offered to pay for the pizza. I was about to take him up on the offer when Laurel pulled some money from her pocket. Mom had given her the cash before she left. I ignored the niggling feeling that it was odd that Mom hadn't given the money to me. Was this how things were going to be from now on? Laurel is the oldest, after all. She insisted on being the one to call for the pizza; she'd never done that before.

There was a pause and then she said her name. I winced and looked over at Martha—she knew the score. Thomas was too busy flicking through the channels on the TV to notice. Laurel said yes in answer to a question that was almost definitely something along the lines of "Laurel Logan? *The* Laurel Logan?" I went to grab the phone from her, but she waved me away. Her face lit up. "Thank you. That's very kind. Yes . . . Yes. It's wonderful to be back. I really appreciate that." There was another pause as she listened, then she laughed. "Thank you! Have a good evening, Phil. Bye . . . Yes . . . I will do. Bye!" She pressed the button to end the call and then turned to us, triumphant. "He said he'd throw in some free garlic bread and a bottle of Sprite."

"Why?" I asked.

Laurel shrugged and said, "I don't know. He saw me on TV. He said I was pretty."

I wasn't about to lecture Laurel about the dubiousness of getting freebies from strangers who've seen you on TV and "feel a connection with you." (That's what they always say—all the strangers who stop us on the street or who've sent cards and letters and presents. They all feel this mysterious "connection.") Anyway, Thomas was pleased about the Sprite. He raised his glass in Laurel's direction. "Cheers, Laurel!"

My sister smiled at him, and I tried to ignore the pointed look that Martha was aiming in my direction. When the pizzas arrived, Laurel insisted on going to the door. I'm not sure "giving money to the pizza-delivery guy" counts as one of the essential life skills her counselor is always going on about.

There were a couple of awkward moments when we were

trying to choose a film to watch. Thomas scrolled through all the options on Netflix, and Laurel kept on suggesting this film or that film, even though she had no idea what they were about. And that was the problem. You'd be surprised by how many films include abduction or a sinister psychopath or sexual abuse or some kind of family trauma. I kept having to say no to Laurel's suggestions, which made it look like I was being difficult.

Thomas was getting annoyed. He handed me the remote control. "Why don't *you* choose, then?!" So I did. A romantic comedy that none of us had seen. Thomas despises romantic comedies. He despises most films, in fact. Unless they're four hours long and subtitled. He kept on bitching about the one we watched, which was fine because it was dire. It didn't matter, though, because Laurel loved it. She cried at the end and then laughed at herself for crying.

Laurel thanked me when Martha and Thomas had gone home.

"What for?" I nibbled on a leftover pizza crust.

She looked so serious. "Letting me into your world."

I wasn't quite sure what she meant by that. She saw my confusion and started again. "I mean, I really appreciate you letting me spend time with you and your friends. It can't be easy for you . . . having a brand-new sister appear out of nowhere, turning your life upside down." She looked shy all of a sudden, embarrassed by what she was saying.

I put the pizza crust down and shook my head. "You've got it all wrong."

"What do you mean?"

"My life *was* upside down. Before. You've . . ." Was I

really going to say this? It was a line so cheesy it wouldn't have been out of place in the film we'd just watched. I looked at Laurel, and her face was so open and honest and expectant. "You've turned my life the right way up again."

Laurel's smile made me glad I'd said it.

Sometimes it's okay to be cheesy.

CHAPTER
16

It starts almost as soon as we arrive at the market. It's the first time Laurel's come with us. The last two Sundays she stayed home with Dad. Martha wanted to come along, too, which was weird because she's never been remotely interested before. **Maybe next weekend?** I texted her. She didn't reply.

Maureen runs the stall next to us, selling fancy vinegars—strawberry balsamic is her latest obsession. She's really friendly, always cheerful no matter how bad the weather is or how few customers there are.

"Got another little helper today, Michael?" She never calls him Michel; he never bothers correcting her.

Michel nods and says good morning. He's forgotten his beret, so he's looking slightly less French than usual; his ears are already turning red from the cold. Maureen stops lining up bottles of vinegar and comes over to our stall, where Laurel is busy laying out the plastic tablecloth (red and white checked, of course).

"Hi! I'm Maureen, but you can call me Mo. Nice to meet . . . Oh my god!" She turns to look at Michel. "Is this . . . ?" Then she turns back to Laurel. "Are you . . . ?"

Michel stops unloading the car and walks over to Maureen. "Yes, but could you keep it to yourself?"

Maureen snorts. "Keep it to myself? You do know she's probably one of the most famous people in the whole country right now, don't you?"

Laurel is watching this little exchange, yet to say a word. Sometimes I wish I could read her mind.

Maureen asks if she can give Laurel a hug. Laurel shakes her head and apologizes. "You don't need to say sorry. You poor, poor girl," murmurs Maureen, wrapping her arms around herself instead of my sister. I turn away, grabbing my beret from the dashboard.

It's a disaster from the start. The first customer recognizes Laurel, even though she's at the back of the stall wearing my beret, with a scarf covering half of her face. No one knew who we were before. We were just Faith and Michel, purveyors of the finest macarons this side of Paris. I was not Little Laurel Logan's sister and he was not Little Laurel Logan's almost-sort-of stepfather. Maureen keeps shaking her head in wonder, even while she's serving her own customers. She called Michel a dark horse for not telling her about Laurel.

By half past ten, there's a crowd of people around our stall; no one is buying macarons. One woman pushes to the front. She wants her daughter to have her photo taken with Laurel. The daughter (maybe ten years old, stuffing her face with Doritos) doesn't seem bothered either way. Laurel takes her hat off and hands it to me. She goes around to the front of the stall and stands next to the girl. The smile on her face seems to be genuine, but how *can* it be? The woman doesn't even thank her.

More and more people ask to have their picture taken with my sister, as if she's some contestant from a TV talent show. It doesn't matter to them that she's a teenager emerging from an awful ordeal; she's *famous*. They'll be able to go home and tell their families over lunch. They'll say that she's thinner than she looks on TV or prettier or taller or nicer. They'll say that you'd never guess what she'd been through, if you didn't know. They'll say her sister wasn't very friendly, and nowhere near as pretty, and what on earth does she have to be so grumpy about? Shouldn't she be happy that her sister is back?

A creepy-looking old guy tries to put his arm around Laurel, and she jumps as if shocked. This whole thing was clearly a huge mistake. I quickly maneuver myself between Laurel and the old guy and steer her away from him. Michel looks as freaked out as I feel. "I think we should get you home, Laurel. What do you think?"

Laurel nods mutely, and I tell him I'll look after the stall. I hear someone shouting a question at Laurel: "Laurel! Aren't you afraid he's still out there somewhere?"

Someone else—an older woman, it sounds like—says, "Oh my goodness, she's right. He could be watching right now!" It's as if some kind of madness has crept over these people. Maybe when they left their houses this morning they were normal, reasonable people who had an idea of the kinds of things that are appropriate to say, but now they're rude and obnoxious and have no qualms about scaring a girl they don't know.

People are still taking photos when I open the car door and practically push her inside. No doubt they'll be posting them on Twitter and Instagram in a matter of minutes. Michel asks if I'm going to be okay and promises he'll be back as soon as he can. It takes him forever to reverse the car through the crowds, because more and more people stop to see what's going on.

As soon as they're gone, the crowd starts to dissipate. A too-tanned woman in her twenties approaches the front of the stall and asks if she can ask me a question. "I'm not talking about Laurel, so you can just get lost, okay?"

But it turns out she only wanted to ask if I'd recommend the salted caramel over the chocolate and passion fruit. I apologize profusely and end up giving her one of each so she can choose.

Maureen brings me a cup of tea and says she'll watch the stall for a few minutes if I want to get away for a bit. She's a nice person, really. There's just something about Laurel—about her story—that seems to turn people into idiots. I shouldn't blame them; it's not their fault.

I go and sit on the steps in front of the church, sipping my tea even though it's still far too hot. I hope Laurel's okay. My heart is still thumping from the stress of it all.

Dad's furious when he finds out. Laurel cries because she thinks she's done something wrong, so Dad has to reassure her that it's other people he's angry with, not her. He calls them parasites.

Laurel feels bad about how things turned out.

"It's not your fault," Michel and I say at the same time.

Laurel looks down at her lap; her hair falls in front of her face. "It *is,* though, isn't it? If it wasn't for me, none of that would have happened. I should have . . . I don't know. I should have told them to go away instead of posing for pictures."

I kneel down in front of her, trying to get her to look at me. "Hey . . . listen to me. You did the right thing. You *have* to be nice to them. I can just see the headlines if you weren't—'Laurel Logan Swore at My Mom!' " Laurel's mouth twitches into a smile. "But you know what's really cool? *I* don't have to be nice to them. I can say whatever the hell I want because no one's ever going to write a headline about me. So if that kind of thing happens again, I'll handle it, okay?"

Laurel looks up. "It was scary . . . all those people. That man . . ."

"How dare they? How *dare* they?" Dad goes off again, ranting about invasion of privacy. Michel ushers him over to the kitchen, suggesting a cup of tea might be a good idea.

I get up from the floor and sit next to Laurel on the sofa. She thanks me.

"You're going to have to stop thanking me, you know."

"Why?" She looks worried, as if she's just committed some sort of dreadful faux pas.

I smile to let her know that there's nothing to worry about. "You don't have to thank me for every little thing. We're family. We look out for each other."

"That sounds good to me." She bites her lip and tucks a few strands of hair behind her ear. I'm slowly—too slowly—starting to learn some of the signs. Some of the little tics that belong to her. The lip-biting and hair-tucking mean she's unsure about something. (Or maybe they just mean she's got chapped lips and is fed up with her hair falling in front of her face.) She looks to check that Dad and Michel aren't listening, then whispers, "I'm sorry I haven't been here to look out for *you*." A knotty lump sprouts in my throat. "That's what big sisters are supposed to do, isn't it? They're supposed to *be* there. And I wasn't."

"You're here now, and that's all that matters." This is a lie. It all matters—every little bit of it. But the truth is there's nothing we can do to change the past. I surprise myself by making a silent vow to be the best sister possible—to do everything in my power to make up for those lost years. It's the least that I can do, really.

CHAPTER 17

Silent vows are ridiculous. You shouldn't have to keep a promise you only made inside your head. It shouldn't count if you didn't actually say it out loud. But for some reason I feel like I have to keep my promise to Laurel, which is why I find myself in a TV studio, in front of an audience of giddy middle-aged women, sitting on an overstuffed sofa next to Mom and Dad. Laurel gets her own chair, right next to Cynthia Day. It is my worst nightmare, fully realized.

Dad didn't want to do it, either, even though he and Mom had appeared on *The Cynthia Day Show* twelve years ago to try to drum up publicity for Laurel's case, which was waning as the first anniversary approached.

We're doing this for Laurel. I just have to keep reminding myself of that, with every banal, pointless question Cynthia asks, trying to extract tears from us. That's her specialty: making people cry, then showing how much she empathizes with them by crying, too. For some bizarre reason (and completely unbeknownst to me, otherwise I'd have done something about it), Laurel has been watching *The Cynthia Day Show* religiously for the past month or so. A producer got in touch with Mom right after Laurel came home, asking if Laurel would go on the show. She said no, but she must have told Laurel about it, which was probably why Laurel started watching. When the producer got in touch a month later, offering an obscene amount of money for the whole family to appear on the show, Laurel really, really wanted to do it. So we sat down as a family to discuss the pros and cons, which was a waste of time, as the only thing that really mattered to any of us was what Laurel wanted. Her eyes were bright and brimming with excitement as she talked about wanting to see a real, live TV studio, and wanting to meet Cynthia (*She's so nice!*). The decision was made. The money would go straight into a bank account for Laurel.

Thomas was appalled. He couldn't fathom why I would agree to be a part of something like this. He only stopped going on about it when I snapped at him, telling him he had no idea what I was going through. He clammed up, barely spoke for the rest of the day. Martha was more supportive, which was reassuring because I feel like I've barely seen her recently. We've still been hanging out together at school, but I've been spending so much time with Laurel that Martha's fallen by the wayside a bit. I haven't been to her house since Laurel came back, and she's invited me at least four times. Martha understands, though—she gets it. I've still replied to *most* of her texts. And she's been to our house a couple of times, so it's not like I've been neglecting her.

It's too hot under these lights. I'm sweating. No one else seems bothered by the heat. Mom and Dad have been on

TV loads of times, so this is nothing new to them. They didn't even seem nervous. And Laurel was just excited to be here. When we came on set earlier, she pointed out a picture that had been drawn by a kid the week before. Laurel told me all about it.

"It was amazing! You should have seen it, Faith. He was only little—maybe five or six. And he sat on the floor and drew a portrait of Cynthia while she interviewed his parents. It only took him a few minutes, and then Cynthia cried when she saw it and said she would treasure it forever, and the little boy just shrugged and said she should probably sell it. Oh my goodness, it was so funny. The people in the audience were going crazy!" Laurel realized I wasn't reacting to this story with as much enthusiasm as she was expecting and asked me if I was okay. I told her I was nervous. When Mom and Dad had asked, I said I was fine. For some reason I don't mind admitting weakness to Laurel. She put her arm around me and said there was no need to be nervous. "Cynthia is so nice. There was this woman on the show yesterday, and she'd started this charity that . . ." I tuned out.

The wardrobe woman tutted when she saw me. "No, no, no, that won't do at all." The clothes that Mom and Dad and Laurel were wearing were all fine, apparently, but mine were not. I'd wanted to be comfortable, so I'd opted for one of my favorite sweaters—a black V-neck. There's nothing wrong with the sweater, but the wardrobe woman said it "wouldn't do me any favors on camera." I asked what she meant, but she wouldn't elaborate. That's how I've ended up wearing an orange top with purple stripes on the sleeves. When Laurel saw me in it, she said I looked nice, so I didn't kick up a fuss.

Cynthia Day came into the dressing room half an hour before the show started. The first thing I noticed was the smell that wafted into the room with her—the most cloying perfume you could imagine, heavy and unbearably floral. The second thing I noticed was her gravity-defying hair. Bouffant and *then* some. It doesn't move when she moves her head—not even a little bit. Laurel whispered, "Oh my god, it's really her," under her breath while Cynthia was saying hello to Mom and Dad. "It's okay. Remember she's just a normal person," I whispered back.

"She's a *famous* person."

"So are you," I reminded her.

Then Cynthia turned her attention to us, and she clapped her hands together. "Laurel! I can't tell you what an *honor* it is that you agreed to come on my little show." She went to kiss my sister on both cheeks. I thought Laurel might freak out, but she didn't. She just stiffened slightly, waiting for it to be over. Progress, I guess.

Cynthia turned to me. "And this must be Faith. Thank you so much for being here." She didn't kiss me, and I was glad because the choking perfume was even worse close up. Cynthia perched on the edge of a table and told us what to expect. She said there was no need to be nervous, that the questions wouldn't be anything we hadn't heard a million times before. "Just tell your story. That's all my audience wants to hear." And then she was gone. Unfortunately the stench of her perfume remained.

The audience is 95 percent women. They lean forward in their seats, straining to get closer to Laurel. They nod when

111

she speaks and turn to each other and smile in a sad, sympathetic sort of way. Laurel's doing a fantastic job. She takes her time answering Cynthia's questions, thinking before she speaks. She looks over at Mom and Dad and me every so often as if to check that she's doing okay; Mom and Dad nod encouragingly.

Cynthia introduces some footage on the big screen behind her. "As you all know, we are very lucky to have had the Logans on our little show before. I just want to take a moment to remind you of what they've been through. Twelve years ago, Olivia and John sat on this very sofa." She smiles and corrects herself. "Well, not this *actual* sofa. This sofa is brand-new—I chose it myself. . . . Do you like it?" The audience members clap, showing their approval for Cynthia's choice of furnishings. "Anyway, where was I?" This is one of Cynthia's tricks—acting ditzy. I guess she thinks it puts people at ease.

The footage shows Mom and Dad on a sofa very much like the one we're sitting on now. Cynthia's interior-decorating tastes clearly haven't changed in over a decade. I've seen this interview before in one of my YouTube missions. I only watched it once, though, because it wasn't very interesting. My parents looked sad and worn-out. There had been no new developments in the case. They talked about how it felt to have been without Laurel for a whole year. Mom said she couldn't put it into words, and Cynthia nodded even though you could tell that she really, really wanted Mom to at least *try.*

The clip finishes with Cynthia talking straight to the camera. "Laurel, if you're watching this . . . your parents love you very much, sweetheart." That was just weird—the idea that Laurel would be watching. I think she probably said that on the spur of the moment, unlike everything else, which seemed to be so carefully orchestrated. It made her look stupid.

The screen goes blank, and Cynthia says nothing for a moment or two, letting everyone stare at my parents and marvel at how different they look today.

"So, Laurel, how does it feel being back with your family?"

Laurel shakes her head, beaming widely. "It feels like a miracle." The audience loves that. They clap and whoop and cheer. Everybody loves a happy ending.

Cynthia smiles and waits for Laurel to elaborate. Laurel takes a deep breath and looks over at us. "I used to dream about it. About seeing my family again. Those dreams were *so* real. And then I would wake up in total darkness . . . in that basement, and it felt like my heart was breaking. It happened all the time at first—the dreams. But over the years, they happened less and less until I just . . . stopped dreaming." She bows her head and there's total silence in the studio, until someone in the audience sneezes and ruins the moment completely. Laurel looks up at Cynthia again. "All I know is that seeing them again, after all this time, well, it's even better than those dreams I had. Knowing that they never forgot me, knowing that they never gave up hope . . . it's"—she shrugs and holds up her hands—"a miracle! Sorry, I'm repeating myself. I'm not so good with words. Sorry." She might be blushing, but it's impossible to tell under all the makeup she's wearing.

Cynthia puts a hand on Laurel's knee. Her nail polish is burgundy, and she has rings on almost every finger. A huge diamond adorns her ring finger. (She just got engaged to a man half her age; it will be her third marriage.) "I think we can all agree that you're doing just fine, Laurel."

Laurel smiles. "Thank you. Can I just say . . . I'm such a big fan of your show. I watch every day. Sometimes even twice!"

The audience makes an *Awwww* sound; it's as if each person has been programmed to react in exactly the same way. "Well, that is very lovely to hear." Cynthia keeps her hand on Laurel's knee. "And can *I* just say . . . I'm such a big fan of yours!" She laughs and looks at the audience, who is lapping this up.

Cynthia asks some more questions, varying the tone between light and dark. A question about clothes (*I love your top. You must be having so much fun, going shopping, doing the usual things girls love to do?*) is swiftly followed by one about Laurel's captor (*If you could say something to him right now— anything at all—what would that be?*).

I can feel Mom tense up beside me. I don't think the police would be too happy about it; what if Laurel's answer provokes him in some way? What if he decides to come back and take her from us again? I've been having nightmares about that. I haven't told anyone. I dream about Laurel and me in the front yard of the Stanley Street house, but this time we're all grown up. We're sitting on a polka-dot picnic blanket, eating BLT baguettes. A man opens the front gate, and it creaks on its hinges. He stands over us and holds out his hand to Laurel. She looks up at him, and she's not scared.

I look up at him, too, but for some reason his face is blurred, like Vaseline smeared on glass. Laurel takes his hand, stands up, and walks away. The gate creaks again. I start to cry, but I'm not sure why. I think I've lost something. I usually wake up the moment I realize what's happened—when the horror engulfs me.

Laurel's answer to Cynthia's stupid question about Smith isn't so bad after all. "I have nothing to say to him." She has a neutral expression on her face, and her voice has a neutral tone. It's perfectly judged.

Cynthia nods, as if this was the answer she was expecting. "I bet you don't." A hush descends on the room, and Cynthia shakes her head slowly, trying to convey sympathy for Laurel and disgust for her captor, all at once. "I just *bet* you don't."

Cynthia turns towards the camera. "Now we're going to take a short break, but don't go anywhere. When we come back, we'll be talking to Olivia and John about their ordeal, and let's not forget Faith, reunited with her big sister at long last. See you in three!"

CHAPTER
18

Cynthia tells us we're doing great. "This is *gold*," she says. I presume someone has switched the microphones off, because Cynthia burps. Not a full-on belch—it's slightly more ladylike than that. She smiles and apologizes. She leans toward us and confides, "Cauliflower always gives me gas, but do I ever learn? No, I do not!" I find this far too funny, because apparently being on live TV reduces my sense of humor to that of an eight-year-old boy. Cynthia looks at me as if *I'm* the odd one for laughing so hard.

Dad asks how I'm feeling and I tell him I'm okay. I'm not, of course. I'm unbelievably nervous. Cynthia's going to talk to me, and I'm going to be expected to say words that make sense, maybe even stitch some of them together into whole sentences. I really, really need the toilet, but there's not a whole lot I can do about that now.

I keep thinking about Martha, sitting at home watching me humiliate myself. And Thomas, *not* watching. I can't believe he said he wasn't going to watch. Part of me is glad, relieved that he won't see me wearing this disgusting top and smiling and simpering at Cynthia Day. But I'm also a little bit hurt. He should *want* to watch; it's not every day your girlfriend appears on the third-biggest talk show in the country. He should have said he wanted to watch, and I should have told him not to. *That's* how it should have worked.

I wonder if Penny's watching, too. We talked about it at our last family counseling session. She let Laurel go on and on about this stupid show, wasting our time when we should be talking about other things. Anyway, Penny didn't come right out and say that she thought it was a terrible idea, but I bet she disapproves. She's just too busy listening and nodding and oozing empathy all over the place to say how she really feels.

A girl wearing black rushes onstage—a makeup ninja. She powders my face and runs off just in time for the count-down to the end of the commercials. No one else's face needs powdering, because no one else is sweating as much as I am.

Cynthia talks to Mom and Dad next. She talks to them as if they're still together, making no reference to the fact that Dad doesn't live with us. There's no mention of Michel, or Dad's "lifestyle," as some of the papers insist on calling it. She asks what it's like having Laurel back home, and they say it's wonderful. At one point, Mom cries and Dad gives her a handkerchief.

An image pops up on the screen behind Cynthia, and she turns to look at it. It's the last age-progressed image of Laurel; the one that was supposed to show what she might look like at age fifteen. I watch as the people in the audience stare up at the picture, then stare at Laurel, then back at the picture again. Then I do the same. It's not as bad as I thought, actually. But the girl in the picture has a bland, regular sort of face. It's the kind of face that's easy to forget. Laurel does not have a forgettable face. There's something about her face that makes you keep looking. It's the eyes, I think. Of course, it doesn't help that the picture on the screen is in black and white, while the real Laurel is full color, not to mention 3-D.

Cynthia comments on the image, saying it didn't do Laurel justice, but that the police had done the best they could. She asks Dad how he feels about the police, knowing that they weren't able to find Laurel and don't seem to be able to find her captor despite receiving "literally hundreds of calls from the public."

Dad is at his diplomatic best, saying, "Olivia and I are grateful for all the hard work they've put in—and continue to put in—every single day." Cynthia tries to get him to say something juicy, tries to put words in his mouth (those words being "police incompetence"), but he's a pro at this.

Finally, Cynthia turns to me. I wonder what would happen if I vomited right now. Would it be best to just puke on the floor in front of me, or should I try puking over the back of the sofa? Would they cut to a commercial break?

I'm concentrating so hard on not vomiting that I only start listening toward the end of Cynthia's question, which doesn't appear to be an actual question. ". . . *such* an appropriate name. That's what we all clung to, wasn't it? *Faith*."

I don't roll my eyes even though I really, really want to.

She's not the first person to talk about my name like that. People think it's so poetic; I think they're fools.

"So tell me, Faith, what's it been like for *you*?" She smiles encouragingly.

All eyes are on me; I preferred it when all eyes were on Laurel. "Good . . . it's been good." Oh god. Could I possibly sound *more* stupid?

Cynthia laughs, but not in a mean way. She turns to the audience. "Well, I suppose that just about sums it up! Now, Faith, I have a big sister of my own—hello, Diane, if you're watching!—and if there's one thing I know for sure, it's that I couldn't cope without her. What does it feel like, having your big sister back after all this time?"

I look over at Laurel. She's sitting back in her armchair, looking perfectly at home. She winks, but no one else can see because her face is angled away from the cameras and the audience. It puts me at ease, that wink. It says, *This is all bullshit, but let's play along.* I start to relax.

"It's the best thing that's ever happened to me."

While Cynthia's saying, "Bless!" and the audience is going, "Awwww," and Dad's patting my leg, I examine that statement from all possible angles, picking it up with tweezers and looking at it under a microscope. I come to the conclusion that it's actually the truth. Having Laurel back *is* the best thing that's ever happened to me. This surprises me more than it should.

Laurel's grinning at me, and I grin right back at her. Cynthia asks me what it was like growing up "in the shadow of this terrible crime." She says it can't have been easy for me. A couple of months ago, I'd have jumped at the chance to tell

119

my side of the story for a change, to moan about how awful it's been, how no one could ever understand what it was like.

Today I shrug. "It was nothing compared to what my sister went through. Mom and Dad did their best to protect me from it all, to try to make sure that I had a happy childhood."

Cynthia pounces. "And did you?"

I glance at Mom, then Dad. "I did."

I half expect Mom to call me a liar, which would certainly make for interesting viewing. Instead I hear her catch her breath. She's crying again. Cynthia's not going to miss an opportunity like that.

"Olivia, are you okay? Can you tell us why that makes you so emotional?"

Mom breathes deeply, trying to pull herself together. "It . . . means a lot, to hear that. We tried so hard to make sure Faith had a normal childhood, but it was hard. And sometimes I think . . . I think we failed her."

I turn to look at her and reach past Dad to take her hand in mine. "You didn't." And suddenly Mom and I are standing and hugging, and it's the oddest thing to be hugging your mother in front of a studio audience, knowing that millions of people are watching all over the country. It's even odder not to feel embarrassed about it.

Cynthia appears to wipe away a tear; she's loving this. She asks me a few more questions, and it's really not that bad if you just focus on what she's asking and forget about the rest. I end up almost enjoying myself. It's quite nice having someone absolutely focused on you, asking about your feelings and opinions. It makes you feel like you *matter.*

Cynthia turns to Laurel. "And what's it like for you, getting to know your baby sister again? Is she different from how you expected her to be?"

Laurel takes a moment to think. I probably should have done more of that—weighing up what I was going to say instead of just blurting out the first thing that came to mind. "In some ways, Faith's exactly how I expected her to be. I used to lie awake at night and think about what she would be doing and how she would look. It got harder, as the years passed. But she was always here." Laurel taps her temple. "I never let go of her." There's a perfect pause and Cynthia nods her approval. "But Faith's also different from how I expected her to be. I could never have hoped for her to be so supportive and kind and loving toward someone she can barely even remember. Having a sister like that is . . . Well, I feel like the luckiest girl in the world." Cheers and clapping from the audience. "She's teaching me so much—it feels like she's the older sister and I'm the younger one!"

Laurel looks at me when she says, "I just wish everyone was lucky enough to have a sister like Faith."

CHAPTER
19

My English teacher, Mrs. Truss, asks me to stay behind after class. I'm sure she's going to complain about the essay I handed in last week—the one I'd rushed so I could teach Laurel how to make spaghetti carbonara. Instead, she asks me what Cynthia Day is *really* like. She empathizes with her because she's been married three times, too. Mrs. Truss thinks that it might be third time lucky—for her and for Cynthia.

Laney Finch finds me at lunchtime; she *always* finds me. She's alone this time. She tells me how beautiful my sister is (*like,* really *beautiful*), and how brave she was to go on *The Cynthia Day Show.* "If I'd been through something like that, I think I'd want to hide away forever." I nod instead of telling her how offensive she's being. As an afterthought, Laney says, "You were really good. . . . It was nice to see you looking so happy. And I *loved* your top. Where's it from?"

Martha was less kind. She called me when we were driving back from the TV studio. "What's with the personality transplant? Did they give you some happy pills or something? Is that one of Cynthia's little tricks?" Martha took my silence as a sign to continue bitching. "And that top? Jesus Christ, I'm not sure my eyes will ever recover."

I didn't really mind Martha mocking me—not much, anyway. After the madness of the previous few hours, it was refreshingly normal. I couldn't say too much in the car, though. Mom and Dad were thrilled with how it had all gone. "Better than I expected," Dad had said when they took off his microphone. Laurel had barely said a word since we'd got into the car. Mom and Dad didn't seem to notice, but I nudged her and mouthed, "Are you okay?" while Mom was busy talking about Cynthia. Laurel nodded and whispered that she was just tired. She spent the rest of the trip staring out the window.

We picked up some Thai food on the way home, calling in the order from the car when we were twenty minutes away. I asked Laurel if she wanted to make the call, but she shook her head. I wasn't worried—not exactly. It had been a lot to process—all that attention, all those crazy women in the audience with their damp eyes and scrunched-up tissues.

As soon as Dad left, I went up to my room to call Michel. I couldn't imagine what it must be like to watch the person you love on national TV, acting like you don't exist. He sounded exhausted. I can always tell when Michel is tired because he sounds more French. It's the only time he ever struggles to find the English word he's after, and it frustrates the hell out of him. He prides himself on his perfect English.

I asked him what he thought of the show; he'd taken the afternoon off work to watch it. But it turned out there had been an emergency at the hospital—a Rhodesian ridgeback had eaten a shoe (brown leather brogue), and Michel had been called in for the surgery. So Michel had missed the show; I was glad. He asked how it went, and he said he was proud of me. "For what?" I asked.

"For going on that awful show in the first place. You didn't have to do that. No one would have blamed you." He was wrong about that; Mom would have blamed me.

We talked for a little while, about the Rhodesian ridge-back (doing well, expected to make a full recovery) and the cooking show we both watch (not doing so well after a format change for the new series). It was nice to talk about something that didn't involve Laurel. I heard Michel say hi to Dad when he arrived home, but he didn't hang up until he was quite sure that there was nothing more I wanted to say. He asked whether he should watch *The Cynthia Day Show* online, and I told him not to bother. I hoped curiosity wouldn't get the better of him.

Curiosity gets the better of *me,* and I watch the whole show again a couple of days later. It's strange, how different it is from the way I remember. It's all a bit soft-focus, for one thing. Cynthia probably insists on that so her wrinkles don't show up on camera. It's excruciatingly embarrassing, watching myself—and, even worse, hearing myself speak. I almost don't recognize that girl wearing the orange top and sitting up too straight. At least you can't tell I was sweating profusely, thanks to the makeup ninja. Laurel comes across really well, although she looks at the camera a lot instead of looking at Cynthia. It feels like she's talking directly to the viewer sometimes. I can just imagine people up and down the country, snacking on chips or chocolate chip cookies, watching my sister. It's no wonder people feel like they know her.

Since Laurel came home, people have been sending emails and cards and presents. Mom set up a PO box years ago, so luckily most stuff goes straight there. But some people always manage to find out our address. It's not exactly hard to figure out after watching all the outside broadcasts filmed on our doorstep. Google Maps Street View is the stalker's friend. Not that these are stalkers; they're just people who sometimes come across that way. Laurel's had seven marriage proposals since she came back. What kind of weirdo sends a letter or email asking to marry some girl they've never met before? Three of them sent photos. One of the guys was buck naked.

Mom doesn't tell Laurel about the crazies. She goes through every bit of correspondence before it gets anywhere near Laurel. Lots of people are still sending teddy bears, forgetting that Laurel is a grown woman now. At least Barnaby has plenty of new friends.

Many of the letters say the exact same words: *I feel like I know you.* I would never dream of writing to a stranger and saying something like that. Laurel doesn't seem to find it as odd as I do. She says it's nice that people are so thoughtful. Mom says that the people who write these letters usually have some reason to write them—some tragedy or misfortune in their own lives that leads them to project their feelings onto Laurel. I'm not convinced.

Laurel has replied to some of the letters—just a short note to thank them. Mom bought her a hundred thank-you cards, and she's already written thirty or so. It will take her forever at this rate, so last night we went on the laptop. I helped Laurel set up a template of a basic thank-you letter that she can amend as she sees fit; then she can print them off in the study and sign them. She wasn't convinced at first.

"Wouldn't people prefer to have a handwritten card? It seems more . . . personal." She came around to my way of thinking when I pointed out exactly how many letters she had to reply to, and the fact that she could copy and paste the template into emails, too. We set up two email accounts— one for her to reply to all the emails that were pouring in every day, and a personal one. Mom's going to start forwarding her the messages that aren't weird or offensive or upsetting or perverted, and she'll keep intercepting the mail from the PO box. Hopefully the deluge will die down soon. Interest will wane; it always does.

I like helping her with this sort of thing; it's nice to feel useful. Laurel *needs* me; no one has ever needed me before. Thomas never says that he needs me. He never says *I can't live without you,* or *I would die if you left me,* or any of those devastatingly romantic/downright weird things people in love are supposed to say. But then I suppose I never say that sort of thing to him, either.

Laurel doesn't know what to do with her personal email account. She has no one to email. "You will," I told her. She smiled, but I could tell she didn't believe me.

I was brushing my teeth last night when I realized she was standing in the doorway, watching me. "How do you get friends?"

I spat out the toothpaste foam and watched it as it trickled down the drain. "What do you mean?"

Laurel was wearing her pajamas—an old T-shirt of mine that she'd taken a liking to and a pair of red-checked pajama bottoms. Her face was scrubbed free of makeup, and her hair was twisted into a messy ponytail. She looks better without makeup; I think it makes her look too old. She's a better color already—she was pale as a ghost when she came back. I bet she tans really well in the summer. She straightened the towels hanging on the rail. Mom's always doing that, too. Like mother, like daughter. "How do you become friends with someone? How do you even find people to be friends with in the first place?"

I splashed cold water on my face, giving myself time to think. Laurel has a lot of questions about a lot of things, and I try to answer each one as best I can. I only lost my patience with her once, when I really needed the bathroom and she was asking me to explain something about the Internet and search engines. I snapped at her—nothing too bad; I just asked if she could give the constant questions a rest for *one* minute. She took a step back, bumping into the banister, and for an awful second I imagined her plummeting over the side and breaking her neck on the stairs. I apologized straightaway, but the stricken look was slow to leave her face. The trouble was, I was still bursting, so I told her to wait outside the bathroom. When I came out, she was gone. I found her sitting on the floor behind the door in her bedroom. I apologized again, but she said nothing. She only started talking to me when I said that Thomas would be a better person to ask about computer stuff. I think he must have been a real computer geek before he decided that being into poetry and philosophy was probably cooler. (If not cooler, certainly more likely to attract girls—not that he would ever admit that was one of the deciding factors.) She asked me if I would ask him to help her. Then she apologized for asking questions all the time. That made me feel lower than low, so I apologized to *her* and she apologized to me again, and we eventually laughed and agreed to stop apologizing. Now I try to answer every single one of her questions, whether my bladder is about to explode or not.

How *do* you become friends with someone? It's not something I've ever been particularly good at. It was okay when I was little, before I realized that kids usually only wanted to talk to me because of Laurel. I had plenty of friends up until the age of eight or nine. That was when things changed. That was when girls started whispering about me and boys started teasing me. That was when some of the girls in my class started playing a game at recess. One of them would pretend to be Laurel, playing innocently in the front garden (a patch of grass in the courtyard, well away from any patrolling teachers). One of them would be "The Shadow," who had to try to get to her by dodging past the other girls (who were supposed to be "The Detectives"). They asked me to play once; I said no.

Martha was the first real friend I ever had. She wasn't interested in Laurel, which was enough to make me interested in her. She made me laugh. I didn't realize how important laughter was until I was friends with Martha. My childhood hadn't exactly been brimming with the stuff.

Thinking about Martha made me feel bad. I suppose I have been neglecting her a little. Thomas too. But weirdly,

I don't feel as bad about him, even though I probably should. Things will get back to normal soon, though. I'm sure of it. I'm just still trying to get used to this new life of mine.

Laurel was waiting for an answer.

"I suppose you usually make friends at school. You find someone who likes the same things you do and you talk to them." Laurel had only had one year of school before she was snatched from us. "And I suppose it works the same way when you leave school. I don't know. . . . Maybe you have a hobby and you meet up with other people with the same hobby. Or you can meet people on the Internet. There's a girl at school who met her best friend *and* her boyfriend on an online forum for her favorite band." Then I had to explain about Internet forums. I didn't tell Laurel that there are a lot of forums about *her*. They used to be all about the abduction and solving "the crime that shocked the nation," but they've diversified since she came home. I found one the other day that was all about the clothes she wears. People post photos of her and then comment on "the style choices of the lovely Laurel Logan." It no longer surprises me that people have nothing better to do with their lives.

"I'd like to have friends." Laurel didn't say this in a self-pitying way. She said it in exactly the same way I would say that I'd like to have a cookie with my cup of tea.

"You *do* have friends. You have me."

She shook her head. "That's different."

"You have Thomas and Martha."

"They're *your* friends."

"They're *our* friends now."

Laurel wasn't sure about that; she wasn't sure they liked

her. Of course they liked her, I said. I promised Laurel she would have plenty of friends. It would just take a bit of time, that's all. And she would have to be careful about who she trusted, because some people would want to be friends with her because she's Laurel Logan—the Girl Who Came Home. It will take a while before she can spot them, though—the ones who are interested for all the wrong reasons. But I'll be there, watching. I won't let anyone take advantage of her.

CHAPTER 20

Thomas and Laurel are sitting at the kitchen table, shoulders almost touching. He's explaining something exceptionally boring about the Internet while he taps away on my laptop. Laurel is hanging on his every word, nodding and asking questions. Thomas is loving it; boys seem to really like *knowing* things.

I made them both tea and even put out a plate of cookies. That was two hours ago. Since then I've read the magazine section of the Sunday paper, two chapters of the new Stephen King book, and an article about Laurel on my phone. The article raves about her "performance" on *The Cynthia Day Show*. I don't like how the journalist calls it a performance—*appearance* is surely the right word.

I can't seem to settle. It's weird not being at Dad and Michel's. They've gone to France for a long weekend. A couple of days in Paris before they go visit my grandmother in Nice. I think it will be good for them to get away for a bit. Hopefully Dad will stop neglecting Michel. He seems to be over here all the time these days. Whenever I ask where Michel is, Dad says he's at work or out with friends. According to Dad, Michel is perfectly fine, busy getting on with his life. And according to Michel, that's actually the case. He says he doesn't mind, that he understands that Dad wants to spend as much time as possible with Laurel.

Martha texts and asks if I want to meet up. I'm about to say that I can't make it, but then I change my mind and tell her I'll meet her at our favorite coffee shop in half an hour. Thomas looks panicked when I announce that I'm leaving them to it. "But . . . but . . . I thought we were going to . . ." He can't finish this sentence, because he can't very well say that I'd hinted we would have some "alone time" after he'd helped Laurel with computer stuff.

We haven't had sex again—not since the night before Laurel was found at Stanley Street. We haven't even been on a date. He's been really patient; he understands that Laurel's my priority right now. But I'm well aware that his patience has its limits. And I *do* want to spend more time with him, just as soon as Laurel is properly settled in. I *do* want to be alone with him. Definitely before his birthday. And definitely *not* in his van.

I'm grabbing my coat from the hall closet when it suddenly hits me that maybe Laurel doesn't want to be left alone with Thomas. She's only met him a couple of times—he's little more than a stranger to her. I kick myself for not thinking this through. "Laurel? Can you come here for a second?"

She pops her head around the living room door.

"Are you . . . ? I can stay if you like. I don't have to go out. I didn't think . . ."

132

Confusion clouds her features for a moment before she nods in understanding. "No, you should go. It's fine. Really. I'll be fine." I watch her closely, searching for any hint of a lie. "You don't need to be so overprotective!" She smiles.

"I know. I'm sorry. I just thought . . . you haven't been alone with a—"

"Don't." The word comes out harsh and flat, but she does her best to soften it with a hand on my arm. "Faith, I said it was fine, okay?" She looks over her shoulder, then turns back to me and whispers, "I like him. I trust him."

"Why?"

She smiles as if that's a stupid question. "Because you do."

I told Laurel to text me if she wants me to come home. She rolled her eyes and said, "Yes, *Mom!*" Then she hugged me and told me to have fun with Martha.

But it doesn't turn out to be very much fun at all. It starts to go wrong almost immediately, when Martha tells me that the girl serving the coffee recognized me from *The Cynthia Day Show* and asked her if it would be okay to ask for my autograph.

"Bullshit! You're lying." I risk a glance at the girl in question. She's rearranging the muffins on the top shelf of the cabinet.

"Don't stare! She'll know we're talking about her!"

I ignore Martha. The girl doesn't look over—not even once. "You're hilarious, Martha. Really."

"I'm not lying! She wanted to know if I'd met Laurel. I told her to mind her own business . . . *after* she'd made the coffee. I didn't want to risk a serving of saliva in my latte. Look, you're just going to have to face facts: you're famous now." She sips her drink but fails to hide the sly smile on her face. Normally I don't mind Martha, but I'm really not in the mood for her snarkiness right now.

Things take a turn for the worse when I tell her I've left Laurel and Thomas at home together. She doesn't say anything, but she raises her eyebrows and widens her eyes.

"What?" I ask.

Martha tears off a piece of blueberry muffin and pops it into her mouth. Then she gestures that she can't talk because her mouth is full. I wait, impatiently, before repeating the question.

"Nothing!" All wide-eyed innocence.

I wait her out.

"It's nothing . . . honestly. I was just thinking that if *I* had a boyfriend, and if I had a sister who looked like Laurel . . . well, I probably wouldn't . . ."

Martha has never had a boyfriend. "Probably wouldn't what?"

She shrugs and takes a sip of coffee. I don't think she has any idea of how infuriating she's being. "I probably wouldn't want to leave them alone together."

I knew that was what she was going to say, but that doesn't make it any easier to hear. It's not the words themselves, but the fact that Martha's the one saying them. It's the kind of stupid thing I wouldn't be surprised to hear spouting from Laney Finch's mouth. *"What?"*

"You *asked*! I was just being honest." She's looking at me as if *I'm* the unreasonable one. Then she tries to backtrack.

134

"It was a stupid thing to say. I'm sorry. I wasn't thinking. Of course it's fine to—"

"What the hell is *wrong* with you? As if Thomas is going to pounce on my sister, after everything she's been through! *God,* Martha." I realize too late that I'm speaking far too loudly. People are staring—including the girl behind the counter.

Martha seems taken aback by my reaction. "That's not what I was . . . Look, can we just talk about something else? This is silly."

"You're the one who started it."

Normally she'd say something sarcastic—that I have the argumentative skills of a five-year-old, perhaps—but today she just apologizes. I accept her apology and we try to move on.

It's the strangest thing, but I can't think of anything to say. I'm still furious about what she said. The thought of anything happening between Thomas and Laurel is too ridiculous for words, so I should have just been able to laugh it off. But for some reason it's lodged in my brain like a splinter. I look across the table at Martha, who's looking back at me, waiting. What do we usually talk about? I can't even remember. I can't remember how to have a conversation that isn't about Laurel.

"Um . . . how's it going with your mom's job?"

One look at Martha's face confirms that this was the wrong thing to ask. She puts her mug down. "She got laid off last month."

"Last *month*? Why didn't you tell me?"

"I don't know. I tried, but you were so busy with Laurel

135

and everything. I told you she had that meeting with her boss, remember?"

"No, you didn't." Did she? Maybe she did. The day before Laurel came home. A text message.

"Look, I'm not going to argue with you, Faith. You've had a lot to deal with recently. I *get* that. I don't blame you."

Why does Martha saying that she doesn't blame me give me the distinct impression that she *does*? "I'm sorry." An apology seems like the best way to defuse the situation.

Martha downs the last of her drink. "It's okay. Thomas was really nice about it."

It feels like ice water trickling through my veins. People always say that anger is hot, but for me it's so cold that it burns. "You talked to Thomas about it?" My words are clipped, my mouth barely able to open enough to force them out.

She shrugs, and it seems like the sole intention of that shrug is to infuriate me. "Well, *yeah.* I had to talk to some-one."

"And I suppose that someone had to be my boyfriend?"

Another shrug. Martha looks up at the wall next to us, suddenly interested in the blander-than-bland art.

I grab my phone and put it in my bag. "I have to go."

Martha looks at me, and for a second I think she's going to apologize, but instead she says, "Since when have you been bothered about me talking to Thomas? Why are you being so weird, Faith?"

I stand and look down at Martha. Her hair is a mess. She really should think about at least running a brush through it once in a while. Maybe then she might be able to get a boyfriend of her own instead of trying to borrow mine. I want to tell her to fuck off. I want to tell her that she has no idea what I've been going through, and that I *do* care about what's going on in her life, and I *do* care about her mom losing her job.

In the end, all I say is, "I'll see you at school."

"Fine." She gets her phone out and pretends to look at something.

I walk out of the coffee shop with as much dignity as I can muster. It was hardly a screaming fight. There were no tears, there was no swearing, there were no real insults to speak of, but it's still the first argument Martha and I have ever had. Why did it have to happen now, when things are going so well with Laurel?

CHAPTER
21

I'm not jealous about Martha talking to Thomas. I'm not. I've always liked the fact that they get along okay. It makes things easier for me. But the thought of her confiding in him doesn't sit well. That's not meant to happen. They are supposed to talk about books and films and people at school— not things that actually *matter*.

It doesn't take long for me to realize that my feelings have more to do with guilt than jealousy. I've hardly spent any time with Martha since Laurel came back. I seem to have forgotten that other people have things going on in their lives, too—that the whole world does not in fact revolve around Laurel and me. Of course I should have remembered to ask Martha about her mom; I knew how worried she was about her.

Maybe Martha shouldn't have said that stupid thing about leaving Laurel and Thomas alone together, but she didn't mean anything by it. I should have just brushed it off. That's what you do with your best friend, isn't it? You forgive them for making mistakes. When did I forget how to do that?

A worrying thought nudges at the edge of my brain. It won't go away no matter how hard I try to ignore it. That whole conversation with Martha was all wrong—like we'd forgotten how to be friends. Like *I'd* forgotten how to be a best friend. It's the same with Thomas, too. I feel as if I've forgotten how to be his girlfriend.

I've forgotten how to be anything other than a sister.

I text Martha from the bus: I'm sorry I've been a crappy friend. Let's not fight. We're really not very good at it.

She doesn't text back right away, and I don't blame her for leaving me hanging. I'd probably do the same. I'm just getting off at my stop when she finally texts: I'm sorry too. Should have told you about Mom. Still besties?

That makes me smile. Martha would never ever use the word *besties* in normal conversation—unless she was making fun of someone.

Still BFFs, I text back.

She has the last word: Squeeee!!!!

The *squeeee* might have been sarcastic as hell, but the sentiment is still there. We're okay.

The news vans left weeks ago. This story is over as far as they're concerned—all neatly wrapped up, with a polka-dot bow on top. Of course, I know better than to believe they're gone for good—they'll be back as soon as anything happens. They'll be back when the police catch that monster. They *will* catch him; he can't hide forever.

In the meantime, the neighbors are happy to have their

parking spaces back, and I'm happy to be able to walk down my own street and not have to worry about what my hair looks like or whether I'm wearing the same top I had on yesterday.

There's laughter coming from the living room. I expect to find Thomas and Laurel where I left them—sitting at the dining room table—but they're lounging on the sofa. The laptop and mugs of tea have been abandoned, the cookies left untouched. There's a movie on the TV. I can't place it at first, but then one of the actors says something in French, and I realize it's *Three Colors: Red*—Thomas's favorite film.

I stand in the doorway for a couple of seconds before Thomas looks up. "Hi! You're back early." He sits up straight as if I've just told him off for slouching, when I have, in fact, said nothing.

Laurel pats the space next to her on the sofa—the space between her and Thomas—and says I should sit down. She asks if I had a nice time with Martha and if I've seen this film before. Clearly Thomas forgot to mention that we went to see it together on one of our first dates.

"I need a cup of tea. Do either of you want anything?"

Laurel says, "No, thanks."

Thomas shakes his head. He's watching me closely, trying to work out how I'm feeling. I turn my back to him and head into the kitchen. He joins me a minute later, just as I'm switching on the kettle to boil. He closes the door behind him. "Hey," he says as he leans against the counter.

"Hey," I say.

"Are you annoyed?"

"Why would I be annoyed?" I take my mug from the cupboard above the kettle and open the ceramic jar labeled COFFEE, which is where we keep the tea bags. I broke the jar labeled TEA a couple of years ago, smashing it into hundreds of pieces on the kitchen floor. On purpose.

Thomas shrugs and I feel my shoulders tense up. If one more person shrugs at me today, I will not be held responsible for my actions. "I don't know. You just seem . . . annoyed."

"Well, I'm not."

"Okay," he says in that sarcastic whatever-you-say tone. "How's Martha?"

I turn away from him and open the fridge. The milk carton is almost empty. We always used to have plenty of milk, but Mom hasn't adjusted how much she buys now that there's an extra person in the house. I pour the last dregs into my mug, even though it's not enough for a decent cup of tea.

"Faith? I asked you a question." Thomas hates being ignored. He thinks everything he has to say is of the utmost importance and should be listened to with a bowed head and a serious expression on your face.

"I've got a question for you. Why didn't you tell me about Martha's mom losing her job?"

He wasn't expecting that. "What are you talking about?"

"It's a perfectly straightforward question." I take a teaspoon from the drawer—the one that doesn't match the rest of the set. I always used to use it to eat my yogurt because I felt sorry for it; I thought it must be lonely, being the odd

141

one out among the rest of the cutlery. "Martha told you about her mom. You didn't bother to tell me. I'm asking you why."

"I don't know. I thought you knew."

"Well, I *didn't* know." The kettle has boiled. I pour the water into the mug too fast and it splashes onto the counter-top. Thomas grabs a dish towel and wipes up the water. I dunk the tea bag and press it against the side of the mug, making sure the color is as close to perfect as I can get it under the circumstances.

Finally, the tea is made and there's nothing else for me to occupy myself with. "Faith? What's the matter?" Thomas's voice is gentle and coaxing. "Are you annoyed about Laurel and me watching *Red*? Is that it?"

I *am* annoyed about that. That film has always been our thing—mine and Thomas's. We must have watched it at least eight times. "I'm not annoyed about that. . . ."

Thomas moves closer to me and puts his hand on the back of my neck. His fingers start to work their magic. I've almost forgotten what it feels like to have him touch me.

I move away, out of reach. "Did you at least show her all the computer stuff she wanted to know?"

Thomas nods. "Yeah, she picked it up really quickly. She's a natural." Thomas looks at the door as if to check it hasn't suddenly turned transparent in the last couple of minutes. "Can I have a kiss?"

I really don't want to kiss him. I want to go sit in a quiet room with my mug of tea and not talk to another human being until tomorrow at the very earliest. "Okay," I say.

He smiles, and I can tell he's relieved. Everything must

be fine if I'm happy to kiss him. He leans in toward me and the smell of his stale breath assaults my nostrils. I count to ten—slowly—while we're kissing. I don't want to pull away too soon. After all, this is the most action he's had in weeks.

We watch the rest of the film. I sit between Laurel and Thomas on the sofa—Laurel insists on it.

The sofa seems too small.

CHAPTER

22

It was a blip, that's all. One bad day. I must have got out of the wrong side of bed or something. Everything is fine at school the next day. Martha, Thomas, and I have lunch together, and Thomas monopolizes the conversation, talking about a Peruvian poet who's just died. Sometimes I think he scours the Internet searching for the most obscure people he can find to make himself look knowledgeable, but this time Martha's heard of her, too. I nod along with them, just pleased that things seem to be back to normal and no one's talking about yesterday's weirdness.

I can't quite rid myself of the nagging idea that Martha and Thomas might have talked to each other last night, comparing notes. If they have, there's not a lot I can do about it. I should be glad that my boyfriend and my best friend get along so well. I *am* glad.

Things can start to get back to normal now that Laurel has settled in. Soon she won't need me so much, and sometime after *that,* she won't need me at all. And that will be a good thing. That's what we're all working toward—normality. We're getting there, slowly but surely. The other night, Laurel and I disagreed about what to watch on TV. It was nothing serious, and I let her have her way in the end, but I noticed Mom watching us closely the whole time. She didn't look annoyed like you might have expected, and she didn't tell me to give the remote control to Laurel and be done with it. She was smiling.

"What are you grinning at?" I snapped at her.

That only made her smile more. "Nothing." She tried to wipe the grin from her face and concentrate on the television.

"Tell us!" said Laurel.

The two of us stared at our mother until she relented. "It's just . . . it makes me so happy to see you two bickering like that. It's just like me and your auntie Eleanor when we were your age."

"So?" I asked.

The smile slipped from her face. "Well, I never thought this would . . . I mean, I always hoped . . . It's just so nice to see you being sisters. It's all I've ever wanted." Then she dissolved into tears, but she said it was okay, they were happy tears. Laurel and I looked at each other and smiled. I handed her the remote control, and she turned off the TV. I moved over to the sofa so I was sitting next to Mom, then I hugged her. Laurel hugged her, too. Mom had one arm around Laurel and one arm around me, and we stayed like that for a long time. The sofa felt the right size again.

• • •

I know something is up the second I get home from school. Mom and Dad and Laurel are sitting at the dining table. Dad wasn't supposed to be arriving until later. Mom invited him and Michel over for dinner (because I nagged her until she agreed to it just to shut me up). As far as I'm concerned, this will be our first *real* family dinner.

I look at the faces around the table, searching for clues. Mom and Laurel look fine; Dad doesn't look too happy. I dump my bag on the sofa, then sit down on the empty chair. We only have four. I'll have to bring one from the kitchen before Michel arrives.

I ask what's going on. Then I get the strangest flashback to the moment when Mom and Dad told me they were splitting up. They sat me down at the same dining table, in a different house, and spoke to me in soft, sympathetic voices. *(We still care about each other, very much. And we love you just the same as we always have. There's really no need for you to worry.)*

Mom tells me that nothing bad has happened, and Dad raises his eyebrows as if he's not so sure about that. Laurel winks at me, which reassures me more than Mom's words ever could. I wait for someone to tell me what the hell is going on here.

Mom looks at Dad, but he shakes his head and puts his hands up. "I'm having nothing to do with it."

Mom purses her lips. Then she turns to me. "Laurel and I had a meeting this morning." It's the first I've heard of any meeting. "With a publisher. They've got a proposal for us."

"What kind of proposal?" I ask, even though there's only one kind of proposal it could possibly be.

"A book deal. They're prepared to pay a *significant* amount of money."

"They want you to write a book?" I ask Laurel.

Laurel opens her mouth to speak, but Mom gets in there first. "They want *us* to write it." She places her hand on top of mine. "As a family."

"Well, that's weird."

"The editor said it will be the first book of its kind. 'Groundbreaking' was the word she used." It doesn't escape me that Mom used the word *will* instead of *would,* as if this is already a done deal. From the look on Dad's face, it hasn't escaped him, either. "Of course, the lion's share of the book would be about Laurel, but they want to hear the *whole* story—what it's been like for each of us. They've already found the perfect ghostwriter for the project. They're hoping to publish in time for Christmas."

"Why would anyone want a book about us—about Laurel—for Christmas? No offense, Laurel." Laurel is sitting quietly, just watching.

"My point exactly," Dad says triumphantly.

Mom rolls her eyes. "You two are so cynical. It's the perfect book for Christmas—it's a story of hope, isn't it?"

"Anyway," says Dad, "it's a decision we have to make as a family. I've already made my feelings on the matter quite clear. I think the public has probably had just about enough of us by now. It's time to move on." He looks at Laurel, but her face is curiously blank. "But I've agreed to abide by your decision." He looks from me to Laurel and back again.

That is so typical of Dad, taking the easy way out.

"Well, Faith, what do you think?" Mom's eyes are wide

and hopeful even though she knows (she *must* know, surely?) what I'm going to say.

"I think it's a terrible idea." I can practically see the thought bubble coming out of Dad's head: *That's my girl.*

Mom sneaks a glance at Laurel before focusing back on me. "But why? Don't you think it would be good to set the record straight? To tell our side of the story?"

"You've been telling *your* side of the story for years." This sounds worse out loud than it did in my head. I try again. "I just don't see the point of this. Of keeping on talking about what happened. It's in the past now."

There's silence around the table. I stare at the empty mug in front of Laurel—the one with my name on it. I'm not sure why, but she seems to prefer it to the one I bought for her.

"Faith has a point, Olivia."

"Yes, I know she has a point. *Thanks,* John, for stating the bloody obvious . . . as usual."

Dad holds his hands up as if he's being held at gunpoint. "Whoa there! There's no need for this to turn nasty."

Mom sighs and leans back in her chair. "We have to think about Laurel's future. The kind of money they're talking about could set her up for life." I wish they wouldn't talk about Laurel as if she weren't here. But it's almost as if she *isn't* here. She isn't reacting to anything anyone says. She doesn't seem bothered by Mom and Dad arguing, which makes me think they were probably arguing before I got here. "And you'd get a share of the money too, Faith. . . ."

I hadn't thought of that. For some reason I assumed it would all go to Laurel. I wonder how much. . . . No. No amount of money is worth that kind of invasion of privacy. I stand; Mom tells me to sit down. I ignore her. "I just want to live a normal life without everyone knowing our business. You three can do what you want, but there's no way I'm getting involved in this."

I grab my bag from the sofa and walk out of the room. Mom and Dad both call me back, but I ignore them. Upstairs, I slam my bedroom door, then flop down on the bed.

Is it always going to be like this? Why can't people just leave us alone? Everyone seems to want their pound of flesh, and Mom seems perfectly willing to carve it up for them and serve it lightly sautéed with a side of béarnaise sauce.

I keep waiting for someone to knock at the door. Dad, maybe, coming to say that he's proud of me for taking a stand against all this bullshit. Mom, coming to apologize and say that she's had a change of heart and realized that the idea of us all writing a book together is truly, truly terrible. Or Laurel. I have no idea what she would say. But no one comes, so after a while, I pick up a book and start reading. Time passes, slowly.

CHAPTER
23

I clear my throat. "Can you pass the salt, please?"

Mom doesn't move, even though the saltshaker is closest to her. Michel reaches across the table, almost catching his shirtsleeve on the candle flame. He grabs the salt and puts it down in front of me. *"Merci,"* I say, under my breath.

Poor Michel. He has no idea what he's walked into. Unless Dad called to warn him. No one's mentioned the book deal since I stormed out of the conversation. It's not the elephant in the room—it's bigger than that. A blue whale, floundering and gasping for air.

There are lots of awkward silences. Michel does his best to fill them, but it's a losing battle. He's already complimented Mom on the food—slow-roasted shoulder of lamb—five times.

Dad's on his third glass of wine already. Mom says it would be nice if he left some for other people. He ignores her and pours himself some more. The glass is so full that he has to lift it to his mouth excruciatingly slowly so he doesn't spill a drop on the pristine tablecloth.

Laurel has barely touched her food. Mom's noticed—she keeps on glancing at Laurel's plate. Laurel moves the food around with her knife and fork, as if that's fooling anyone.

"Is everything okay, love? Are you not hungry? I can make you something else if you'd prefer?" Mom's always fussing over Laurel. She can't leave her in peace.

"No, it's really good, thanks." Laurel eats a tiny bit of potato, which seems to make Mom feel better. She stops watching Laurel like a hawk and concentrates on her own plate for a couple of minutes.

Michel starts telling us about a man who came into the vet's office with baby turtles in his coat pockets. Laurel smiles politely and I even manage to laugh. Dad drinks more wine.

We're having dessert—chocolate mousse served in little espresso cups—when Mom finally crumbles. "Look, we're going to have to sort this out. Zara—that's the editor; she's really lovely, by the way—wants an answer tomorrow."

Michel doesn't ask what Mom's talking about, so Dad must have given him the lowdown after all. Everyone looks at me.

"What are you all looking at me for? I've told you what *I* think. Write the book without me—no one would give a shit about what I have to say anyway."

Mom dabs at her mouth with her napkin. "I think you're being remarkably selfish."

Dad leans forward. "Now, hang on a minute, Olivia. That's not fair. Faith's entitled to her opinion on the matter. Some of us are just . . . more private than others."

"Well, some of us have more *reason* to be private than others," Mom snaps back, tossing her napkin onto the table.

"What's that supposed to mean?" Dad's face is red, and I can't tell if it's because he's angry or drunk or both.

"You know full well what it means."

"How *dare* you? After everything I've been through with the press . . ." He shakes his head in disgust.

Things are getting out of hand. Someone needs to step in and say something. I thought Michel might be the man for the job, but he's always so careful around Mom.

I try to think of something to say to defuse the situation. "Have either of you bothered to ask Laurel what *she* wants to do?"

Mom's lips twitch into a half smile, and that's when I know I've made a mistake. She wants to do it; Laurel wants us to write the fucking book.

"Laurel? Why don't you tell Faith what you told us earlier?"

Laurel's hands are in her lap. She almost looks like she could be praying, if it wasn't for the fact that her eyes are open. The chocolate mousse in front of her has a single spoonful carved out of it. Laurel's mouth is clamped shut, as if she's worried someone will force another spoonful into her mouth if she opens it even a little bit.

"Laurel?"

"Leave the girl alone, Olivia!"

"Can you please stop fighting?" Laurel says, her voice little more than a whisper. Everyone hears, though.

Mom and Dad both apologize, and Michel shoots me a look that I can't decipher. Laurel looks at me, too.

"It's okay," I say. "You can tell me the truth."

"I want to write the book. I want us *all* to write the

book." I half expect Mom to high-five her and run a victory lap around the dining table. But I'm pretty sure my mother has never high-fived anyone in her entire life, and she doesn't "do" running.

"Why?" It's a simple question, but I'm almost certain Mom never bothered to ask it.

Laurel stares at the light above the table—the one that looks like it's made up of three flying saucers from the 1970s. The one Mom's been meaning to replace ever since we moved in. The last time I mentioned it, she said it was "growing on her." Like a fungus.

The silence goes on for too long; it's as if Laurel's gone into some kind of trance, staring at that ugly light. "Laurel?" I reach across the table to touch her hand, and something flashes across her face. I'd have missed it if I'd blinked. Perhaps Mom, Dad, and Michel were blinking, all at the exact same moment. I take my hand away and start to doubt myself immediately, because what possible reason could there be for her to have that look on her face? All I did was touch her. Surely that didn't warrant a look of pure revulsion?

A flashback. That's the only explanation that makes any sense. Laurel's counselor, Penny, told us that flashbacks were more than likely. That they can happen at any time, without any warning. She said there were bound to be things that Laurel had gone through that she might have buried in the recesses of her mind to protect herself. Those things might stay buried forever, or they might just lurk there, waiting to jump out at her when she least expected it.

"Well?" Mom nudges me with her foot under the table.

"Sorry . . . what?"

"The least you can do is listen to what Laurel has to say." I'm not even sure Mom realizes what a bitch she's being.

I look at Laurel and wait. There's no hint of revulsion on her face now. It's hard to imagine the twisting grimace I saw—thought I saw?—only seconds ago. Now her expression is warm and kind and open. "I think . . . I think it would help us heal. As a family."

I say nothing.

Now it's Laurel's turn to reach across the table and take my hand in hers. "I think it would give us closure." *Closure.* That's what you get for watching *The Cynthia Day Show* every day. Cynthia's always spouting that kind of psychobabble nonsense; her audience laps it up like kittens.

Laurel squeezes my hand. "It would be a project that we can all do *together*—as a family." She looks over at Mom, and they share a sad little smile, like they're both thinking of all the things we've missed out on doing *as a family.*

But why does it have to be a *book*? Why can't we do something that normal families do, like go to Disney World? Or IKEA.

Martha would be horrified if I agree to this. Thomas too. Laney Finch would be delighted—and that's putting it mildly. I don't even need to look at Michel to know that he thinks this is a terrible idea, but he won't say anything, because Dad's in an impossible situation here. Dad would do anything for Laurel—anything at all. Because he's spent so many years not being able to do a single thing for her.

Laurel lets go of my hand. "I'll understand if you don't want to do it, Faith. We *all* will." Mom nods in agreement, because that's what Laurel wants her to do. "It's up to you."

One last try. "But can't you do it *without* me?"

Laurel shakes her head. "I wouldn't want to. You can say no, Faith. We don't have to do it. We can forget all about it," she says. I believe her. Mom might hold it against me until the end of time, but Laurel wouldn't.

In the end, it all comes down to one thing: my sister. Laurel's future *with* thousands and thousands of dollars in a savings account, or Laurel's future *without* thousands and thousands of dollars in a savings account. Maybe I'm wrong. Maybe she would be able to get a regular job like a regular person. Maybe she can go to some university and study law and end up being a hotshot corporate lawyer. Maybe she can live a normal life and lock up the memories of what happened to her and store them away somewhere in her brain, never to be found again. But maybe she can't. And if she can't live a normal life, she's going to need money. Lots of it.

Mom's the only one who seems genuinely shocked when I say, "Let's do it. Let's write the book." Shocked but happy. Laurel rushes around from her side of the table and hugs me. "Thank you," she whispers.

Dad's not surprised at all. He knows I feel the same way he does: Laurel is our priority now. Her needs come first.

CHAPTER 24

Michel volunteers to do the washing up and asks me to dry the dishes. Mom, Dad, and Laurel stay in the living room.

"You didn't have to do that, you know," Michel says quietly as he hands me the wineglass he's just washed.

"I did." I wipe the glass with a dish towel, careful to get rid of every last drop of water before placing it on the counter.

"No, you really didn't. It's your life, too." I want him to stop talking. "They shouldn't have pressured you into it."

"They didn't pressure me into anything. I'd already made up my mind to do it." I have no idea why I'm lying to him, especially since it's abundantly clear that he knows I'm lying to him.

He stops washing dishes and turns to look at me. I continue drying because I can't face looking at him. "I'm worried about you, Faith."

"Worried? Why would you be worried about me?"

He's silent for a moment. Either he's choosing his words

156

carefully, or he can't think of the exact English words to convey what he's thinking. "You're not being yourself."

My grip tightens on the stem of a wineglass. I wonder if I could shatter it if I grip hard enough. "I don't know what you're talking about."

"I know you don't," says Michel. He sounds tired.

I'm about to ask him what the hell he's talking about when Mom walks in, asking whether I've seen the fancy cookies she bought at the store last week.

"I haven't seen them." Laurel and I polished them all off on Tuesday night. "Actually, Mom, I've got a bit of a headache. I might just go to bed, if that's okay? I'll put away the rest of the dishes in the morning."

Mom comes over and touches my forehead with the back of her hand. I didn't say anything about having a temperature, so I'm not sure what she's hoping to achieve. She prescribes a tall glass of water and two ibuprofen.

Michel tells me he hopes I feel better soon. I thank him and leave the kitchen. I don't hug him good-bye like I always do.

Dad and Laurel are sitting on the sofa, talking quietly. I tell them I'm not feeling so well and give each of them a hug. Laurel's worried. She asks if she can bring me anything, then she asks Dad if he thinks we should call a doctor. Dad laughs and tells her not to be silly, and I can tell she doesn't like being called silly, but she doesn't say so. I reassure her that I'll be fine, I'm just tired. I don't think she believes me, but she says good-night, and that she'll come up to check on me in a little while.

She doesn't come, though. I lie in bed, listening. I hear

Dad and Michel leaving after half an hour or so. I listen to their footsteps on the gravel outside. Michel will be the one to drive them home—he's *always* the one to drive them home. He says he doesn't mind not drinking, which is just as well because Dad would definitely mind.

I'll apologize to Michel tomorrow, even though I'm not quite sure what I'll be apologizing for. He was only looking out for me when he said I didn't have to be involved in this ridiculous book idea. I know that. He's always the one to look out for me. But what was that nonsense about me not being myself? Where the hell did *that* come from?

It's not true. I *am* being myself. I'm always myself, because what else is there to be? The weirdest thing is that, these past few weeks, I've felt more like "me" than I ever have before. Not that I go around thinking about how "me" I'm being. But since Laurel came home, I've been feeling more settled somehow, despite all the upheaval. It's as if I can breathe again—great, big gulps of air—after a lifetime of feeling slightly suffocated.

Less than an hour after Michel and Dad leave, I hear footsteps on the stairs. Mom's footsteps. I know that, because she always steps over the creaky stair, third from the top, when she thinks I'm asleep. The footsteps come closer and stop outside my bedroom door. I clutch the edge of the duvet, and my whole body tenses up. There's something creepy about someone standing, listening, on the other side of a closed door, even if it is your mother.

Perhaps she wants to apologize. I'd like to think she feels bad for pressuring me about the book deal. But I suspect she hasn't even given it a second thought. I don't necessarily think it's a case of her putting Laurel's needs before my own. It's more like she's putting *her* needs before mine—and Dad's. She's always been more comfortable with the publicity side of things than he has. And she's always claimed that it's because she would do anything in her power to get Laurel back. Since she couldn't go and knock down every door in the country or search every abandoned warehouse or travel around the world looking for clues, it was her only option. Making sure as many people as possible knew about Laurel Logan, and making sure they never forgot her. That was her mission, her obsession.

On my unkinder days—and I've had a lot of those—I used to wonder if maybe my mother enjoyed the attention a little bit. She seemed so comfortable being in the limelight—going on talk shows and speaking in front of huge crowds—that sometimes it was hard to think otherwise. Dad went on the talk shows, too, and read out all the official family statements, but there was always a sense of reluctance about it. He gritted his teeth and did what had to be done—for Laurel. He hated all of it. And, like me, he probably thought those days were over. He probably thought that we could go back to being a normal family. Maybe not quite the normal family we were thirteen years ago, but a slightly different version, with Michel included.

The Cynthia Day Show was one thing, but this book deal is a whole different ball game. This will be big news. This will make sure the spotlight remains firmly fixed on the Logan family for months and months—maybe even years. What was I *thinking*?

Certain sections of the press will have a field day with

this. It won't be the first time that we've been accused of courting attention, but this will be different. Back then, there was always a reason, and no one could really argue with that reason without being vilified themselves—just ask Jeanette Hayes. My parents were desperate to get their daughter back. Who couldn't relate to that? But now Little Laurel Logan is back home where she belongs. Of course people will still be interested in her—in hearing about how she's doing. People want their "happily ever after." But the danger is that they'll soon tire of the story, that we'll be seen to be milking the situation for all its worth. And before you know it, journalists will be digging around for nasty stories about Laurel or Mom or Dad . . . or me.

People will buy the book—I have no doubt about that. But that doesn't mean we should write it. We don't have an obligation to satisfy anyone's curiosity—the most morbid curiosity you could ever imagine. I've agreed to it now, though; there's no going back. I just have to focus on the fact that Laurel will be set up for life—or at least for the next few years. And she'll get to tell her own story, in her own words (well, a ghostwriter's words). If she's happy to talk about it—for everyone to know what that monster did to her—then she has the right to be heard. It's not the choice I would make, in her situation. But Maggie and Penny have both said that it's good for Laurel to talk about her experiences, and that the real danger is in her bottling things up inside.

I lie in bed and wait for Laurel to come and check on me like she promised. I stare at the glowing red numbers on my alarm clock and count the seconds in each minute, trying to catch the exact moment the numbers change. I never get it right, though. The sixty seconds I count out in my head are always faster than the real sixty seconds.

She must be staying up to watch TV. I don't mind that she's forgotten to come and see me. It's not as if I need her to tuck me into bed for me to get to sleep. But for some reason I *can't* sleep. My brain is too busy, flitting from one topic to the next and back again, like a hyperactive housefly. I'm dreading telling Martha and Thomas about the book. Martha will mock me mercilessly, but I've had years of practice dealing with that. It's Thomas I'm more worried about. His favorite insult is *sellout*, and he uses it a lot. He stopped liking his favorite band as soon as they became popular. *(Their new material is far too commercial.)* We argue about it sometimes, but it's more bickering than a real argument. I maintain that he only likes obscure bands that no one's heard of because he likes to be the one who "discovered" them, even though that's total bullshit. He likes to be able to say that he saw them play in some sweaty little back room of a club *long* before they were famous and playing huge arenas. The trouble is, the bands he likes always seem to end up being popular, which clearly means that when it comes down to it, the music he's into is little more than the lowest common denominator.

Thomas will be disappointed in me. Even if he doesn't say it (and he probably *will* say it), I'll know it's true. I can hardly blame him, though—I'm a little bit disappointed in myself. But I'm just going to have to get over that, because I'd rather be disappointed in myself—and have Thomas disappointed in me—than let Laurel down. If Thomas can't understand that, then maybe he's not the right person for me. As soon as that thought pops into my head, a jagged ball of anxiety lodges itself in my chest. It's nothing new; it magically appears almost every time I really let myself think about my relationship with Thomas these days. To be honest, I started having some doubts even before Laurel came back. But I always stomped on those doubts, grinding them down to dust under my shoe.

I don't know if it's normal to feel like you love someone one day and then like you sort of hate them a little bit the next. Actually, that's not even how it is. It's more of a minute-to-minute thing. Thomas can be really, really kind and sweet. I like him the most when we're laughing about something silly—not *at* someone. But then he'll say something so insufferably pompous that I want to slap him.

It can't be normal to have these feelings about the person you're supposed to be in love with. Or maybe it *is* normal, and being in love is a global conspiracy in which everyone vows to keep quiet about the fact that it's actually nothing special.

I'm not sure what would have happened if Laurel hadn't come back. Would Thomas and I still be together? Is having a boyfriend you're not entirely sure about better than having no boyfriend at all?

CHAPTER 25

Just before two a.m., I realize that there's no way I'm getting to sleep. I'm thinking hot chocolate is the way to go. If Laurel hasn't fallen asleep on the sofa, I'll make one for her, too. I put on my bathrobe and creep downstairs, careful to avoid the creaky stair.

The lights are off in the living room; the TV is off, too. Laurel's not on the sofa. A strip of light under the kitchen door confirms her whereabouts. Maybe she's read my mind and has already got the milk heating on the stove. I like the idea that we might have some kind of psychic connection.

I open the kitchen door, and Laurel jumps in her chair. She knocks over the glass that was on the table next to her, and water goes everywhere. "Shit! Faith! I was just . . ."

I rush over to the sink and grab the paper towels. "Sorry, I didn't mean to scare you!" That's when I notice what's on the table: a photo album. Luckily the photos are protected by plastic, so the water hasn't done any damage.

"Why did you sneak up on me like that?" Laurel grabs

some paper towels from me and starts dabbing at the photo album while I concentrate on the water on the table.

"I didn't mean to! I just came down for some hot chocolate." Laurel is breathing hard; her face is even paler than usual. Something's not right here. "Laurel? Are you okay?"

She shakes her head and closes her eyes for a second, trying to compose herself before she speaks. "I'm sorry. I didn't mean to freak out. It just . . . it reminded me of *him*." Oh god. "I . . . I never knew when to expect him."

"I'm so sorry, Laurel." I don't like it when she mentions him. I try my hardest to forget that he's still out here, because it scares me. He could be anywhere. The police have assured us that it's highly unlikely he'll be anywhere within a hundred miles of us, that he'll be lying low, given that he's now the most wanted man in the country. That seems to be good enough for Mom and Dad and Laurel, but it's nowhere near good enough for me. A couple of police officers parked down the street wouldn't be able to stop him—not if he really wanted to get Laurel back. I've been having nightmares about him creeping into our house and taking her.

Laurel walks over to the kitchen window, and her shoulders start to shake. Mom must have forgotten to pull the blinds down, so I can see Laurel's reflection in the window. Her hands are up to her face, as if we're playing a game of hide-and-seek. I hate it when it's dark outside and light inside and you can't see if someone's lurking in the shadows. Whoever is out there can see you, but you can't see them. There's a security light above the back door, but it's been broken for nearly a year.

I go over and put my hand on Laurel's shoulder. She

flinches slightly and it breaks my heart. I rub her back and tell her everything's going to be okay. In between sobs, Laurel apologizes for overreacting. I tell her there's no such thing as overreacting, after everything she's been through. She turns to me, and I go to wipe away her tears, but her eyes are dry. She sniffs and wipes her nose with her sleeve and takes a long, shuddering breath.

"Do you want a hot chocolate? It always makes me feel better." It's true. It's been my comfort drink since I was little. I used to have three cups a day until Mom decided I was getting too fat. She didn't exactly *say* I was getting fat, but I knew she was thinking it. She stopped buying chips and Coke, and suggested I take up a new hobby . . . some kind of sport, perhaps? I was ten years old. She must be happy now that she's got the skinny daughter back, even if she's only skinny because she's been practically starved for the past thirteen years.

"No, thanks. I think I'll just go to bed. Would you . . . ? Oh god, this is going to sound so silly. . . ." Laurel shakes her head. "No, it's okay, actually. I'll just . . ."

"What is it, Laurel?" I ask gently.

She stares at a spot on the wall, avoiding eye contact. "Would you mind staying with me until I fall asleep?" She says this quickly, running the words together.

"Of course I will."

Laurel doesn't look at the table as she walks past it; I do. There are two photos on each open page of the album. Four photographs, all taken at Christmas. A sleepy, pajamaed eight-year-old me standing beside the Christmas tree. Me opening my presents, sitting cross-legged in a scrunchy sea

165

of wrapping paper. Dad carving the turkey, looking proud of himself even though Mom was the one who did all the cooking. An awkwardly posed family picture: Mom, Dad, me (wearing an orange paper hat), Gran and Gramps, Auntie Eleanor.

"What were you doing with those? Looking for tips on how to have the worst haircut in the whole history of human existence?"

Laurel doesn't laugh. "I think your hair looks cute in those pictures."

"Why were you looking at them?" It makes me sad to think of her sitting down here all by herself, poring over photos of things she missed out on. The photos give a false impression, though. Everyone looks happy (even me, with my disastrous hair), but that's because no one took pictures of Mom sobbing in the kitchen or Dad staring into space instead of watching the Christmas film I insisted we watch together every year. Laurel would never know any of that from looking at these photos. These photos make it look like we didn't miss her at all, like everyone just got on with their lives and couldn't care less about her.

"Mom was showing me them earlier."

I nod and close the album. I turn off the light, and we go upstairs. I wait in Laurel's room while she gets changed in the bathroom and listen to the water running as she brushes her teeth. She never gets changed in front of me. Mom's the only one of us who's seen what marks that monster might have left on my sister's body.

Laurel gets into bed, and I perch on the stool in front of her dressing table. We talk for a little bit, then I turn out the

light and wait for her to fall asleep. It's at least fifteen minutes before I hear the change in her breathing, and I sneak
out of her room and into my own.

It's a long time before sleep comes for me. I keep replaying the scene in the kitchen. Laurel lied to me. She looked
me in the eyes and lied. Mom didn't show her that photo
album, I know that for a fact. Because Mom didn't know
where it was.

Two days before Laurel came home, I took the photo
album from the bookshelf next to the fireplace. I sat in bed
staring at the photos, trying to make sense of everything
that I was feeling. Thinking about the past and wondering about the future. The next morning, I didn't take the
album back downstairs. I wanted to keep it close to me, so
I put it in one of my bedside drawers—the bottom one. It
lay there on top of a couple of old swimming certificates, a
pair of Mickey Mouse ears, and a "book" I'd written (and
illustrated) when I was eight years old.

Mom stopped rooting around in my room years ago. She
wouldn't dare go through my stuff. There's only one explanation: Laurel has been snooping in here. I know it. And
she must *know* that I know it. So why didn't she just say she
found the photo album while she was looking for something
in my room? I'd probably have believed her. Even if I hadn't
believed her, I wouldn't have been annoyed. There are a
couple of things in there that I wouldn't be too happy if
Mom found, but I've got nothing to hide from Laurel.

There shouldn't be any secrets between sisters.

CHAPTER
26

I expect her to put up a bit of a fight when Laurel suggests it, but Mom doesn't bat an eyelid. Penny must have talked to her beforehand, laying the groundwork. "I think it's a great idea. Faith and I can come and meet you for a late lunch, and we could go shopping afterward—just us girls." Mom's been in a good mood since we signed the contract for the book deal. The publisher paid the first chunk of money a couple of days ago: we are now officially rolling in it.

So Laurel is going into town by herself for the very first time today. She's already showered and dressed by the time I come downstairs. It's the first Monday of winter break. I usually sleep in really late during the holidays, but for some reason this morning I woke up at seven-thirty—exactly the same time my alarm is set for me to get up for school. Laurel makes me a cup of tea, and we sit together at the kitchen table.

"Wrong mug," I say, stifling a yawn.

"What?" Laurel seems edgy this morning, distracted.

I hold the mug up for her to see her name.

"Oh. Do you want to swap?"

"Nah. How are you feeling about this morning?"

"Fine," she says. But she's drumming her fingers on the table.

"You don't have to do this if you're not ready, you know. I can come with you." I take a sip of tea. Laurel makes good tea.

Her eyes widen. "No." It's too loud, that word. Too forceful, given that I was only offering to be nice. "No," she says, more softly this time. "Thanks, but I'm ready. I should have done it weeks ago. You and Mom must be sick of the sight of me."

"That's not true."

Laurel shrugs. "I need to be more independent."

She's right, I suppose. And maybe she's feeling stifled, hardly ever being alone. It hasn't occurred to me before, that maybe it's hard for her to have people around *all* the time. With Smith, she was left alone for hours on end—sometimes even days. She's used to her own company. Maybe she even prefers it that way.

"Don't forget to take your phone." I sound like Mom, which makes me cringe. "Text if you need me or if you just feel like some company."

Laurel takes two big gulps of tea, then winces because the tea's too hot for gulping. "Thanks. I'll be fine, though. Really."

"And you're sure you know how to get to the sushi place?"

She says nothing. Instead, she stands and takes something out of the pocket of her jeans, unfolding it carefully for me

169

to see. I drew the map last night, only getting it absolutely right on my fourth attempt.

"Sorry. I know you're perfectly capable of finding your own way around."

"Really? Is that why you felt the need to mark which side of the road I should walk on?" She laughs.

"It's only because there's a building site there at the moment, and the pavement's closed. . . . I didn't want you getting run over." I sound ridiculous. I *am* ridiculous. Laurel is nineteen years old. "Sorry."

"It's okay! You don't have to keep apologizing! It's nice that you care."

"What exactly are you planning on doing this morning, anyway?"

Laurel takes her mug over to the sink and squeezes some dish soap into it. She turns the tap on too fast, and a spray of water shoots up from the sink, splashing her. "Shit! Shit shit shit shit!" She slams the mug down on the counter so hard I'm worried she might have cracked it.

I get up and help her, dabbing at her shirt with a clean dish towel. "It's okay. It'll dry in a few minutes."

"Are you sure? Maybe I should change my top." She looks at her watch; Mom bought her the same one I have. I swear sometimes she forgets that Laurel and I aren't actually twins. "Yeah, I'm going to change."

I explain that there's really no need. She can just keep her jacket buttoned up till the shirt is dry. Laurel doesn't seem convinced, but I manage to persuade her. I make her check that she's got enough change for the bus, then she's out the door.

Mom comes downstairs a couple of minutes later and asks where Laurel is. "But nothing's open at this time! Why didn't you tell her?"

I should have known this would somehow be *my* fault, despite the fact that Laurel is a grown woman. I say as much to Mom and she apologizes. The apology throws me off; normally we'd be gearing up for an argument right about now.

"She'll be fine," Mom says distractedly as she opens the fridge. "She'll be absolutely fine."

"Of course she will."

"There's really nothing to worry about."

"No, there really isn't."

"Okay, then! Breakfast . . . Did you finish the milk again?"

Now it's time for an argument. *You're so selfish, you never think of others, if only you could be a little more thoughtful some-times.* I don't even bother to hide the smile on my face. There's something profoundly reassuring about hearing the same old spiel. There's no point telling her it was Laurel who used the last of the milk to drown her cereal. I'm happy to take the blame, so the argument sort of fizzles out before it's even started.

While she's waiting for her toast to pop up, Mom tells me that she's got a surprise for Laurel and me. I ask what it is, and she says I'll have to wait and see. I tell her she's infuriating, and what's the point of telling me there's a sur-prise if she's not going to tell me what it is? She should have just kept her mouth shut in the first place. So she gives in and tells me: she's treating us both to a shopping spree.

A thousand pounds each to spend this afternoon, from her share of the book-deal money.

Mom looks so pleased with herself that I don't tell her it's a crazy amount of money to fritter away in one afternoon. She's arranged for us to meet a personal shopper at the fanciest department store in town—the one where you have to run a gauntlet past terrifying women intent on giving you a makeover or spritzing you with perfume that would give Cynthia Day's a run for its money. She asks me if I think Laurel will be happy about it, and I say that I'm sure she will be. "It's every girl's dream, isn't it?" she says, sounding hopeful.

I bet she hasn't told Dad, because I'm pretty sure he wouldn't approve. He'd be thinking about how it might look if the story gets into the papers—us cashing in on what happened to Laurel. A photo of Laurel emerging from the shop, laden with bags emblazoned with designer logos. Jeanette Hayes would have a field day.

I suppose we'll just have to hope the photographers stay away—that no one in the store calls them to tip them off about Laurel's presence. And that none of the sales assistants or other shoppers think to snap a picture of Laurel on their phone. Perhaps we'll be lucky.

I don't want to spoil this for Mom; she looks so happy. The physical changes in her are almost as noticeable as those in Laurel. Before Laurel came home, there was something pinched and angular about Mom's face. Her eyes had this haunted, sometimes vacant quality. The angles are still there, but it's as if they've been softened somehow—someone has smudged those hard lines, rounded off the corners. Her eyes are starting to look like the eyes of a normal person with a normal life. I'm not the only one to notice. The *Us Weekly* website printed two pictures of her side by side last week. Before and after. Complete with commentary from three different beauty experts. One of them was certain that Mom has "had some work done" and suggested she'd be better off using a different shade of blush.

I spend the rest of the morning in my bedroom. It's easier to stop myself from saying something mean to her that way. I scroll through the usual suspects—the websites most likely to have mentions of Laurel. I've got it down to a fine art now—no more than twenty minutes. There's nothing interesting today—there hasn't been much for the past couple of weeks. I know I should stop checking, that it might seem a little obsessive, but I can't help myself. Besides, no one else has to know. Mom's stopped reading the papers altogether, which is why she has no idea about that stupid *Us Weekly* feature.

I'm always careful to delete my search history so that Laurel can't see what I've been looking at. For some reason it feels like a betrayal—reading what people are saying about her and not telling her. But that hasn't stopped me.

It seems like Laurel is on my laptop all the time since her little tutorial with Thomas. I don't mind, but she doesn't seem to realize that I need it for schoolwork. She never uses Mom's desktop, even though Mom's hardly ever on it. I have a brain wave and Google to see if the store has an electronics department. With a thousand pounds to spend, Laurel can buy a much better computer than mine. Or maybe I should buy one and give her my old one. It's not like I'll find any clothes there that I would ever actually wear. I just have to get Mom to agree to it, because I'm pretty sure that's not what she had in mind when she planned this little shopping spree.

When Mom calls from downstairs, I realize I've lost track of time down the Internet rabbit hole, and I won't even be able to have a shower before we leave. A few extra sprays of deodorant will have to do.

"We have to go *now!*"

"All right, all right, I'm *coming!*"

"I don't want your sister arriving at the restaurant before us. I *told* you to be ready by twelve-thirty!"

I ignore her and chuck my phone into my bag. A quick look out the window, then I put an umbrella in, too. I'm heading out the door when I realize I haven't deleted my history. Best to do it now, just in case I forget later.

I do it as fast as I can, ignoring Mom's increasingly annoyed shouts.

I stop when I get to the first site I looked at this morning. The next link on the list isn't one of mine. I'm not sure what makes me click on it, particularly when it sounds like Mom's head is about to explode if I keep her waiting any longer. But I do.

It's a map of Blaxford, a town about an hour away. I've never been, but I recognize the name. One of Aunt Eleanor's ex-boyfriends lived there. She hardly ever stayed over at his place—apparently the police sirens kept her awake at night. (Mom told her not to be such an insufferable snob.)

It must have been Laurel; Mom never touches my laptop. But why would Laurel be looking up a map of Blaxford of all places? I check the next link. Another map, the city this time. That makes more sense. Still, I wouldn't have bothered drawing her a map if I knew she'd already looked at a proper one.

I clear the history, deleting all the links. I close the lid of the laptop, then shove the computer under my pillow. Laurel will have to ask if she wants to use it again. I don't mind sharing, but maybe it's time I stopped making allowances for her. She needs to learn that she can't always have her own way, that people won't always be falling over themselves to make things easy for her. The sooner she realizes that, the better.

CHAPTER
27

Laurel steps in front of the three-way mirror and examines herself from every possible angle. Mom has tears in her eyes; the personal shopper has dollar signs in hers. You'd think she was trying on a wedding dress, the fuss they're making. The dress is nice—there's no denying it. It's red and short, but not too short, and the fabric clings in all the right places, but in a classy sort of way. Still, it's not worth five hundred bucks. No dress is worth that much.

"Doesn't she look *wonderful,* Faith?"

I smile and nod. She *does* look amazing. Mom suggests Laurel take her hair down, so she shakes it out of the ponytail, and it's almost like a slow-motion shot from a commercial.

"Oh *yes!*" says the personal shopper.

Laurel giggles and twirls around. The Laurels in the mirror giggle and twirl, too.

"It's too much," Laurel says when she's stopped twirling. "I can't . . ."

"You can and you must!" says Mom emphatically, as if we're talking about something really important here. My suggestion that Laurel buy a laptop with her money didn't exactly go down well. I should have known. Mom said that today isn't about buying things we *need*—it's about having fun, apparently. She said there would be plenty of time—and money—for boring things like computers.

The personal shopper (who seems to think that Laurel looks amazing in everything, even the things that really don't suit her) says that she sold the exact same dress—in the same size!—to a basketball player's girlfriend last weekend. When Mom asks which one, the personal shopper says a name and Mom pretends to know who she's talking about.

The dress is wrapped up in tissue paper and carefully placed in a shiny black bag with ribbons for handles. Laurel hugs Mom and thanks her. Then Mom turns to me. "It's your turn now, Faith!"

The personal shopper looks about as happy as I do at the prospect; Laurel clearly makes a better mannequin than me.

We spent a fortune at the sushi place, piling up the plates. Laurel was a bit dubious about raw fish to start off with, but she soon got over her squeamishness. She loved the conveyor belt, just like I thought she would. That was the main reason I'd suggested we go there for lunch. She couldn't stop staring as the dishes went by. "And we can just take *whatever* we want?" she said, shaking her head in disbelief.

I kept on expecting Mom to ask the question, but she

kept on not asking the question. In the end, I had to do it. "So . . . Laurel . . . what did you do this morning?"

"Nothing much. I just wandered around." She took the last slice of miso eggplant—the one that I'd had my eye on.

"For *four* hours?"

She shrugged. "I went to a café, too."

"Which one?"

Mom gave me a sharp look, but I pretended not to notice.

"I can't remember. Starbucks, maybe?"

"They all look the same, don't they?" Mom says helpfully.

"So you didn't go to Blaxford, then?"

"Why on earth would Laurel go there?" Mom laughed as if it was the most absurd idea in the world.

Laurel's brow furrowed in confusion. "Where?"

Mom told her about Eleanor's ex-boyfriend (*such* a good-looking man) and that he tried to get Eleanor to move in with him and his three kids in their tiny apartment but Eleanor said no and broke up with him. "She said she just couldn't see herself living in a place like that, but I think it was more about the children, really. Three kids under ten? Not exactly Eleanor's cup of tea, and *that's* an understatement. I mean, she likes children—she really does. But she's never wanted any of her own." A pause for a long, wistful look at Laurel, barely a glance in my direction. "She doesn't know what she's missing out on. I think it affected her quite deeply—what happened to you." She squeezed Laurel's hand. "She saw what it did to me, losing you like that." Laurel put her arm around Mom's shoulders, and it made me wish that I were the one sitting next to Mom.

Laurel had arrived at exactly the same time as us in the

end, so Mom's worrying about being late had been completely unnecessary. There had been one booth free next to the conveyor belt. I slid in to one side (with my back to the door, knowing that Laurel would want to sit facing it), Laurel scooched into the booth on the other side, leaving Mom with a choice. Which one of her daughters would she choose to sit next to? No contest.

Later in the afternoon, Mom insists that I at least buy something, and in return I insist that we go to a different shop. The personal shopper makes a (very) halfhearted effort at stopping us: "I'm sure we can find something you'll like!"

Mom thanks her and stage-whispers, "Oh, you know what they're like at that age! No appreciation for the finer things in life." I don't even mind because at least she's agreed that we can finally leave this awful place teeming with awful women buying awful clothes.

We go to the Gap, and yes, it's boring, but at least the clothes are normal here. I buy a pair of gray jeans exactly the same as the ones I'm wearing, ignoring Mom's suggestion to look at the other colors they have. Laurel decides to buy the same jeans as me, and suddenly Mom's saying, "You can't go wrong with gray, can you? Classic." The sales assistant clearly recognizes Laurel but is trying her best to act like she doesn't. It's exactly how Martha and I acted when we saw someone from *The Voice* at the Olive Garden last summer.

We stop for coffee at around four-thirty—an independent coffee shop, at Mom's insistence. We end up in another booth, and yet again Mom sits next to Laurel. They're talking about clothes, and I'm bored out of my mind. Laurel tries to persuade Mom to buy something—to treat herself to a new coat or handbag.

"No, no, I don't need anything."

Laurel elbows Mom gently and says, "You deserve to be spoiled, too, you know! You're so busy looking after the rest of us that you forget to look after yourself. What do you think, Faith?" She looks at me in that chummy, conspiratorial way that usually makes me feel happy.

"Yeah, I suppose so." I don't have the energy to fake enthusiasm. I have a killer headache and my feet are sore, and I'm starting to feel like an outsider in my own family.

Mom says, "I think *someone* got out of the wrong side of bed this morning."

"What are you talking about?"

"Nothing! No need to be so touchy!" Mom laughs and takes a sip of her coffee. "Now, where shall we go next? I've nearly run out of that conditioner I like, so I was thinking we could pop into the drugstore, if you don't mind. Maybe you could get some nail polish to match your new dress, Laurel?"

"Sounds good to me!"

Laurel always says the right thing. She never seems to be grumpy or tired.

Mom can't find the conditioner, so she sends me off to ask someone if the line has been discontinued. I have no idea why she doesn't just ask someone herself. Maybe she's testing me, trying to push me until I snap. I interrupt a couple of sales assistants barely older than me, and one shoots me a hate-filled look before she turns her back to stack some shelves. The other one is helpful but has more to say about hair products than I would ever want to hear. All I want to know is whether they have Mom's conditioner or not, but she's busy telling me about limited editions and argan oil.

While the sales assistant is droning on, I catch sight of Laurel at one of the makeup counters. A flicker of movement catches my eye, and I lower my gaze to Laurel's hand. It glides over the counter, over the shiny tubs and bottles and compacts. Her fingers curl around something—mascara or eyeliner, perhaps?—and she drops it into the bag from the department store. Then she does it again, watching the two women behind the counter the whole time.

The sales assistant finishes her spiel by suggesting we try another branch, and I thank her. She wanders off, but I stand stock-still, staring at Laurel. She picks up something else, but this time she doesn't drop it in the bag. She twists the cap off and draws on the back of her hand, testing the color. Finally, she turns away from the counter and sees me. She smiles and waves.

I turn my back on her and go to find Mom to tell her the bad news about her conditioner. She sighs and says, "Back to the drawing board," and goes to choose another one. I'm tempted to tell her what I saw. What would she think about her darling daughter shoplifting? She probably wouldn't believe me, but the proof is right there in Laurel's bag.

I'm going to tell her. "Mom?"

"Yes, darling?" she says distractedly.

I'm trying to decide the tone I should adopt—shocked?

Sympathetic? Shocked *yet* sympathetic?—when I realize it's too late. You can always tell when someone's standing right behind you.

"Mom? Will you come and help me choose a nail polish? I think I've narrowed it down to two—one of them is a slightly better color match, but the other one says it lasts for seven days." Laurel's voice is the very essence of breezy.

Mom looks up, and her face breaks into this huge smile. "Oh, they tell such *lies*! Maybe one day they'll invent a nail polish that doesn't chip as soon as you look at it, but until then we'll just have to make do."

Laurel and Mom walk off arm in arm, and I trail behind them. They spend at least ten minutes choosing between colors that look identical to me. From time to time, they ask my opinion, and I say whatever they want to hear. Eventually, Laurel makes a decision and the two of them go to the checkout and pay. *Laurel* pays. I watch as she takes some money out of her purse and gives it to the guy at the register.

I hold my breath as we're leaving the shop, fully expecting the alarm to go off. It doesn't.

CHAPTER

28

Grilled cheese sandwiches for dinner, made by Laurel. Mom compliments her on grilling the cheese just right.

After dinner, Mom goes upstairs to call Eleanor. Laurel and I sit in front of the TV. Laurel's recorded *The Cynthia Day Show;* today it's all about a woman who was badly burned in a house fire. Her husband started the fire on purpose. Cynthia Day has just announced that she's sending the woman and her kids to Disney World and everyone in the studio is crying. I glance over at Laurel; she's not crying.

"I saw you."

"Saw me what?" She doesn't bother to look at me.

"Stealing."

Now she looks at me. "What are you talking about?" She looks genuinely baffled.

"I saw you stealing that makeup in the drugstore."

She laughs, and I want to smack her in the face. How dare she laugh at me?

"Why would I do something like that?"

"I was going to ask you the same question. You know you could have bought those things if you really wanted them."

"I didn't steal anything." She folds her arms across her chest and turns her attention back to the TV.

Mom comes back downstairs, and we spend the rest of the evening watching mindless TV shows—all Laurel's choices, of course.

I'm getting ready for bed and replaying my conversation with Laurel in my head. She was very convincing—not even a hint of guilt or embarrassment. Could I have been mistaken about what I saw? Maybe Laurel picked up the makeup and put it right back down again, but I was in such a weird mood and so desperate to see something to tarnish the image of the golden child that my eyes tricked me into believing that I'd seen her stealing.

The fact that I'm even attempting to second-guess myself about something like this is revealing. I'm not delusional. I know what I saw. I just can't make sense of it, that's all.

My phone buzzes with a text message. It's probably Martha. I was supposed to text to tell her all about the big shopping trip. She'd thought it was ridiculous, too, wasting all that money. And she'd actually been quite understanding about the book deal, when I'd explained it all to her. Thomas had been a dick about it, but no more than I'd expected.

The message isn't from Martha or from Thomas—the only two people who ever message me. It's from Laurel: Can you come here?

That's weird. Why didn't she just knock on the wall like

she usually does? I take my time getting changed and brushing my hair before I go next door.

Laurel's room is dark, the only light coming from Egg the Penguin. I flick the switch next to the door, flooding the room with brightness. At first I think she must be in the bathroom, but then I catch sight of her head. She's sitting on the floor on the other side of the bed, wedged into the small space between the bed and the wall. I thought she'd stopped doing that. I've been checking the space underneath the dressing table every few days, to see if she's still using it as a hiding spot.

"Laurel? Are you okay?"

"They're on the bed." Her voice has a dull, mechanical quality.

Liquid eyeliner and a tube of lipstick. I perch on the edge of the bed to examine them. The eyeliner is electric blue, and the lipstick is an unappealing shade of purple.

"I'm sorry."

"Why did you do it?"

No answer.

I get off the bed and kneel in front of her. She won't look at me. Her hair hangs down over her face so I can't see her expression. "Laurel? You can talk to me, you know. I'm not going to tell anyone." I'm feeling more charitable now that she's admitted it.

"I don't know why I did it."

I wait for her to come up with something better, and eventually she looks up, pushing her hair behind her ears. "It's the *truth*!"

It doesn't make sense. People don't just steal things for

no reason; they steal things because they can't afford to buy them, don't they? "I don't think the colors will go with your new dress." When in doubt, try to lighten the mood.

A trace of a smile flickers across her face. "I can't explain it. . . . It was . . . I don't know. I wanted to see if I *could* do it. I didn't think I'd get away with it, and I wanted to see what would happen. Does that make any sense at all?"

I shrug because it doesn't. "You know if you'd been caught, it would be all over the newspapers, don't you?"

She nods. "Maybe that's what I was hoping for."

"Why would you want that?" I'm starting to realize there's more to my sister than meets the eye.

Laurel stares into space, focusing on a spot on the wall. "Because maybe then they'd see that I'm . . . normal. That I'm a regular person who makes mistakes sometimes. I'm not someone to look up to. Little kids shouldn't be asking for my autograph or wanting to get their pictures taken with me. It's not right."

I thought she loved all that stuff—she certainly does a good job of smiling and *looking* like she's enjoying herself. "You don't need to do those things, Laurel. No one's forcing you."

"I want to take it back. The makeup. I'll go tomorrow."

"You can't! They'd probably catch you sneaking it back onto the shelves and think you're stealing!"

"Well, I'll just tell them what I did. Talk to one of the sales assistants." She looks like a little girl determined to get her way, jaw jutting, eyes defiant.

"No. You won't. Look, let's just forget all about it. Pretend it never happened. I understand why you did it, but there's no need for anyone else to find out about it." The lie is instinctive; I still don't understand why she did it—not really. "It would only upset Mom." That's the truth.

"I could explain—"

"No. She wouldn't get it. Trust me on this."

Laurel asks if I'm sure, and if there's anything she can do to make amends. There are no amends to be made, I tell her. I'm pretty sure the drugstore isn't going to go under because someone stole some makeup. In that little-girl voice she sometimes adopts, she asks if I'm angry with her.

"Of course not," I say.

"Are you sure? It's just . . . the last few days I've had the feeling that"—she shrugs, and I don't want her to finish this sentence—"that maybe you resent me a little bit."

My mouth opens to issue a denial. My mouth shuts again. When I finally speak, I tell the truth. "You're right." The look on Laurel's face just about breaks my heart, so I rush ahead. "No, no, it's nothing you've done! Honestly, it's *my* issue, not yours. I think I maybe got a little bit used to getting my own way . . . while you were gone. And now you're back, and I suppose it's just taking me a little longer to adjust than I thought."

She nods slowly. "It must be hard for you."

I feel ashamed, hearing her say those words, seeing her looking at me with sympathetic eyes. It must be hard for *me*? Compared to everything she's been through? I start to cry, and she comforts me, which makes me feel even more ashamed. I am the worst person in the world.

CHAPTER
29

It was Laurel's idea, to get up early and make breakfast for Mom. She asked me what Mom would like, and I said bacon and eggs, with toast cut into triangles and served on the toast rack. In truth, Mom would probably prefer something a bit healthier, but the only fruit we have in the house are three tasteless apples and a speckled banana.

I teach Laurel how to fry an egg and how to get the bacon just the right side of crispy. She prepares a tray, complete with one of the napkins that we only use at Christmas and Thanksgiving. We make a pot of tea and pour a glass of orange juice, then Laurel carries the tray up the stairs. I knock on Mom's door and we go in. She's sprawled across the bed like a starfish, which always makes me wonder how she ever used to manage to share a bed with Dad. It takes her a few seconds to wake up, but she finally sits up and props a pillow behind her. Her sleepy smile makes me feel good inside.

"What's all this?" she says as Laurel places the tray on her lap.

"We made you breakfast!" Laurel says proudly.

"Yes, I can see that! But what have I done to deserve the royal treatment?"

Laurel looks to me for an answer, but I don't really have one. "We just thought it would be nice."

Mom takes a slice of toast from the rack and munches on the corner. "Mmm, I could get used to this."

Laurel and I perch on either side of Mom, and we talk while she eats her breakfast. Mom says it's the best breakfast she's ever had, and that's including the one she had the morning after she got married, when she and Dad stayed in a very expensive hotel. "My two girls," she says. There's so much love in her eyes that it almost hurts to look at her. The shame from last night bubbles up in my throat again, threatening to spill out of my mouth and onto the duvet cover.

Laurel starts quizzing Mom about her wedding, and I learn things that I never knew before. Dad was so nervous he threw up in the bushes outside the church; he had to ask around for chewing gum so that he didn't have vomit breath for the "You may kiss the bride" moment. Mom had a blazing fight with Gran the night before the wedding, but she can't remember what it was about now. The first dance was some terrible song from the eighties, which Mom insisted on having even though Dad hated it.

Mom doesn't seem to mind talking about it, which surprises me. I'd have thought she'd want to forget all about the day she married my dad. I say something to that effect, but Mom shakes her head. "I could never regret marrying your father."

"Why?" Laurel asks. By this point, she's lying on the bed next to Mom.

Mom gives Laurel a look as if to say, *It's obvious, isn't it?* But it's not obvious to us.

"Because of you two, of course!"

The three of us smile at one another, and I wonder if I'm the only one thinking that if she hadn't married Dad, Mom would have been spared thirteen years of unhappiness—the kind of unhappiness that no one should ever have to endure in their lives. I quickly come to the conclusion that, yes, I am definitely the only one thinking that.

Thomas's patience has finally run out; it's hardly surprising. He hasn't come right out and said that we need to have sex again soon or he will break up with me, but I bet that's what he's thinking. The hints he's been dropping haven't exactly been subtle, and they've been getting harder and harder to ignore. I'm amazed he's waited this long, to be honest. He's not like other boys our age—or rather, he *is* like other boys our age, but he would rather die than admit it.

I can't exactly explain to him that he's sort of dropped down on my list of priorities since Laurel came back. He wouldn't understand; no one would. Having my sister back shouldn't mean that everything—and everyone—else in my life falls by the wayside. I know that. I do. It's just that Laurel coming back has changed everything. It's changed *me*.

Still, I do want to have sex with Thomas again. Just to see. The truth is, I haven't missed him all that much. I've been happy just to see him at school, mostly. And I'm sure that can't be right. I'm sure I'm supposed to miss him, to be pining for him, aching for the touch of his skin on mine. So this is an experiment—to test my feelings once and for all.

When Mom announced that she was going away for a spa day (and night) with Eleanor, the plan popped into my head right away, as if it had been lurking in the wings just waiting for the right circumstances to present themselves. This time, the sex will be happening in the proper place—in a bed—just to see if that makes any difference. Laurel and I are going to start watching a new TV series that Martha told her about. Then I will say that I'm tired and want to have an early night. I'll make sure that Laurel goes to bed at the same time, which shouldn't be too hard. Things have been really good for the last couple of days. We've been going out of our way to be nice—both of us falling over ourselves to make sure the other one is happy.

As soon as I'm in my room, I'll text Thomas to let him know that the coast is clear. Or maybe I'll get him to wait half an hour—or even an hour—to make sure that Laurel is asleep. He will text when he's outside, I'll creep downstairs to let him in; the two of us will creep back upstairs and get down to business. We'll have to be quiet—definitely no laughing this time. As soon as the sex is over, he'll have to leave. I can't risk us falling asleep and him still being there when Laurel gets up the next day.

Of course, I could just *tell* Laurel. She would probably be fine about it. It might even bring us closer together, hatching a plan, keeping a secret from Mom. But it doesn't feel right. The idea of her in the next room, knowing what Thomas and I are doing. Even if she agreed to sleep in Mom's room so she wouldn't accidentally hear anything, it still wouldn't feel right.

I haven't told Martha, either. I have a good excuse, though: she's away for a couple of days, staying with some family friends. But that's not the real reason I haven't told her. She would ask too many questions, and I'd probably end up telling her how unsure I am about Thomas. A few months ago, that would have been fine and we could have talked about it and she would have understood. But now she actually *likes* him, rather than thinking he's a bit of a pretentious wannabe. I bet she would stay friends with Thomas if I broke up with him, and I bet I wouldn't be as cool about that as I would have to pretend to be.

CHAPTER 30

The plan goes smoothly, and Laurel falls asleep halfway through the fifth episode of the TV show. Laurel goes to bed, and I text Thomas just after eleven. His reply arrives with lightning speed; he's clearly raring to go.

I was going to change into my pajamas, but they would definitely spoil the mood, and it's not as if I have any sexy lingerie hiding at the back of my dresser. So I decided to keep my clothes on—for now.

Thomas leans in to kiss me as soon as I open the front door. He tastes savory, but not in a bad way. Still, it means he hasn't brushed his teeth in the last few hours. I brushed mine till my gums bled. He grins. "Is she asleep?"

I nod. I listened outside Laurel's door for long enough to hear the snuffly breathing sound she makes when she sleeps. Thomas and I creep upstairs. He mutters something about the van being a much simpler option, and I shush him. I follow him into my bedroom and shut the door.

• • •

The lighting is low—I put my bedside light on the floor just in case Thomas decides he wants to do this with the lights on. I didn't bother to change the sheets, because Mom changed them two days ago and, besides, Thomas isn't exactly fastidious when it comes to personal hygiene.

It's only the third time Thomas has been in my bedroom. Mom always insists that we stay downstairs when she's around—and up until recently, she's almost always been around. He doesn't waste any time, launching himself at me and kissing me hard. Too hard—our mouths slam together and for a moment I think I might have chipped a tooth. I tell him to slow down, that there's no rush.

"Easy for you to say," he murmurs in between kisses on my neck.

I pull away. "What's that supposed to mean?" I ask, forgetting that we're supposed to be keeping the noise down. I repeat the question in a whisper when Thomas doesn't answer.

"Nothing," he whispers, pulling me into his arms again. "I just . . . I've been looking forward to this."

It's such an innocent thing to say that it makes me smile. Thomas seems to have this ability to say the right words to turn things around. He doesn't always find the right words at first, but he gets there in the end.

There's a brief moment of worry when Thomas thinks he's forgotten to bring condoms; I start to wonder if maybe God (I don't actually believe in God) just doesn't want us to have sex again. That he's putting too many obstacles in our way. It's a *sign*. But then Thomas remembers that he put the condoms in his jacket pocket because his jeans were in the wash.

He pulls his T-shirt over his head to reveal his skinny, hairless chest. He's not self-conscious about his body at all, unlike me. He pulls down his jeans and stands in front of me, with his socks and boxers still on. He looks at me and waits. "Well, aren't you going to . . . ?" He gestures to my clothes.

I take off my top slowly. Reluctantly. All of a sudden, I'm not sure that this is the best idea in the entire world. It doesn't seem fair to Thomas to be doing this with him when I can't seem to make up my mind about how I feel about him. But then he comes closer to me, and he tells me I'm beautiful. I look into his eyes and I believe him. I'm sure about his feelings for *me,* and shouldn't that count for something?

I lean into him and tuck my head into that space between his head and his shoulder—the space that I always thought was custom-made just for me. He holds me tight and tells me that we don't have to do anything if I don't want to. "I can just hold you for a little while." I can't see his face to check, but it feels like the truth. He really *wouldn't* mind. And that's when I realize that I do care about him. I *want* to do this.

I kiss him fiercely to get the message across, then I push him toward the bed.

It hurts more this time, which doesn't seem fair. I close my eyes and try not to feel. It will be over soon. I wonder if Mom is having a nice time at the spa with Eleanor. If I know Eleanor, it will be more champagne and massages than wheat-germ juice and Bikram yoga. Then I wonder if it's normal to think about what your mom is up to while you're having sex with your boyfriend. Probably not.

Thomas's breathing is getting faster and noisier in my left ear. Hopefully it won't be long now. I'm completely silent, unlike the last time. I run my fingers up and down his spine, and it reminds me of the bumpy back of a dinosaur I saw in the Natural History Museum on a school trip. How old was I then? Eleven? Twelve? No, definitely eleven.

I don't know what makes me open my eyes. I didn't hear anything. But I look over to the door, and it's open—just a few inches. I'm sure I closed it behind us.

She's there, watching. A scream rises in my throat but lodges there like a thorn before it can escape from my mouth. My body jolts in shock and I gasp, but Thomas is too close to coming to notice.

My gaze catches Laurel's and she doesn't even flinch at being caught. I expect the door to slam shut, but it doesn't. I don't know what to do. I want to look away, but I can't. Any second now.

Thomas's orgasm seems to take an age. Then he lies perfectly still on top of me and the whole weight of him is on me, and I feel like I'm being crushed even though he hardly weighs anything at all—certainly less than I do.

Eventually he raises himself up on his arms and kisses me; his face has a fine sheen of sweat and a couple of red blotches have appeared on his cheeks. I look back toward the door. It's closed. She's gone.

• • •

I let Thomas lie next to me for a few minutes. He asks me what I'm thinking. Nothing, I say. He asks me if I'm happy. I say yes. He gets dressed and tells me he loves me. I say that I love him. He leaves.

I lie in bed, naked. I clutch the comforter with my fingers and pull it right up to my neck. I'm acutely aware of her presence next door, just as she must be aware of mine. I feel hot with embarrassment, cold with confusion. Why didn't I push him off me the second I noticed her? Why didn't I tell him afterward?

What the hell was she *thinking,* spying on us like that? What am I going to say to her? Should I go and talk to her now?

I don't move. I watch the door and hope and pray that it doesn't open again.

CHAPTER
31

I get up early after a restless night. If I slept, I don't remember. I get dressed in jeans and a hoodie, careful not to make a sound. I open my bedroom door and stand and listen. I hear cars passing outside, the gurgling from the radiator on the landing, a dog barking. No sounds from Laurel's room.

I don't risk brushing my teeth, because the noise from the pipes will almost certainly wake her. I go downstairs and out the front door. I end up in a café, rushing to use the restroom before I join the line at the counter.

I sit in a corner, facing the door. I drink two cups of dreadful, swill-colored tea and check the time on my phone every couple of minutes. I can't stay away forever; Mom will be back at lunchtime.

Just before nine I get a text from Martha asking if I want to do something when she's back this afternoon. She doesn't specify what that something might be, so it's probably nothing, but we'd be doing nothing together, at least. I reply and say I'll go over to her place at three. Anything to get out of the house.

Another text arrives, from Laurel this time. She wants to know where I am; she's made breakfast. I reply and say I'll be home soon, that I just went out to buy some milk. She texts again: OK, I'll get the coffee on!

I forget the milk, but Laurel doesn't say anything when I walk into the kitchen empty-handed. But there's plenty in the fridge—Mom stocked up before she went, buying enough groceries for us to endure a three-month siege even though she was only going to be gone for twenty-four hours.

Laurel's trying her hand at scrambled eggs today. "I figured they would be the easiest to do on my own." She smiles warmly. Her hair is tied up in a ponytail. She hasn't showered yet, either.

I look in the pan that she's stirring; the eggs have been seriously scrambled. The toast pops up from the toaster, and Laurel asks me to butter it. She's put our matching mugs out on the counter.

I concentrate hard on the task at hand. The scraping sound of the knife on the toast scratches at my nerves; I wonder which one of us is going to be the first to crack. Someone has to bring up the subject, and I don't think it should be me. Laurel pours the coffee.

We sit down at the table—she's already put out the cutlery, and even a couple of sheets of paper towel to use as napkins. The eggs are rubbery and weirdly crusty in places. I don't want to eat them, but I don't want to hurt Laurel's feelings. Cooking is one of the things she seems to really enjoy. I blame Michel—he keeps going on about her being a natural and saying maybe she should look into a career that involves food. Dad always shuts down this kind of talk; he thinks she has no chance of having a normal job like that.

I eat a corner of toast with the tiniest bit of egg I can get away with. I realize that Laurel's looking at me, eyebrows raised in expectation. "Delicious," I say, talking with my mouth full because Mom's not around to moan about it.

"Liar. But that's okay. They'll be better next time."

We eat in silence for a couple of minutes. The toast is hard to choke down, so I start eating more eggs to aid in the process.

"So . . . did you sleep well?" she asks.

That's when I realize how we're going to play this. In true Logan style, we are not going to talk about it. We are going to bury it, hope that a cement mixer comes along and pours concrete over the issue so that it will never see the light again.

"Fine, thank you," I say with a smile. "How about you?"

"Like a baby," she says. "That's a weird saying, isn't it? Slept like a baby. Babies are always crying."

I smile again and agree that it is a weird saying. Then I ask Laurel about her plans for the day.

All the time we're talking I'm wondering what she's really thinking. She knows that I saw her, so she must be scared that I'm going to say something—accuse her of spying on Thomas and me. She saw me notice her. There was eye contact—*prolonged* eye contact. But I suddenly remember something Martha once said about her mom's eyesight, that she can't see more than a few inches in front of her face without her glasses. I rack my brain to remember if Laurel's had an eye test since she's been back. I'm not sure. Being kept in a basement for all those years would surely have an effect on your eyesight. How could it not? So maybe—just maybe—Laurel *doesn't* realize that I caught her watching us. And I'm not sure whether that's a good thing or not. Perhaps she's blind as a bat and no one's bothered to check? Maybe there's a chance her eyesight is so bad she didn't even realize what Thomas and I were doing. (Nice try—*of course* she knew what we were doing.)

It's a relief, in a way. Not to have to talk about it. Not to have to stutter and stumble over my words as I try to explain why I'd been so secretive about Thomas coming over. I'd have to beg her not to tell Mom, too. Mom would not be happy to find out that Thomas and I are having sex. It doesn't matter to her that it's legal, or that we're in a serious, long-term relationship, or that we're using protection. What matters to her is that she doesn't like Thomas and never will. If she found out, she'd never leave Laurel and me alone in the house again. I'm sure that Laurel would agree to keep it a secret from Mom, but now I can't ask. She won't tell her; I'm almost certain of that. Because if she did, then she'd have to admit that she was watching us, and that would just be awkward.

It's better this way, brushing it under the carpet, pretending nothing odd—nothing excruciatingly, embarrassingly weird—has happened. Now I just have to try to erase the memory from my head. If only it were that easy. I have a funny feeling I will never be able to forget the shock of seeing her standing there, watching. Judging.

• • •

Mom comes home sporting a pair of sunglasses, accompanied by a vaguely winey vapor. "Never again," she says. "She's a bad influence on me, you know."

Laurel says she'll make Mom a sandwich, but Mom winces at the mention of food. "Thanks, love, maybe later. I think I'll have a little nap first. Anyway, did you two have fun last night?"

"We had a lovely time, thanks. A really nice, girly night," says Laurel. I'm almost sure that she puts a slight emphasis on the word *girly*. And if I'm right, then Laurel is toying with me. Perhaps it amuses her to see me squirm.

Mom trudges toward the stairs with her overnight bag, taking careful steps as if she's on a boat in a storm. Laurel catches my eye and shakes her head, smiling. This is supposed to translate as something like *Parents, huh?* or *What is she like?* I'm supposed to return the look in kind, or maybe roll my eyes and laugh. Instead, I ignore it completely. My eyes pass over her as if she's not even there.

Mom stops on the third stair. "Oh, I nearly forgot! How could I forget?" I refrain from remarking on the obvious correlation between alcohol consumption and memory loss. "You'll never guess who called me last night! Well, she called, but I didn't answer because I was . . . Anyway, she left a voice mail, and when I listened to it this morning, I could hardly believe it. Talk about a blast from the past!"

"Who was it?" I hate guessing games.

"Dana Fairlie!" Mom looks at me expectantly. I have no idea who Dana Fairlie is, which is quite obvious from the confused look on my face. "The Fairlies? Number Twenty-Four?" Nope. Not a clue.

Mom heaves a big sigh as if I'm being deliberately dense. She comes back down the stairs. "Laurel, you remember little Bryony? The two of you used to be inseparable. Always in and out of each other's houses, making mischief."

Laurel nods, vaguely at first and then more decisively. "Yeah. Yes. I remember."

It turns out that the Fairlies used to live a couple of doors down from us on Stanley Street. They had two daughters around the same age as Laurel and me, so they became friends with Mom and Dad. They moved to Australia a month before Laurel was taken. I remember now, but the memory is of a photograph I saw a long time ago. Laurel and another girl. Two little blond girls, as alike as sisters (*real* sisters). Their hair in matching pigtails, heads together, faces tilted at an angle, big smiles. I remember what I thought when I saw that picture. Why couldn't the other little girl have been taken away instead of my sister? And now I know why: because she was thousands and thousands of miles away. Safe, on the other side of the world.

"Anyway, they're *back*! Well, they're not *back* back, but they're here for a month or so. Kirsty wants to go to college over here—just think of that, little Kirsty, all grown up and off to college! It's hard to believe. . . ."

In typical Mom fashion, she's arranged for us all to meet up tomorrow without bothering to check with us first. I mean, it's one thing to do that to Laurel—she never has any plans—but I actually *have* a life. I agree to it, though, because I'm curious to see these people who could have so easily been us. Say the paperwork for the emigration hadn't come through yet, or Mr. or Mrs. Fairlie had to stay in the country for an extra month to finish some big project at work; they would have still been on Stanley Street that day when our lives fell apart. Bryony and Kirsty could have been playing in their front yard, and maybe Laurel and I would have been inside because one of us wasn't feeling very well. We would have been snuggled together on the sofa watching a Disney film when the shadow passed our house. Bryony Fairlie's face would be on the front page of every newspaper, and my parents would feel terrible about it and do everything they could to help the Fairlies through their ordeal, taking care of Kirsty and making lasagnas that Mrs. Fairlie could reheat after yet another press conference. Mom and Dad would join the search party and put up posters that read HAVE YOU SEEN THIS GIRL? and try their hardest to remember in case they might have noticed something significant that day. A car that didn't belong on the street or a man acting suspiciously. And all the while, as Mom hugged Mrs. Fairlie and told her everything was going to be okay, and Dad exchanged grim looks with Mr. Fairlie, they would be thinking the same thing. Over and over again. *Thank god it wasn't one of* our *daughters. Thank god.*

CHAPTER
32

Every surface in Martha's kitchen is covered with jars. There are two huge pots bubbling away on the stove, and Martha's mom is dipping a metal thermometer into one of them. She looks happier than the last time I saw her. Being unemployed seems to suit her.

Martha drags me away from the kitchen and upstairs to her room. "The jam-making is completely out of control! She thinks she can make a business out of it, even though I told her it's a stupid idea."

I shrug. It seems like an okay idea to me. Customers at the farmers' market think nothing of spending a crazy amount on a jar of artisanal jam. But I let Martha rant and moan, because that's what best friends do.

I almost tell her about what happened last night, but it's all too complicated. Plus, I don't want Martha thinking I'm weird. She wouldn't understand why I didn't confront Laurel for spying on Thomas and me. I don't even tell Martha about the shoplifting, but I do talk about Laurel. I tell

Martha about the dress, and she agrees that it's an obscene amount of money to spend on one item of clothing. I moan about the book deal and the fact that I have to go and meet the ghostwriter next week. They've decided that I should be the first one to be interviewed, probably because I have so little to say. At least I got to choose the meeting place; the editor (Zara Double-Barreled) told Mom it should be somewhere I feel comfortable. Mom said I should do it at home, thinking I would be reassured by her presence. I suggested a café bar near the canal—where it's highly unlikely I'll see anyone I know.

It starts with the dress and the book deal, and before I know it I'm telling Martha (almost) every little thing that Laurel's done to annoy me over the past couple of weeks. "She's just always *there,* you know?" Because that's what it really comes down to: Laurel is around *all* the time. Unless you count her twice-weekly visits to the psychologist and random sessions with Penny. But other than that, there's no respite, no escape.

"So having a big sister isn't all it's cracked up to be, then?" Martha says with a smirk.

And there it is again: the guilt. It's always there, too, shadowing me, just like Laurel. I feel like I have to be grateful *all* the time, that any negative feelings—no matter how small—are not allowed. Sometimes, late at night when sleep eludes me, I worry that something awful will happen to Laurel. That she'll get run over by a car or choke to death on a fish bone or drown in the bath, all because of me. Because I haven't been grateful enough to have her back. I worry that Laurel is going to be taken away again just to punish me.

I tell Martha that I didn't mean it, that I do like having a big sister, honestly. She laughs and says, "It's okay, you know. You don't have to pretend with me." She leans over and squeezes my knee. "This is a *safe* place," she says with a fake sympathetic expression on her face.

I know she's making fun of me, but I'm so grateful I could cry. Just knowing that she doesn't mind listening to me whine, and that she doesn't think I'm a terrible person, makes me feel a whole lot better.

I tell Martha about the Fairlies and how weird it's going to be. Martha reassures me that however weird it is for me, it's going to be ten times weirder for Laurel. Everyone will be focused on her anyway; they always are.

"What are you going to wear to the party?" Martha's sitting at her desk with her back to me. She always sits up straight, like a character in a costume drama. People her height usually slouch.

"What party?" I'm sitting on the floor with my back against the bed, deleting old messages from my phone. It's been a bit of a waste of an afternoon. We could have at least gone to the movies, but Martha said there was nothing she wanted to see. Still, it's been good to get away from home for a few hours. God knows how I'll get through the rest of the week with my sanity intact.

"Thomas's party." She doesn't turn and look at me, and I'm not sure whether it's because she's worried about my reaction or because she doesn't realize that I have no idea what she's talking about.

"I'll say it again: What. Party?"

Now she turns, unable to ignore my frostiness. She looks confused. "His surprise party? For his eighteenth? How can you not . . . ? Hasn't his mom . . . ? She said she was going to get in touch with you last week."

There are so many things wrong with what Martha's saying that I really don't know where to start. First of all, Thomas hates parties *and* surprises. Put the two together and you pretty much have his worst nightmare. Second of all, how come Martha knows about this before I do? Last, but by no means least, what the hell was she doing talking to Thomas's mother?

Martha rushes to explain, trying to get the words out as quickly as possible—the words that will remove the look on my face. "Oh . . . wow . . . okay, I was sure she'd have talked to you by now. Anyway, I can fill you in. So she's planning a surprise party. She's already invited all the family. She knows that it's not really Thomas's thing at all, but she said this was her last chance to throw a party for 'her little baby,' and he hasn't let her do much to celebrate his birthday for the past couple of years, so she decided to just go for it. I did say it might not be the best idea, but she thinks he'll probably secretly love the attention. She said that he might pretend to be all cool and intellectual, but underneath he's just a little boy whose favorite food is jelly and ice cream. Did you know that? I thought his favorite food was sashimi." Finally, she pauses to check how she's doing. Is the look on my face still unimpressed, or has it morphed into something friendlier?

It has not. "When were you talking to his mom?"

Martha shrugs. "Last week? Or maybe the week before.

I can't remember exactly." She's going to have to do better than that, and she knows it. "I needed to borrow a textbook. Thomas went upstairs to get it, and she cornered me in the kitchen." Thomas's house is nowhere near Martha's. For her to get there, she would have to get a bus that passes right by the end of my street. There are no textbooks that Martha would need to borrow from Thomas that she wouldn't be able to borrow from me. "You were out," she says, answering a question I didn't ask.

"He didn't mention it."

"Why would he? Anyway, what are you going to wear? Mrs. Bolt said 'smart-casual,' whatever that means. Do you think it means we can't wear jeans?"

She's making a decent effort to distract me, or rather, she would be if we were the sort of girls who have conversations about clothes. The fact that we're *not* the sort of girls who have conversations about clothes makes me realize that she hadn't been able to find a better entry point into a conversation about the party, and that she was therefore fully aware that I knew nothing about it. My head hurts.

I do a good job, I think, of acting like I don't mind about Martha having cozy little chats with Mrs. Bolt—the kind of chats that Mrs. Bolt has never shown any interest in having with me. Martha watches me closely for signs that I'm pissed off, but after my initial failure to hide my feelings, I'm back on track.

A surprise party for Thomas's eighteenth is a terrible, terrible idea. He will hate every minute. He will hate the presents people give him—the presents that prove that they don't know him at all. He will hate the music, having his

209

photograph taken, blowing out the candles on his cake (which, Martha informs me, will be in the shape of a pile of books). It will be funny to watch him squirm. In a way I'm glad his mom didn't talk to me about it, because I probably would have managed to talk her out of it. I wouldn't miss this for the world.

I ask Martha who's invited. Thomas has a few friends at school, but no one really close. Mrs. Bolt will be getting in touch with them over the next couple of days, leaving it until the last minute so they don't "ruin the surprise." It seems to me that leaving it so late is much more likely to mean that they won't be able to come. It's not as if people will have cleared their social calendars just in case there's an outside chance they'll get an invite to the coming-of-age of Thomas Edwin Bolt. (I tease Thomas about his middle name on a regular basis. Not that Thomas is much better; why can't he just be Tom like a normal person?)

While we're talking, I get a text message from a number I don't recognize. Speak of the devil. Thomas's mom has finally bothered to inform me about the impending celebration. She doesn't even apologize for leaving it so late. The message answers the next question I was about to ask Martha: the venue. The Bolts have booked a room above a bar near their house. Another text arrives before I've finished reading the first.

"She's asked if I want to bring Laurel."

"So?"

I sigh. If I have to explain this to Martha, it means she doesn't get it.

Martha shrugs. "You know . . . it might be a good thing,

210

Laurel coming to the party. It's the perfect opportunity for her to make some friends, don't you think?"

Martha could be right. As long as there are some half-decent people coming, there's bound to be someone Laurel can hang out with. I think Thomas mentioned something about a cousin who's studying at Oxford; she might be a good place to start. It's times like this that I'm grateful to have a friend like Martha—someone who sees things slightly differently. I smile. "You're a genius."

Martha sighs dramatically and flops down onto the bed behind me. "I *know*. A brain like mine is *such* a burden. You have *no* idea."

CHAPTER
33

Laurel's *really* happy about being invited to the party, and I can tell from the look on Mom's face that she's happy about it, too. Mom probably thinks that this is a *beginning,* that maybe Laurel can start to live something close to a normal life after all. I swear them both to secrecy, explaining that Thomas knows nothing about the party.

Laurel looks at me with wide eyes. "I don't know how you manage not to say anything to him! I could *never* keep a secret like that."

I don't tell them that I've only just found out about it myself, and I haven't talked to Thomas, so keeping the secret has been easy as pie so far. I should have known about this weeks ago and been fully involved in planning it. That's what people would expect—and what Mom and Laurel clearly think—so I'm not going to tell them any different.

"Thomas doesn't really strike me as the type of person who'd like a surprise party," Mom says coolly, sipping her wine. She's clearly decided that hair of the dog is the only way to deal with her hangover.

"He's not," I say. They both look at me, waiting for me to continue. "That's what makes it such an amazing idea!" I laugh, and Mom laughs, too, and says I'm terrible.

Laurel's face is blank, and I realize this is one of those everyday human interactions that seem to baffle her. She can't understand why I would be so gleeful about something that Thomas will hate. I try to explain, but it doesn't do any good. Laurel narrows her eyes and looks thoughtful. "Do you mean you think he'll actually secretly enjoy it? He'll just be pretending to hate it?"

A quick glance at Mom, who nods almost imperceptibly. "Yes, that's exactly what I mean."

Laurel seems nervous about meeting up with the Fairlies. While we're waiting for Mom to get ready, she keeps on getting up and staring at herself in the mirror above the fireplace. For reasons known only to herself, she's decided to wear her hair in pigtails today. Mom raised her eyebrows when she saw her, but said nothing.

I ask Laurel if she's okay, and she nods and smiles and says of course she is. I don't believe her. It's understandable that she's anxious, I suppose. I'm a little nervous, too, but Mom's really excited. Yesterday's hangover is a distant memory and the prospect of lunch out with "her girls" seems to make her happy. She eventually comes downstairs wearing far too much makeup. There's no point in saying anything, though—it would only upset her. I can understand her wanting to look her best to see a friend she hasn't seen in years. I just wish that she would understand that she doesn't need to wear that much makeup these days.

213

Now that the trauma of Laurel's disappearance is starting to erase itself from her face, she doesn't need to wear a mask anymore.

I spy them on the other side of the restaurant. They're in a big, curved booth that reminds me of a clamshell; I wish they'd sat at one of the normal tables instead.

None of us have been to this restaurant before; I have no idea why Mom chose it. On the way over to the booth, I look at the other customers and notice that they're mostly well dressed, a lot of women with bags from fancy shops. So *that's* why Mom chose this place: she's trying to impress.

The Fairlies file out of the booth, and Mrs. Fairlie hugs Mom. "Olivia! It's so wonderful to see you!" She comes over to me next, which surprises me. Most people notice Laurel first. "Little Faith! Oh my goodness! Look at you!" I never understand what that means: *Look at you.* It's the kind of thing you say when someone has a new haircut. It's neither positive nor negative, but people tend to take it positively. They hear what they want to hear, rather than what's actually been said.

Over Mrs. Fairlie's shoulder, I see the two girls. Bryony and Kirsty. They're both smiling shyly and looking about as awkward as I feel. Then Mom hugs them, too, and we all keep getting in one another's way in our efforts to greet everyone.

Nobody tries to hug Laurel; Mom must have warned them, I guess. Bryony embraces me in a loose sort of hug—

the kind where you barely touch the other person. Kirsty and I sort of wave at each other from a couple of feet away.

Eventually we go to sit down. Mom and Mrs. Fairlie make sure that Bryony and Laurel are sitting next to each other.

"Well," says Mrs. Fairlie, "long time no see!" Her accent is odd—with a slight upward lilt at the end of each sentence. Bryony and Kirsty have full-on Australian accents. It suits them. They *look* Australian: tanned and blond and beautiful.

As soon as the drinks have been poured, Mom raises her glass. After a moment's hesitation, we all do the same. "To old friends!" We all clink glasses and take a sip of our drinks. Then there's a pause before Mom launches into a barrage of questions about the Fairlies' "life Down Under," as she calls it. I see what she's doing: trying to divert the focus from Laurel and pretend that this is just your standard reunion with old neighbors.

Before long Mrs. Fairlie and Mom are deeply involved in a discussion about the benefits of the Australian outdoor way of life *(We eat outside eight months of the year!)*. Laurel and Bryony are talking quietly on the other side of the booth. I can't hear what they're talking about, because Mom and Mrs. Fairlie are being so loud.

Kirsty keeps staring at Laurel, as if she can't quite believe Laurel is real. I mostly concentrate on my plate—a salad with three different varieties of beets. The food is really good, actually.

"So . . ." Kirsty has a mouthful of food, but she's clearly not going to let that stop her from speaking. "What's it like, having her back? It must be *weird*!"

I want to hate Kirsty for being so blunt, but I can't. She's one of the only people to recognize the strangeness of the situation. I only wish she'd said it louder so Mom could hear that there are other ways of looking at Laurel's return—it's not all smiles and hugs and rainbows.

"Yeah, it is. It's good, though."

She snorts loudly and Mrs. Fairlie looks over, disapproval etched on her face. Kirsty ignores the look. "You don't sound so sure!"

"I *am* sure . . . but you know what it's like having a sister."

Kirsty looks across the table at her sister, and I look across the table at mine. Their heads are close together, as if they're sharing secrets. "Do I *ever*? I always wanted a brother, you know? Someone who'd shove me or smack me if we had an argument, rather than give me the silent treatment for three days."

"Bryony seems nice, though?" I whisper, subconsciously mimicking the inflections in Kirsty's voice.

Another snort from Kirsty. "Yeah, that's what everyone thinks. They have no idea what a raving *bitch* she can be— especially when she has her period. Fucking nightmare!"

Mom must have heard the swearing, because she turns her attention to us. "What are you two gossiping about?"

"I was just telling Kirsty about us going on *The Cynthia Day Show*." The lie trips off my tongue.

"Oh my goodness, is that woman not dead yet?" says Mrs. Fairlie. "I used to watch that show when I was in college! I can't believe it's still running. . . . Who watches that garbage?"

Thankfully Laurel doesn't seem to hear Mrs. Fairlie bad-mouthing her favorite TV show. Mom doesn't seem offended even though Mrs. Fairlie has essentially lumped us in with the garbage. Mom tells her that *The Cynthia Day Show* has actually got a lot better in recent years. "It's less about teen pregnancy and paternity tests and more about human-interest stories." She can tell herself that all she wants, but it still won't be true. Laurel told me that yesterday's show featured a woman who wasn't sure about the identity of the father of the baby she was carrying, but she was "ninety percent sure it was either her fiancé or his twin brother."

Kirsty keeps asking me questions about Laurel, but I don't really mind, because the questions are different from the ones people usually ask. She's actually interested in what it's like for me and how it's changed *my* life. At one point, she admits that she used to wish *her* sister would disappear, but then she sees the look on my face—or rather the absence of the look she wanted to see—and apologizes. I'm surprised to find that I sort of like Kirsty. Maybe if the Fairlies hadn't moved to Australia, we would have been friends.

The waiter brings the dessert menus, and Mom and Mrs. Fairlie both say something along the lines of "Oh no, I *shouldn't,*" before ordering deconstructed sticky toffee pudding and raspberry crème brûlée respectively. I don't order anything; I do my best to ignore the approving look from Mom. Kirsty orders the same as her mom, and then everyone turns to Laurel and Bryony.

Laurel smiles and says she's not hungry. The smile is a bad photocopy of a real one, blurred and smudged. It's not as simple as they say—that you can tell a fake smile because it never reaches the eyes. No, Laurel's better than that. But there's a strained quality, as if she's working the muscles in her face so hard they might go into spasm any second now. It's in her voice, too—slightly too loud, slightly too chirpy. She is *not* happy. I'm sure I'm the only one who notices; the Fairlies don't know her well enough, and Mom has a tendency to only see what she wants to see.

The interesting thing is that Bryony doesn't look too happy, either. She says she doesn't want any dessert, and Mrs. Fairlie nudges her and says, "But sticky toffee pudding is your favorite!"

Bryony scowls and says, "I *said* I didn't want anything." Then she looks up at the waiter (who is being remarkably patient, waiting to take our coffee order) and asks him where the bathroom is.

"I'll go with you," Laurel says quickly, and you can tell Bryony isn't too thrilled about that, but she doesn't say anything.

Laurel and Bryony head off in the direction the waiter pointed, and Mom and Mrs. Fairlie look at each other and smile.

"Like two peas in a pod, those two," says Mom.

"Going to the bathroom together!" says Mrs. Fairlie, laughing at her own terrible joke.

"God, you're *so* embarrassing," says Kirsty, rolling her eyes.

CHAPTER
34

"That was lovely. Wasn't that lovely?" Mom turns to look at me. The bus is packed with commuters and shoppers. There was one double seat available—for Mom and Laurel, of course—so I'm sitting behind them, next to a skinny guy wearing jeans, a denim shirt, *and* a denim jacket. He keeps looking at me out of the corner of his eye.

"Yeah, it was nice." I want Mom to stop turning around. I don't want Triple Denim listening in on our conversation and having the chance to figure out who Laurel is.

Mom turns to Laurel next. "Such a nice family. I was so upset when they moved away!"

Laurel says all the right things—how much she enjoyed the lunch and how wonderful it was to see Bryony. I can only see the side of her face as she talks to Mom, but it's her voice that's the real giveaway. Too polished, too shiny.

When Bryony and Laurel came back from the bathroom, the other three were engaged in a pointless debate about the sexuality of some middle-aged actor Mom's always had a thing for. No one else noticed the awkwardness between the two girls, or the fact that instead of talking to each other, they spent the rest of the meal focusing on Mom and Mrs. Fairlie's conversation. Bryony was sitting as far away from Laurel as she could possibly get, perched right on the edge of the bench seat. Mom and Mrs. Fairlie were probably too distracted by the desserts—they both kept on making *ooh* and *mmm* sounds with each spoonful.

I caught Laurel's eye, arching my eyebrows in a silent question. *Is everything okay?*

Her response was half a nod—a brief raising of the chin. *Everything's fine.*

The good-byes were less awkward than the hellos. Kirsty suggested we exchange numbers, given that she's going to be at college over here next year. There were tears in Mrs. Fairlie's eyes. "This has been *so* special. . . . I'm so glad everything turned out okay." She glanced at Laurel, but Laurel was busy staring out the window. Mom and Mrs. Fairlie vowed to keep in touch, and Mom said we might even go to Australia on vacation sometime in the next couple of years. She neglected to mention who was included in that *we*. There had been no mention of Dad during the meal, I was pretty sure of that.

I seemed to be the only one who noticed that Bryony and Laurel didn't really say good-bye to each other.

As soon as we get home, Laurel announces that she has a headache.

Mom says, "Why don't you go upstairs for a nap? There's Tylenol in the bathroom cabinet if you need it."

Laurel's halfway up the stairs when I call up to her. "I'll bring you up a glass of water if you like?" I get an approving look from Mom for that.

Laurel says there's no need, that she can swallow the pills dry, but I insist.

She's sitting on her bed when I come in. I ask her if she wants me to get the Tylenol for her.

"No, thanks," she says.

"You don't really have a headache, do you?"

"No."

I sit down next to her on the bed. "What's the matter?" I don't say that I noticed the awkwardness at lunch; it's better if people don't know that you can read them so easily.

"Nothing. I'm just tired, I think." I'm about to quiz her further about Bryony and what was said, but she says, "The nightmares have been bad the last few nights."

"I'm sorry." There's not much else I can say. My nightmares are bad enough. They're horrible at the time, but the horror recedes as soon as I wake up. Laurel's nightmares are different, obviously. She's lived inside a nightmare for most of her life. I'm not sure she'll ever be able to truly escape.

I'm dying to find out what happened with Bryony, but I can't ask Laurel while she's sitting there looking so desolate.

I've started to notice a pattern, if you can count something happening three or four times as a pattern. There are times when someone—usually me—asks Laurel a question or says something to her, and out of nowhere she'll mention Smith or something that happened to her in that basement. It's almost as if she feels the need to remind you (me) about what she's been through. As if there are some things she doesn't want to talk about, and shouldn't *have* to talk about, solely because of what that man did to her. The strange thing is, the questions that spark this reaction rarely have anything whatsoever to do with what happened to her. I try to remind myself that any little thing could trigger a memory for her. But I can't get rid of the niggling feeling that sometimes she uses her ordeal as a sort of Get Out of Jail Free card when she wants to shut down a conversation.

CHAPTER
35

The ghostwriter is late; I was twenty minutes early. I chose a couple of sofas next to the window in the corner, putting my coat and bag next to me so she would have to sit opposite me. Mom arranged to meet a friend for lunch in town so she could give me a lift. She invited Laurel, too, but Laurel said she wanted to stay home.

"I hope you're going to do something other than watch TV?" Mom said, and it was the first truly Mom-like thing I've heard her say to Laurel. It was nagging, pure and simple, and I was very, very happy to hear it. Laurel didn't seem to mind, either. She promised she'd only watch one episode, then she would start on dinner. She's going to have a go at making pasta from scratch, which she's been excited to try ever since she saw some TV chef making it in his pretend apartment.

"Are you sure you're going to be okay on your own?" Mom asked. "Don't answer the door to anyone you don't know, remember."

"I'll be *fine*. Stop worrying and go and have some fun!" She hugged Mom, then turned to me. "Thank you for doing this."

"For doing what?" But I knew what she was talking about. Of course I did.

"The book. It means a lot to me. You know that, don't you?" I nodded. "I hope it won't be too painful for you to talk with the writer. All those memories . . ."

"I'll be *fine* . . . as long as I have a decent dinner to come home to! By the way, there's regular pasta in the cupboard if it all goes horribly wrong."

Mom waited till she heard Laurel locking the door behind us before getting in the car.

I feel pretty good about things. The last couple of days have been okay. I've spent most of my time hanging out with Laurel and Mom, and everything has been normal, even though it's a new kind of normal. Thomas and I went for a walk yesterday, and it was nice even though the weather was awful. We huddled under his umbrella and talked—really, actually *talked*—for the first time in ages. We talked about things that had nothing to do with my sister.

I thought I would be more nervous about meeting with the ghostwriter. I *am* nervous—of course I am; it's a weird thing to have to do—but I'm glad I'm doing it. Laurel is so grateful; I like her being grateful. And the money will come in handy, even though Mom says I can't get my hands on my share until I'm eighteen. She's put my money in a special savings account, but at least she's increased my allowance.

Laurel's getting a much (MUCH) bigger share of the money from the publisher, and she has access to hers now. It makes sense—it is *her* story. Martha asked me if it bothered me—Laurel getting so much more cash than me—and I said it didn't. She called me a liar. I knew she could never understand. Laurel needs this money; I don't.

A woman walks into the bar and cranes her neck to look around. I don't wave just in case she's not who I'm waiting for. In my head, the ghostwriter is short and thin and mousy, rounded shoulders and rounded glasses. She's the kind of woman who fades into the background. I realize my mistake as soon as this woman starts striding in my direction. She covers the distance in remarkably few steps.

"You must be Faith. Kay Docherty. Lovely to meet you." She holds out a hand, and I shake it. She must be at least six foot tall—even taller than Martha. White-blond hair in a severe bob with equally severe bangs. She's dressed in lots of complicated layers in varying shades of gray, finishing off the look with a pair of black leather Converse.

"Nice to meet you," I say as she starts unwinding a very long scarf.

She takes one look at my bag and coat before picking them up and putting them on the other sofa along with her coat and scarf, not even bothering to ask if I mind. I watch as she takes out a notepad, a pen, and a tiny recording device and lays them out on the table, then sits down and grabs the cocktail menu. She flicks through it, then puts it down again.

She calls the waitress over and says, "Bombay Sapphire, tonic, three ice cubes, and a wedge of lime, please." The waitress doesn't seem to think this request is anything out of the ordinary. I'm half tempted to order a cocktail, just to see what happens, but I go for a Coke instead. Some alcohol might help loosen me up a bit, but I can just imagine it ending up in the book—*Laurel's ordeal drove me to drink!*

I have to turn in my seat to face Kay, and she does the same. She places the tape recorder between us, switches it on, and tells me to ignore it. Easier said than done. She explains a little bit about how it's going to work, that I can just tell the story in my own words or she can ask questions to prompt me. We'll probably need a couple of sessions like this, depending on how much I have to say. Then she'll go away and write it up and send it to me for approval.

"So you'll write it like you're pretending to be me?" It feels dishonest somehow. That people will read this book and think they're reading *our* words.

"Sort of. I like to think of it as something like channeling your spirit."

She laughs at the skeptical look on my face. "Okay, okay, that sounds like bullshit. But it's actually not far off. Last year I worked with a very famous athlete—not mentioning any names! It was a fascinating project, trying to work out how *he* would write the story, trying to nail his voice. . . . It's about capturing the essence of a person—the essence of their story. Anyway, you don't need to worry about all that now."

"Wouldn't you rather write your own story?"

The waitress arrives with our drinks and sets them down on little black napkins. My Coke has three ice cubes and a wedge of lime, just like Kay's drink. The waitress glances at the recording device on the sofa, then looks from me to Kay and back again, trying to work out what might be going on here. Maybe she thinks that Kay is famous and I've won a competition to interview her for my school newspaper. The waitress asks if we would like anything else and goes on to list the available bar snacks. She's clearly just dragging things out, waiting to see if we'll give anything away, but we both say, "No, thanks," so she has to go away.

"My own story? You know, in all the years I've been doing this, no one has ever asked me that question. No one whose book I've worked on, anyway." She can't have been doing this job for *that* long; she looks quite young. "I'm afraid my story wouldn't sell many copies. . . . There's nothing much to tell."

For some reason I'm interested in Kay Docherty. I ask her if she's ever written any novels, and she claims not to have the imagination for it. "No, it's real lives that interest me."

"But isn't it annoying to do all that work on a book and have someone else take the credit for it?" I would hate it.

She shrugs and shakes her head. "Not at all. It's . . . rewarding, helping people to tell their stories. Plus, the money is *insane!*" She leans back and laughs, then shakes her head and frowns. "Nice try, Faith." She smiles as if she's got the measure of me.

"What do you mean?" I take a sip of my Coke.

"Asking me all these questions, trying to distract me. We're here to talk about *you,* not me. So . . . why don't we start at the beginning. What—if anything—do you remember about life *before* Laurel was taken?" She leans closer to me and cocks her head to one side.

I look at the recording device, then back at Kay. She nods encouragingly. I start to talk.

227

I'm hesitant at first, stumbling over my words, forgetting things or not saying them the right way, then having to go back and correct them. Kay is patient and tells me not to worry, that there's no need to apologize if there's something I can't remember. She asks about Mom and Dad and their relationship, which I try to gloss over as quickly as possible. I'll leave that to *them* to explain. Kay asks me about the day Laurel went missing, about any memories I have of the man who took her. She asks a lot of questions about how I felt at various times, asking me to describe my emotions in as much detail as I can.

I start to relax. Kay orders me another Coke. She asks for some wasabi peas, too. I've never tried them before. They're vile, but for some reason I keep popping another one into my mouth every couple of minutes.

After an hour or so, I realize I'm actually enjoying myself, even though most of the stuff I'm talking about isn't exactly cheery. But Kay is really nice. She doesn't mind when I go off topic and start talking about something that has little or nothing to do with Laurel. It almost feels like a normal conversation—like we're friends just catching up on each other's lives.

Kay is very sympathetic about everything I've been through. She asks if I ever felt neglected or ignored by my parents, in the aftermath of Laurel's disappearance. I tell her the truth: yes. All the time.

She asks whether it was hard for me to make friends, and I tell her the truth: it was.

I'm honest about everything, which surprises me. I'm used to editing my thoughts and feelings when I talk to people—particularly when talking to strangers. It feels good, to talk about this stuff with someone I've never met before. Therapeutic, almost. I try not to think about the fact that there might be some things that Mom and Dad will wish I'd been slightly less honest about. But I can always ask Kay to take those bits out when she sends me the rough draft to read through. Besides, it's not as if I've said anything particularly earth-shattering. Laurel's the one with the real story. People will probably skip my chapters to get straight to hers; I know I would.

I surreptitiously check the time while reaching for another wasabi pea. Mom will be waiting outside.

Maybe I wasn't so surreptitious with the watch-checking after all, because Kay says, "Well, I think that's about it for today. I know how tiring it can be, dredging up all these memories." She downs the rest of her gin. "You've done really well. There's some good stuff here," she says, tapping the recording device. "I think one more session should do it. Whenever you're ready. There's no rush."

She gives me her card and tells me to call her to set up our next meeting. She goes up to the bar to settle the bill—the publisher is paying, apparently.

We put on our coats, and Kay air-kisses me and thanks me again. I have this strange urge to tell her that we should stay here and carry on with the interview. I could call Mom and tell her I'll meet her at home. Instead, I tell her that I was actually a bit reluctant to go ahead with the book, and that I'd been a bit nervous, not knowing what to expect.

"You're a natural storyteller, you know," Kay says as we walk toward the door.

I laugh and feel a blush creeping up my cheeks. "No, I'm not. You're just good at asking questions."

Kay shakes her head and holds the door open for me. "Well, that may be true, but you've got a gift, young lady. Trust me."

A natural storyteller? The words keep popping into my head while Mom is quizzing me about how it went. What did Kay mean by that? Was it a compliment? Or was it a round-about way of calling me a liar? I can't decide. I'm going to have to ask her the next time I see her.

I should be relieved that there's only one more session. But I can't help feeling offended, if that's even the right word. Kay thinks that after sitting down with her for another couple of hours I'll have nothing more to say. After five hours of talking to me, she will have me all figured out. She'll know the sum total of all that is interesting in the life of Faith Logan, aged seventeen and a half.

Of course Kay will spend days and days talking to Laurel, finding out every minute detail about her time in captivity and how she feels now that she's home. This is *The Laurel Show* and my role is nothing more than a bit part.

"You seem quiet, love." Mom glances over at me. We're stuck in a traffic jam. I always start to feel claustrophobic after being in the car with Mom for more than a few minutes. There's no escape if she decides to start an argument.

"I'm just tired. I don't think I've ever talked so much

in my life." This is the truth. I'm much more likely to be sitting in a corner, watching and listening. I thought I preferred things that way, but I'm starting to wonder if maybe that isn't the real me. Perhaps the real me—the me I would have been if my life hadn't been completely overshadowed by Laurel's abduction—*likes* being the center of attention. Perhaps she likes having people hang on her every word.

"I wonder how your sister's getting on with the pasta," says Mom.

I'd forgotten all about that. I'd forgotten all about Laurel, in fact. Even though I've been talking about her all afternoon.

CHAPTER
36

We hear the laughter coming from the kitchen as soon as Mom opens the front door. The kitchen door is closed. Mom and I exchange a look. Laurel's laugh is loud; the other laugh is quieter, and deeper. I recognize it immediately.

Mom takes off her coat and hangs it on one of the pegs next to the front door. I head straight through to the kitchen, opening the door with such force that it bangs against the wall. Mom *hates* it when I do that.

The scene in front of me can only be described as chaos. There is flour *everywhere*. Broken eggshells litter the counter. Laurel is kneading a big lump of dough; Thomas is standing next to her, holding a glass bowl. He has flour on his nose. Thomas freezes when the door slams open, but Laurel doesn't even blink.

"You're back! How did it go?" She carries on kneading as if this is a perfectly normal situation.

"It went okay, thanks," I say coolly.

Laurel smiles and says, "I'm so glad! Hey, can you pass me some more flour?"

I get the open bag from the table, she lifts the lump of dough, and I scatter some flour on the counter. I don't tell her that I think adding more flour is a mistake, that the TV chef she's so fond of always warns you not to use too much.

Thomas looks very uncomfortable with the situation. He seems to not want to let go of the bowl, which is probably a good thing, because I have a sudden urge to smash it over his head. "Hi," he says, "we were just . . ."

"Hello, Thomas. I didn't realize you were coming over this afternoon." Mom comes into the room and stands next to me. "Oh my . . ." She's a bit of a neat freak, especially when it comes to the kitchen.

Laurel preempts Mom's dismay. "It's okay, it's okay! I'll clean it up in a minute! I just need to leave the dough to prove . . . or rest or whatever it's called."

"I didn't say a word," Mom says with a smile.

"But you were going to!" Laurel laughs.

Laurel is babbling away about making pasta not being as easy as it looks and something about egg yolks. Mom gets a cloth out of the cabinet under the sink and gets started on the cleanup operation, even though Laurel tells her she has it under control. Thomas finally puts down the bowl. I think he's deciding whether to come over and kiss me, or hug me at least. Instead he asks if anyone would like something to drink. Mom and Laurel say yes please; I say no.

Mom keeps glancing over at me. She can tell I'm not exactly thrilled with the situation, but she would never say anything in front of Laurel. Thomas is watching me like you might watch a poisonous snake that's escaped from its cage and is slithering its way toward a group of unsuspecting children. It's amazing that Laurel doesn't sense the atmosphere in the room. So amazing, in fact, that it makes me wonder if she *does* sense it, but is choosing to ignore it.

Laurel places the dough in the bowl and wraps plastic wrap over the top. "Thomas was just saying he thought we were *awesome* on *The Cynthia Day Show.* Isn't that nice of him to say?" This just gets better and better. Either Thomas lied to me about not watching it, or he lied to Laurel just now. The answer is clear from the look on his face and the fact that he's concentrating so hard on the tea bag he's dunking. Why didn't he just admit that he'd watched it? That's just plain weird.

"I'm just going to the bathroom," I say, and walk out of the room before anyone can say anything else to piss me off.

I go up to my bedroom. I sit on the bed. Thomas joins me a couple of minutes later, bringing two mugs. "I thought you might have changed your mind about the tea."

"I haven't."

He puts both mugs down on the bedside table. He's given me the one with Laurel's name on it. "Is everything okay? You seem annoyed. Are you annoyed?" He sits down next to me and takes my hand in his. I don't snatch my hand away. That's something, at least.

"Why would I be annoyed?"

"Is it the Cynthia Day thing? I'm sorry I lied. I didn't want to make you more nervous about it." I don't want to look at him. I'm doing such a good job of *not* looking at him. But I can't work out if he's telling the truth. I risk a glance, and he maintains eye contact, nodding ever so slightly as if that's going to convince me.

Silence seems like the best policy. I count to twenty-seven in my head before Thomas speaks again. "She texted me, asked me to come over to help with the pasta."

"Because you're so *renowned* for your cooking skills?"

"Well, um . . . I suppose no one mentioned to her that I'm useless in the kitchen. I told her as much, but she sounded stressed. She really wanted to cook you something nice for tonight. I think she feels bad about you being pressured to do this book."

He thinks he's saying the right things, but with every word he utters, I feel myself getting more and more wound up. "I wasn't pressured into doing anything. I can make my own decisions, you know. But it's nice to know that you two talk about me when I'm not there."

"We don't! It's not like that." He lets go of my hand. "God, I should have *known* you'd be like this. I can't seem to do anything right these days."

"What's that supposed to mean?"

"Nothing," he mumbles. "Forget I said anything."

"No. Tell me what you're talking about."

He sighs and stands. "I think I should go. I don't want to fight with you."

"We're not fighting." I'm not sure why I say this. Perhaps because I really want it to be true.

He almost smiles. "I'm sorry if you're annoyed that I came over when you weren't here, but I wanted to see you after your meeting with the writer. I was worried about you." He reaches out and touches my cheek, and I find myself leaning into his hand.

Everything Thomas is saying sounds reasonable enough, and every feeling I've had since I got home suddenly seems petty and small and paranoid. I look up at Thomas, and he's looking at me with so much patience and understanding that I feel ashamed of myself. I'm fed up with feeling ashamed of myself. "I'm sorry." I think Thomas is as surprised as I am to hear me say those words. He crouches down in front of me and tells me that he loves me. "I know," I say.

"Now, are you sure I can't tempt you with that tea? I made it just the way you like it." He arches his eyebrows and looks at me expectantly.

"No one makes it just the way I like it except me . . . but I will sample your pitiful attempt." Thomas laughs and says that I'm incorrigible. I like the way the word sounds when he says it.

We sit side by side on the bed, drinking our tea. "Not bad at all," I say, even though it's a lie. The tea is too strong and too cold, but Thomas can only be blamed for one of those things.

"We're okay, aren't we?" I ask after downing the last dregs from my (Laurel's) mug.

"Of course we are," says Thomas. "I'm really looking forward to my birthday, you know."

"Me too." A romantic meal. Just the two of us, sitting at a table bathed in soft lighting, gazing into each other's eyes, eating fancy French food. That's what Thomas is expecting, anyway. The restaurant he thinks we're going to is next door to the bar we're *actually* going to. Thomas's mother roped me in as the bait to get Thomas to where he needs to be for the big SURPRISE! moment. The poor boy has no idea what's in store for him.

CHAPTER
37

She's done a good job with the pasta, I have to admit. Mom and I both have second helpings. Laurel doesn't eat much, taking ages to twirl the fettuccine around her fork only to let it fall back onto her plate. "Not hungry, love?"

Laurel shrugs. "It's not as good as the pasta you get from the store, is it? What's the point of going to all that effort if it's not better than the ready-made stuff?" She seems genuinely upset about it.

"Ah, welcome to my world!" says Mom with relish. "That's why you'll never find me making my own pastry. . . . Life's too short." She doesn't seem to realize how upset Laurel is, so I give her a nudge while Laurel is staring forlornly at her plate. She clears her throat. "Honestly, sweetheart, this is delicious. The best meal I've had in ages. And it is better than the store-bought stuff . . . because it's made with *love*."

I manage not to laugh at Mom's cheesy line, which is just as well, because it's made Laurel smile. "Really? You're not just saying that? You promise?"

Mom smiles indulgently. "Really. Honestly. Truly. I *promise.*" She looks to me for backup and I nod enthusiastically, which is all I can do, given that my mouth is full of pasta.

Mom puts her spoon and fork down. "It's amazing how far you've come in such a short time, Laurel," she says, and I can tell she's about to get all emotional again. You'd think she'd be over that by now, but no, these little scenes are still happening on a daily basis. "I'm so proud of you." It's not that I roll my eyes or pretend to gag or anything obvious like that, but Mom must sense my irritation, because then she says, "I'm proud of *both* of you." We all clink our water glasses together. And Laurel finally starts eating her dinner.

Later, Laurel and Mom are downstairs watching some trash on TV. I have to get started on research for a history essay. That's the reason I go upstairs. There's nothing on my mind apart from wondering if I remembered to take the right book out of the school library last week. I'm almost sure I *did,* but now that I think about it . . .

Laurel's bedroom door is open and the bedside light and main light are both switched on. Mom obviously hasn't given her the lecture about saving electricity yet. Or maybe she never will, given that Laurel has spent so much of her life in darkness.

I could kid myself that something caught my eye in Laurel's room, that *that's* the reason I find myself in there, looking around. But nothing caught my eye. I don't have an excuse. If she came upstairs right now and saw me, I'd be able to think of something. Looking for my laptop? That would do. Except we both know full well that she doesn't have my laptop—I've been hiding it in a different place every day, just in case. She hasn't asked to borrow it, so I guess the novelty of using it must have worn off.

The night-light is still there, but not switched on. Laurel's one concession to saving the environment, perhaps. The room is tidy. Laurel has yet to accumulate the little possessions that make a room look like it belongs to someone. Most of the gifts people send her get donated right to the children's hospital. That was her idea, one that made Mom positively glow with pride. I didn't point out that most of the gifts are teddy bears and other cuddly toys, so it would be weird for her to keep them. When are people going to start remembering that Little Laurel Logan is a nineteen-year-old woman now? It's as if the entire country—my family included—has a mental block about it. She's kept a couple of cuddly toys, though. One Winnie the Pooh and a random reindeer.

There's only one teddy bear that means anything to Laurel—Barnaby. I look over at Laurel's bed, neatly made, pink and purple cushions lying at a perfect angle in front of the plumped-up pillows. No sign of Barnaby. He's usually there, isn't he? Nestled in between the two cushions, tucked in under the duvet. I go over for a closer look, careful to step softly so Laurel and Mom don't hear that I'm in here. I pull back the duvet, but he's not there. He's not stuck between the pillows or behind the cushions. I put everything back just the way I found it—or as close to it as I can get.

I kneel down and look under the bed, just in case Barnaby has taken a tumble and is awaiting rescue. He's nowhere to be seen. This is odd. I briefly wonder if Laurel might have taken him downstairs with her. For the first week or so after she came home, she often carried him around with her, sitting him down next to her on the sofa. I could tell it broke Mom's heart, seeing her clutching that scruffy old bear.

Barnaby has disappeared. I have no idea why this bothers me so much. I stand back and look at the room, trying to work out where he could be hiding. The closet is the only option. This definitely counts as snooping. If Laurel catches me looking in there, the only option I have is to say that I want to borrow an item of clothing, which I haven't done once the whole time she's been back.

The closet is a mess. Now her tidiness makes sense—everything has been crammed in here. I smile, reassured that Laurel isn't so perfect after all. There's only one clothes hanger in use; the red dress lording it over all the other clothes. T-shirts and tops and sweaters and jeans are all crammed on the shelves. The ones on the bottom of the piles are folded neatly; the ones on the top are not. In the space underneath the hangers, there is a heaped pile of shoes. A shiny shoe box sits in the corner. A quick peek inside confirms my suspicions: a pair of very expensive red shoes. They match the dress perfectly. Mom and Laurel must have been on another shopping trip without bothering to tell me. Not that I blame them—I was clearly spoiling their fun the last time.

I wrap the shoes back up in the black tissue paper and put the lid back on the box. The lid won't go on properly—one of the corners is being stubborn—so I go to pick up the box. That's when I see the leg. A brown furry leg with a bald patch just above the paw.

Barnaby the Bear has suffered the same fate as the Wicked Witch of the West, except he's been subjected to Death by Designer Shoes instead of Death by Tornado-Dumped House. I pick up the box to survey the damage. Actually Barnaby hasn't been completely flattened by the shoe box, and he still has three out of four limbs intact. But that doesn't stop the sight of him from hurting my heart. His head is at an unnatural angle, as if his neck has been broken; he looks *wrong*.

Why is he stuffed into the bottom of the closet like this? Laurel *loves* that bear. He's her prized possession—one of the only things that truly belongs to her. But he didn't toddle into the closet on his own, lift up the shoe box, and snuggle under it. Mom wouldn't have done this—no way. So Laurel must have put him here.

I know what I'm about to do is stupid. And I know it means Laurel will know that I've been in her room, rooting around in the bottom of her closet. But it feels like I have no other option; I can't stand to leave him where I found him.

I put Barnaby the Bear back where he belongs, tucked in on Laurel's bed, snug between the pillows. "There," I whisper to the battered bear. "That's better, isn't it?" For the first time, I start to wonder if there might be something wrong with me, because it feels like maybe my brain isn't working quite as it should. But it's pointless, thinking that way. I'm fine. *I'm* not the one with the problem.

I switch off the bedside light and the main light.

Laurel will know for sure that I've been in here. The question is: what is she going to do about it?

CHAPTER
38

Nothing. That's what Laurel does about it. I hide out in my room for the rest of the evening, with a brief trip downstairs to say good-night. So I don't see Laurel until the next morning. I'm sitting on the sofa, flicking through catalogs, when she comes downstairs. It's one of my favorite things to do when I'm anxious. I have no idea why staring at pages and pages of terrible jewelry and cheap furniture soothes me, but it does.

"Morning," she says.

I'm slow to look up from the catalog, busy gawking at the price of an outdoor trampoline. "Morning." When I finally do look up, I see Laurel smiling down at me. Already dressed, with her jacket and bag in her arms, too. There's a short silence—a moment when either of us could mention Barnaby or the fact that I've been through her stuff. A look passes between us, neither friendly nor unfriendly, and then it's over and she's putting on her jacket. "Where are you off to?" I ask.

"Nowhere special." She picks up her bag and puts it on her shoulder.

"I've heard it's really good there."

A brief, baffled look before she gets the joke. "Ha," she says.

"Want some company?" I don't want to go with her, wherever she's going, but I do want to see what she says.

"No, thanks. Not today. Penny says it's time I started being more independent. Anyway, I'd better get going." She turns away and heads toward the door.

"What's the rush? Is Nowhere Special open this early?"

She doesn't even bother with a *ha* this time. She doesn't even turn around. "I'm not rushing. I'm just ready to go, that's all. See you later, okay?"

I say good-bye, but the door is already closed.

I jump up from the sofa, and the catalog falls on my foot. I hobble over to the window and watch Laurel walk down the street. I'm ready to duck down out of sight in case she suddenly turns around, but she doesn't. I press my nose up against the window and lean as far as I can so that I can watch her for as long as possible. She walks with her shoulders straight—with an easy confidence I've never even attempted let alone mastered.

As soon as Laurel's out of sight, I rush to the front door and open it. The ground is wet, and the damp starts soaking through the soles of my slippers the second I step outside. I peer around the hedge, not caring how suspicious I look. I'm just in time to see Laurel reach the end of our road. If she turns left, she'll be going to the bus stop where you take the bus to the city center. I seem to spend half my life waiting at that bus stop.

Laurel turns right. Unless she's going to the crematorium (which seems highly unlikely), she's probably catching a bus in the opposite direction, away from town. Why would she be going that way? The only time I ever go to that bus stop is when I'm going to Thomas's house and he refuses to come and pick me up.

A light drizzle begins to fall as I stand on our front path in my pajamas. The mail carrier is walking down the street toward me, back bent under the weight of the mailbag. He says a cheery "Morning" as he hands me two letters and a postcard (both addressed to Laurel).

"Morning," I echo. He doesn't comment on my clothes or look at me as if I'm crazy; I guess he must see all sorts of odd things, doing a job like that.

The drizzle turns into a steady rain, and I realize I should probably get inside. My legs want to go the other way, though—they want to follow Laurel, to check if she's waiting at the bus stop and maybe even to wait and see if she gets on the number 67, which stops five minutes away from Thomas's house. I stand rooted to the spot for a few seconds before my brain finally wins the battle. My brain knows that there's no way Laurel's going to Thomas's house. She doesn't even know his address. Unless he told her.

I go upstairs to get my phone, texting Thomas to see what he's up to this morning. I ask if he wants to meet up. His reply arrives about an hour later: Can't this morning. Sorry. Mom wants to go shopping for my bday present. Tonight?

Thomas's mom wants to buy him a watch for his birthday, but she knows she wouldn't be able to choose the perfect one by herself. Thomas already told me this. They're even going to get it engraved. So there's no reason to think he's lying. I text back to say I'm suddenly not feeling very well so I'd better stay home tonight. He says he hopes I feel better soon.

Laurel must have gone somewhere else. Maybe she's just planning to hop on a bus and see where she ends up. That's exactly the kind of weird thing she would do.

I decide to put it out of my mind completely. I will not allow myself to turn into a paranoid wreck. I tell myself that I don't care where Laurel has gone—it's none of my business. Anyway, I'm only a third of the way through my favorite catalog.

When I eventually go to get dressed, I pop my head into Laurel's room. The bed is neatly made, cushions in place.

Barnaby the Bear is not there. He's not in the closet, either.

CHAPTER
39

The week has been drama-free. I haven't mentioned Barnaby. Laurel and I had a good weekend at Dad and Michel's. Since being mobbed at the farmers' market, Laurel has stayed home. Business is booming, probably because people feel they can't come up and ask questions about Laurel without buying something. Michel is happy to take their money, but he never tells them anything about Laurel.

The only awkward moment was when Dad sat Laurel down to tell her that the DNA test the police keep going on about has been scheduled for a week from Thursday. They can't put it off any longer, apparently. He'd tried his best to convince them it wasn't necessary, that Laurel had been through enough. But they wouldn't budge. At least they've agreed that Mom can be the one to do the cheek swab, to minimize Laurel's distress.

Laurel asked why they needed to do the test, and Dad said that Sergeant Dawkins had told him they needed to double-check something in their files. She'd left three messages on his phone about it, so it must be pretty important. Dad told Laurel that there was nothing to be afraid of. She looked like she was about to puke. Dad put his arm around her and asked if it was okay with her. She said nothing for the longest time.

I decided to chip in. "You should do it, Laurel. Get it over with. I'll be with you, if you want."

Laurel looked over at me, sitting in my corner with Tonks on my lap. I nodded encouragingly, and after a second's hesitation, she nodded back. She turned to Dad and said, "Okay."

Thomas has been quiet this week. Martha and I have been teasing him about getting old. I asked him how the shopping trip with his mom went. "Fine," he said.

"So you found a watch?"

"Yeah," he said, before changing the subject. Maybe he was pouting because his mom hadn't bought him the vintage one he wanted. Or maybe he was starting to realize that he should have asked for money instead, like a normal person.

On the day of his birthday, I get to school early and tie a balloon to the radiator near where we normally sit in the cafeteria. The balloon is tacky as anything—silver and heart-shaped, with multicolored letters saying BIRTHDAY BOY. I have his present in my bag, along with a homemade card. I haven't decided whether I'll give them to him at school or at the party. Either way, I'd prefer it if Thomas and I were alone. No one else would think the present was particularly impressive, but I know Thomas will like it. I bought it months ago, long before I started wondering if I still wanted him to be my boyfriend. I remember being so pleased with myself at the time—so smug that I'd found the perfect present for him even though he's impossible to buy for.

Martha arrives a couple of minutes before Thomas. She eyes the balloon with approval and suggests that we start singing "Happy Birthday" as soon as Thomas walks through the door. I'm tempted—just to see his reaction—but he's got enough public humiliation in store for him tonight. We sit with our backs against the radiator and watch the door until Thomas comes in, head down, headphones on, completely oblivious to everything around him. He doesn't look up until he's right in front of us. He smiles when he notices the balloon bobbing away.

"Aw, you guys! You shouldn't have!" he says in an overly enthusiastic voice. Then he gives us a withering look. "I suppose this was your idea," he says, looking at Martha.

"No, no, I couldn't possibly take the credit for this little delight," Martha says as she rummages around in her bag. "But I can, however, take *all* the credit for this!" She produces a huge envelope with a flourish. Inside is the ugliest card I've ever seen, complete with an equally ugly saucer-sized badge that reads 18 TODAY!!!

"Happy Birthday, Mr. Bolt," says Martha, standing and giving him an awkward hug.

I stand, too, feeling almost shy all of a sudden. "Happy birthday," I say.

"Don't I get a birthday kiss?" This surprises me. Thomas

isn't normally one for PDAs. I give him a quick kiss on the lips.

"You know, Thomas, you look different somehow . . . more manly, I think." Martha grabs his upper arm and squeezes it. "Nope, my mistake. Still the same old noodle arms." For a second, I think Thomas is going to be really annoyed, even though he's not particularly sensitive about his body, but he just laughs and says he prefers to think of them as "sinewy."

He fiddles with the badge, and I can't believe he's going to wear it. He twists the pin on the back so that it's pointing outward. Then he looks at me. "May I?"

"You may."

The sound of the balloon popping makes everyone in the cafeteria jump and turn around to see where the noise came from. Laney Finch clutches her hand to her chest and leans on one of her friends to steady herself. One of the boys standing next to the coffee machine shouts *"Dick!"* in our direction, probably embarrassed because he jumped so high his head almost hit the ceiling. Thomas gives the boy a little salute; the boy responds with a raised middle finger.

I decide to give Thomas his present at lunchtime— there's no way I can wait until tonight. We arrange to meet at a little deli around the corner from school. I arrive before him and order our panini. The guy behind the counter knows our order by heart. Thomas doesn't like him, probably because he's really handsome and is always very friendly to me while having a tendency to ignore Thomas.

The guy puts the food down on the table at the exact moment the door opens and Thomas walks in. "Shame . . . I thought I was going to have to join you." He winks at me and stands back to let Thomas sit down. I smile politely and wonder whether it's weird that I don't know the deli guy's name.

Thomas takes a huge bite of his sandwich, and the melted cheese forms oozy strings from his mouth to the panini. It makes me feel slightly nauseous, watching him. I nibble on the edge of my sandwich and try not to look. In between bites, Thomas tells me about his morning. One of his favorite things to do is to embarrass teachers by showing off his superior knowledge on certain subjects; his current number one target is his English teacher. I used to think it was funny, but today it just seems childish. I smile and laugh in all the right places, though—it is his birthday, after all. He demolishes his sandwich in record time, despite the fact that he's hardly stopped talking since he arrived.

"Are you not eating that?" He looks at my sandwich like a hungry hyena.

I push the plate toward him. "Go for it."

"I probably shouldn't. . . . I don't want to spoil my appetite for this fancy meal tonight." He puts his hand on his stomach, which is as smooth and flat as anyone could wish for. Little does Thomas know the most he'll be getting to eat tonight is some chips and dip.

"That's *hours* away! You should eat it." He doesn't take much convincing.

I take the present and card out of my bag when Thomas

has finished eating. At first he says he wants to wait till tonight, that he'd rather open his present in the restaurant than here. Again it doesn't take much to convince him. The card makes him smile. On the front, there's a drawing of us walking hand in hand through a forest. There are wolves and monsters lurking in the shadows of the crooked trees. It took me seven attempts before I was happy with the drawing, and then I had to trace it onto the card. I've never gone to that much effort for *anyone* before.

"I didn't know you could draw! You're really good, you know? This is . . . *really* cool. Creepy, but cool."

Inside the card I've written the kind of thing that a girlfriend writes to her boyfriend on his eighteenth birthday. Thomas leans over the table to kiss me. He calls me a dark horse.

The present is next. He tears into the wrapping paper like a kid on Christmas Day. When he sees what it is, he smiles and says "Wow!" and thanks me profusely, but I can tell something isn't right. He says "wow" far too many times. "Wow" is not a very Thomas-like thing to say. It's a first edition of a book by some poet I'd never heard of before I met Thomas—in mint condition even though it's nearly forty years old. It's the *perfect* gift—for Thomas, at least. If someone gave it to me, I'd probably use it to prop a door open.

Thomas leans over and kisses me again, for longer this time. "It's perfect. *Thank* you," he whispers in my ear. I wonder if maybe I was being paranoid and maybe he *does* love it after all. Perhaps he was so keen to show just how much he loved it that he accidentally went overboard on the enthusiasm and ended up sounding like Laney Finch. But now I feel strange and unsure, and disappointed that the moment didn't go the way I wanted it to go. What is *wrong* with me?

CHAPTER
40

"You're not cutting school, are you?" Kay sips her gin and tonic, raising an eyebrow to make it abundantly clear that she wouldn't care if I *was*.

"Nope, free period."

She was waiting for me this time. Same spot on the sofa, same drink in front of her. For some reason, I find myself telling her that it's my boyfriend's birthday today. I tell her about the poetry book and the surprise party, and the fact that Thomas's mom seems to prefer Martha to me. Kay's amused smile makes me stop talking. "Sorry, we should probably be talking about Laurel, shouldn't we? Um . . . what else do you need to know?"

Kay switches on the recording device. "Well, why don't we pick up where we left off? Tell me about the first time you saw Laurel again after all those years. . . . It was in a hotel room, wasn't it?"

I talk about what it was like seeing this young woman in front of me and trying to reconcile that with the picture of the little girl I had in my head. I talk about when Mom and Dad left us alone, and how it didn't feel like being left alone with a stranger. I talk about how surreal it was, sitting in that suite, watching the press conference going on downstairs.

Then it's on to Laurel's first days back home with us. I can tell Kay is happy with how it's going.

Kay leans back and crosses her legs. "So, Faith, it can't *all* have been sweetness and light since Laurel came home. . . . For all intents and purposes you'd lived the previous thirteen years as an only child. It can't have been easy to have a sister thrust into your life all of a sudden." She sees the confused look on my face and adopts a chummy voice that I find off-putting. "I know what it's like—my sister and I used to fight *all* the time, especially when we were teenagers. Remind me to tell you one day about the time we both liked the same boy." I know exactly what she's doing. She thinks I'm stupid. She thinks she'll get something interesting out of me if she acts like my friend. She probably doesn't even *have* a sister.

I don't know why she's bothering. Even if she did manage to get me to say something juicy, there's no way I'd approve it to go in the book. Maybe she's just nosy or maybe she's looking for a story she can sell to the newspapers on the sly. Or perhaps I'm just being paranoid, and she's just genuinely interested and thinks that a little bit of grit would be a good addition to the story—to make it less sugary, more real.

I take a sip of my drink and shake my head. "No . . . it's been wonderful. We get along so well it's as if we've never been apart. Anyway, I've never felt like an only child.

Even when Laurel wasn't around, she was there." I pause and wonder if what I want to say next would be going too far. Kay seems like the sort of person who can detect bullshit a mile away, unlike Cynthia Day. I decide to go for it anyway. I touch my hand to the middle of my chest and say, "She was always *here*."

Kay doesn't laugh or raise her eyebrows, and she doesn't call me a liar. She just nods thoughtfully, then asks me another question, this time about press intrusion. It's the perfect opportunity for me to get my revenge on Jeanette Hayes, to tell the world exactly what we think of her. But, instead, I say that we've been so grateful that people have respected our privacy and given us the time and space to get to know each other again.

Kay leans forward. "So you're not bothered about what people are saying on Twitter?"

I shake my head. "I never go on there anymore. I've got better things to do." This isn't me. I don't know where this stuff is coming from, but I do know one thing: Mom will be happy. It will be worth it, telling these lies and half-truths, if it makes her happy.

It would almost be funny to see the look on Kay's face if I told her the truth—all of it. If I told her that Laurel gets away with murder—that she can wrap my parents around her little finger without even trying. I could tell her about the shoplifting, about her weird little trips off by herself, and, best of all, that she spied on me and my boyfriend having sex. Now, *that* would be a story people would want to hear. But it doesn't fit with the image they have of Little Laurel Logan, so maybe they wouldn't want to hear it after all. Maybe Laurel would call me a liar and everyone would believe her, because put us side by side, and I can't think of a single person who would take my word over hers.

Kay asks if there's anything else I'd like to say before we wrap up. "Anything at *all*?" She does a decent job of concealing her disappointment when I say I have nothing more to add.

It's Laurel's turn in a couple of weeks. They've scheduled in three whole-day sessions to start off with. "I'm a bit nervous, actually," Kay says quietly, as if she's letting me in on some big secret. "I've never worked on a project quite like this before. Nothing quite so . . . harrowing."

Does she want me to comfort her, when all she has to do is listen to what Laurel went through? That's not going to happen. I just stare at her until she starts talking again. "Well, I think we're done. Thank you so much for your time. I'll let you know when I have something for you to read. I'll probably work on Laurel's sections first, though, so it might be some time."

That's fine with me. I'm in no hurry to read my words filtered through another person's brain. We say our goodbyes. Unlike last time, today I'm glad it's over. I'm glad I don't have to talk about Laurel anymore.

CHAPTER
41

I didn't leave myself enough time to get ready. I'd wanted to wash my hair, but it takes ages to dry. I'll just have to hope that no one notices it's on the edge of being greasy. I always think of it as "on the turn," the way Gran describes milk that's a few days old.

At least I don't need to stress about what to wear, because I already laid out my clothes this morning. Black jeans, boots, a red top. Nothing too fancy. When I go downstairs, Laurel's watching TV. "You look nice," she says. She couldn't have picked a blander word, but I thank her anyway. She asks what time she should get there, and I swear I must have blocked out that she was coming to the party. I have no idea how my brain managed to do that. It's fine, though—I won't have to babysit her. She'll have people hanging on her every word, as usual.

I tell her she should probably turn up around nine o'clock. She looks surprised and says, "That's a bit late, isn't it?"

I shake my head and say most people probably won't be

arriving until then. This is a lie, obviously. It's not that I don't want her there; it's that I'd like a bit of time before she arrives and hogs all the attention.

Laurel says she's nervous, and I tell her there's nothing to worry about. There's no time to give her any more reassurance than that. I can tell she has more to say, that she would like me to stay and talk for a while, but I'm going to be late as it is. "I'll see you later. You know where you're going, right?"

Mom's dropping her off. She'll be fine.

The bus arrives five minutes late, and I spend the whole journey willing it to go faster. I tell myself that I was perfectly nice to Laurel. She can stand on her own two feet now—she doesn't need me to prop her up. Besides, the party will be pretty tame. It's not as if it's some raucous house party with sex and drugs and random strangers. This will be good for her.

Martha's already there when I arrive, moving chairs around under the strict direction of Mrs. Bolt. Thomas's dad is standing on a chair, trying to hang one end of a banner from a light fixture. It looks like he might fall and break his neck any second. That would probably ruin the mood a bit.

Mrs. Bolt spies me lurking in the doorway and calls me over. Thomas's mom doesn't look like the sort of person who's spent most of her adult life in the army. I was surprised, the first time I met her. Thomas teased me about it, asking me what I'd been expecting. I didn't answer, but the truth was I'd imagined short hair, stocky build, maybe some camouflage. I definitely wasn't expecting her to look like she could have had a decent shot at a modeling career. Tall, very slim, long blond hair, nice clothes. At least Thomas's dad conformed to my (admittedly ridiculous and stereotypical) expectations. He looks hard as nails.

Mrs. Bolt gives me a dry peck on the cheek and asks how I am. I mumble that I'm fine, thanks. She looks beautiful tonight. *Elegant* is the word. She intimidates the hell out of me; I never know what to say to her. I still get the feeling that she kind of hates me, no matter what Thomas says (that I'm completely paranoid and she actually thinks I'm lovely). Mrs. Bolt nods and shoos me away to help Martha with the chairs.

Martha has a fine sheen of sweat on her forehead from shifting all that furniture. She's dressed even more casually than I am—faded jeans and a fitted black shirt. Martha doesn't seem to need my help, which is good, because I got sweaty enough rushing from the bus. I look around for something else to do, but it seems like everything's just about ready. I am officially surplus to requirements.

Thomas's mom makes sure the wineglasses are lined up neatly on the table in the corner, then picks up one of the glasses and holds it up against the light. She looks over and sees me watching, so I go and ask if there's anything else I can do to help. Mrs. Bolt looks around the room, and it reminds me of the Terminator, as if she has a computer in her head, analyzing every tiny detail in front of her. "No, I think we're just about ready. Thanks for your help." She smiles and then narrows her eyes. "You haven't told him, have you? You haven't ruined the surprise?"

"No!" I probably should have toned down the indignation a little bit.

She's doing that Terminator thing again, trying to work out if I'm lying. "Good." She turns her back on me without another word and heads over to where Thomas's dad is testing some fairy lights he's strung up over one of those awful stuffed reindeer heads.

There's no doubt about it: Thomas's mother is a straight-up bitch.

People start arriving, most of whom I don't recognize. I've hardly met any of Thomas's family, which is weird when you think about it, because he's met *all* of mine. I sit in a corner with Martha, and we try to guess who everyone is. At last, a few people from school arrive and one of them swipes a couple of bottles of wine and some glasses from the table and brings them over to our booth. I'm pretty sure Mrs. Bolt wouldn't be too happy about that.

Five minutes before Thomas is due at the restaurant, I go over to Mrs. Bolt—because I don't want her coming over to us—and say that I'm going to head outside. She claps her hands together and shouts to everyone to be quiet, then tells them what to do. "Right, off you go!" she says impatiently, practically pushing me out of the room.

I stand in the doorway of the restaurant and look at the menu. I sort of wish we *were* going in there, spending the evening alone together. Maybe that's exactly what we need—to do something different, something special, and reconnect after the weird couple of months we've had. I wonder what Mrs. Bolt would do if we just didn't show up.

"Hey, you." Thomas has snuck up behind me.

"Hey." I turn to kiss him, and I'm so shocked that I can't speak for a second. He looks good—*really* good. He's slicked back his hair so I can actually see his face for a change. His clothes look brand-new—even the shoes. He looks exactly how you should look when you're going to a fancy restaurant for dinner—he's even wearing a tie. "You clean up *well*," I say, standing back to have a proper look.

He's embarrassed to have me staring at him, so he pulls me close and kisses me. "Seriously," I whisper in his ear, "you look great."

"You're just saying that because you're hoping to get lucky tonight. . . ."

He tells me that I look beautiful, and it sounds like he really means it. It's easy to remember why I fell for him when it's like this.

"Shall we go inside?" He puts his hand on my shoulder to usher me in, but I don't move. "What's the matter? You must be freezing out here. . . . Why didn't you bring a coat?"

I have a decision to make. When it comes down to it, it's not even difficult. "Okay, promise you won't be annoyed . . . ?"

Instead of saying what he'd usually say—that he has no intention of doing any such thing until he knows what I'm talking about—he just says, "I promise," and smiles.

I tell him about the surprise party. I tell him everything. His shoulders slump with every detail. "Oh," he says. "Right. Okay."

"And you have to make sure you act surprised when we walk in, because otherwise your mom will know I told you and she'll probably put me in front of a firing squad or something. I'm sorry. I know this is your worst nightmare. I'm so sorry."

He looks gutted—a little boy who's just been told that Christmas is canceled. "So we were never going in there, then?"

"Nope. But we *can* go. I'll call tomorrow and reserve a table, okay? My treat. This was such a terrible idea. . . . I should have said something to your parents. I should have stopped this. Forgive me? Please?"

He closes his eyes for a second, and I wonder if he's going to dump me on the spot. I wouldn't blame him. A couple of weeks ago, I'd have probably been relieved, but something's changed. The knowledge is inside me—it's been there all along, but I wouldn't allow myself to see it. Things have been too confusing, with Laurel being back. I lost focus on what's important in *my* life. I do love him. He may not be perfect, and he drives me crazy on a regular basis, but I *love* him. And if he dumps me now, right here outside this restaurant, I will only have myself to blame.

Thomas straightens his shoulders, and maybe it's because it's his eighteenth birthday or maybe it's because I'm being ridiculous, but I'd swear that he really does look like a *man*. A proper, grown-up man who makes proper, grown-up decisions. He puts his hands on my shoulders and takes a deep breath. "Okay, let's do this thing."

"You mean . . . ?"

"I *don't* blame you. I know what my mother's like when she's got an idea in her head. She's a force of nature. *Hurricanes* get out of her way when she's on a mission. So here's the plan: we will go inside and I will do my absolute best to act surprised, and if that's not working out for me, I'll just hug you so that no one can see my face. We will eat bad party food and have a couple of sneaky drinks, and I will do my best to introduce you to my extended family—if I can remember their names. I will even dance with you, if that's what it takes to prove to everyone that I'm having a good time."

I'm somewhat taken aback by all this. Especially the part about dancing. I have never seen him dance—I can't even picture him dancing. I'm tempted to say, *Who are you, and what the hell have you done with my boyfriend?* but that would be a bad idea. Instead, I go for "But you won't be, will you? Having fun, I mean. I'm so sorry I let this happen."

"Hey," he says softly. "Stop that. Anyway, who says I won't have fun? Maybe a surprise party complete with everyone I've ever met in my entire life is *exactly* the way I wanted to spend my eighteenth?"

"You're kidding, right?"

Thomas puts his arm around me, and we walk toward the entrance to the bar. "Of course . . . but as long as you're with me, I can get through anything."

I push him up against the wall and kiss him. "I love you, Thomas Bolt."

He looks amused as he tells me that he loves me, too.

Through the door and up the stairs, and I hold the door open for Thomas and we enter the darkened room and *SURPRISE!*

CHAPTER
42

Thomas is good at this. Really good. No one seems to have any clue that he knew about the party. He keeps on shaking his head in disbelief and playfully punching his dad's shoulder. As soon as the whole "surprise" bit was over, he hugged his mom and wagged a finger at me to tell me off. Everyone laughed at that. Mrs. Bolt rewarded me with an approving nod.

I start to see a whole new side to Thomas. He's confident and at ease as he introduces me to various members of his family. He keeps a hand on the small of my back, and it reassures me. The weight of it, the warmth of it. Because I am far from confident and at ease. There are too many people, and the room is too hot and it's hard to breathe. But it gets better. And I'm pretty sure it's no coincidence that getting better correlates with Thomas and me sneaking some glasses of wine when Mrs. Bolt isn't looking.

An hour or so in, we are not quite sober. Not drunk, exactly. Not stumbling or falling over or laughing uncontrollably. Just the level where it's easy to talk to strangers and every song you hear reminds you of some happy memory or other. Where smiling is your default state, rather than something you have to think about.

A song comes on, and Thomas and I exchange a look. He starts laughing first, but I'm not far behind. The song was playing on the stereo in his van the night we first had sex. He'd commented on it that night—"how apt"—because the lyrics are filthy. Mrs. Bolt must have delegated the choice of music this evening to one of her minions.

Thomas holds out his hand to me and bows. "Who do you think you are? Mr. Darcy?" I say. He laughs even though it wasn't particularly funny. I take his hand and we head onto the dance floor. No one else is dancing yet. I catch Martha's eye—she's still at the same table with the kids from school. I can tell she's surprised. She knows I hate being the center of attention. But as soon as Thomas and I start dancing, I forget about the fact that people are looking at us. I don't care what I look like, or the fact that I'm sweating, or that my limbs are flailing all over the place.

People join us on the dance floor after only a minute or so, as if they were just waiting for someone to be brave enough to be the first ones up here. It feels good to be brave for once. Martha's still watching, so I call her over. She shakes her head, which is exactly what I would expect her to do. So I grab Thomas's arm, and we make our way over to her table, and I proceed to drag Martha from her seat.

Martha takes a while to loosen up. She's self-conscious at first—halfheartedly moving from side to side, trying to look like she's enjoying herself. But before long, she's really dancing, and after ten minutes or so, Thomas and Martha are engaged in some kind of dance battle with rules that only they seem to understand.

I'd never have believed it could be so much fun, dancing with them. It feels like something we should have done a long time ago.

When Mr. and Mrs. Bolt make their way onto the dance floor, I take it as my cue for a bathroom break. I check to see if Martha wants to come with me, but Thomas's dad is already twirling her around all over the place, and she doesn't seem to be minding one bit.

Getting to the restrooms is a bit of a mission. You have to go downstairs and through the main room of the bar, which is packed full of people watching sports. I recognize a couple of guys from the party hovering at the bottom of the stairs. They probably know full well how Mrs. Bolt will react if she catches them loitering down here. After I pee, a quick look in the mirror confirms that my makeup is just about okay. Anyway, I left my bag upstairs, so there's not a whole lot I can do about it right now.

A woman comes out of one of the stalls, washes her hands, then starts putting on some lipstick. Her face contorts in the mirror and I look away. Not before she catches me, though. "It's Faith, isn't it?" She must be one of the only people Thomas hasn't introduced me to, but it's obvious she's related to Mrs. Bolt.

I nod and say hi before heading over to the hand dryers. Should I have offered to shake her hand? Is that something people *do* in public restrooms?

"SORRY, I FORGOT MY MANNERS! I'M DAWN!

THOMAS'S AUNT!" she shouts, unwilling to wait the extra few seconds for the hand dryer to stop.

"NICE TO MEET YOU!" And of course the dryer stops in the middle of my shouting, making me look like the kind of lunatic who shouts random things in public bathrooms.

"Keep me company for a minute, will you, dear? I've been sweating like a pig on a tanning bed up there! This new powder I've got is supposed to work miracles, but even JC himself would have trouble sorting out *this* face." It takes a moment or two for me to realize she's talking about Jesus. I watch as she powders her face, and it *does* seem to do the trick. I'm sure she'd let me borrow it if I asked, but there is no chance I was going to do that.

It takes me approximately five seconds to realize that Thomas's aunt is one of those people who can have an entire conversation by themselves, with little or no input from the person they're supposedly talking to.

Dawn talks about how she's been *dying* to meet me, but she hardly ever gets to visit because she lives so far away. She tells me all about the farm where she lives and how far it is from the nearest village, and the fact that she insists on going into town at least once a week. Within a couple of minutes, I know more about Thomas's aunt than I do about some members of my own family. I'm hoping for someone else to come into the restroom and distract her so I can make my escape, but the door remains firmly shut. A loud roar erupts from outside, and I briefly wonder if I can feign an interest in soccer, but then Dawn is suddenly saying something that interests me. "It's so funny how things turn out, isn't it? Who would have thought that you two would end up together? God works in mysterious ways, doesn't he?"

I have no idea what she's talking about.

"It was the tenth anniversary that did it, you know."

"Tenth anniversary of what?"

Dawn looks at me like I'm stupid. "Laurel going missing! All those shows and articles. You couldn't avoid the story if you tried . . . not that you'd want to try, but you know what I mean. He read all the books, you know—about all sorts of awful unsolved crimes, not just about your sister. Serial killers and that sort of thing." She shudders at the thought.

I stare at my reflection in the mirror and see myself starting to understand.

"It only lasted a few months, but Cath was a little worried all the same. Such a morbid thing for a young boy to be interested in!" Dawn shakes her head and giggles. "Sometimes you just have to let these things run their course. If there's one thing I know about teenagers, it's that they go through phases. My Kevin dyed his hair bright blue when he was fifteen, and I didn't say a word. Sure enough, three weeks later, he was sick of it and asked me to take him to my salon to get it dyed back! With Thomas it was poetry, wasn't it? He got keen on that and the whole crime thing sort of fell by the wayside. He loves his poems, that boy. I like limericks, myself."

I try to smile, but the muscles in my face seem reluctant to cooperate.

"Laurel's coming tonight, isn't she?" Dawn looks at her wrist; there's a tan line where her watch would be. "I thought she'd be here by now. Everyone's dying to meet her!" Dawn moves closer to me, and I worry that she's going in for a hug. Instead, she brushes her knuckle on my cheek; it's oddly intimate. "I know my sister might not agree, but

I think it's *lovely* that you and Thomas are together. He was so excited when he found out they were moving here, but I bet he never *dreamed* he would end up going out with Laurel Logan's little sister! I think it was meant to be, don't you? Now come on, enough chatting; let's get back to the party!"

She links her arm through mine and leads me toward the door. When we're snaking our way through the crowd of drinkers at the bar, I tell her I have to make a phone call so I'll see her upstairs. "Don't be long—I think they're bringing out the cake soon!"

I stand outside in the cold.

My relationship is based on a lie. It would never have even started—would have been dead in the water—if Thomas had told the truth. I'd honestly believed that he was the *one* person who wasn't interested in my sister. But *of course* he was. Just like all the others.

One question fights its way to the top, clambering over all the others crowding my brain. Was Thomas only interested in me because of my sister? Is *that* why he pursued me?

I'm not even sure I want to know the answer.

CHAPTER
43

I can't stay outside forever and I can't just go home; my bag is upstairs.

Laurel should be here soon. I shouldn't blame her for this. Maybe I should even thank her? If it wasn't for her, maybe Thomas would never have even spoken to me. I would still be waiting for someone—anyone—to take an interest in me. I would still be a virgin.

I need to talk to him. I need to know the truth. Because even if he only wanted to get to know me to find out more about my sister, that can't be the reason he stayed with me. It *can't* be. What we have now, what I felt when I was dancing with him a few minutes ago, that's real. It's real and it's mine, and it has nothing to do with my sister.

I expect to hear the music pumping as I trudge up the stairs, but there's silence. Everyone's gathering around a spot in the center of the room. Thomas is standing next to a cart with an enormous cake on it. Mrs. Bolt is standing next to him, her arm around his shoulders. Thomas's dad is taking a photo of the cake. I can't help thinking that Mrs. Bolt did this on purpose—wheeling out the birthday cake when I was out of the room.

Thomas is looking around, scanning faces. His eyes settle on me, and he smiles and waves me over. People turn and shuffle out of the way to let me pass. I stand next to him while everyone sings "Happy Birthday." Thomas reaches for my hand and squeezes it twice. Two squeezes means: *Are you okay?* I squeeze back twice, meaning: *I'm fine.*

The cake must have cost a fortune. I recognize most of the titles on the spines of the cake books—they're Thomas's favorites. There are eighteen candles on top of the cake. I count them while I sing (mime).

When the singing stops, everybody cheers. Mrs. Bolt leans forward and says, "Go on, then. Blow out the candles. Don't forget to make a wish!"

Thomas turns to look at me, and I have the strangest feeling—the kind of feeling someone like Laney Finch would call a premonition. I can picture Thomas and me standing in a different room, in front of a different cake. This cake is white and tiered. The image is gone before I can get a grip on it, but it leaves my heart beating fast and my head spinning.

A hush descends on the room as Thomas leans over, preparing to blow out the candles. I catch Martha's eye and she mimes a yawn, and I love her for that. Mrs. Bolt says, "What are you waiting for?" and Thomas takes a deep breath, ready to blow out all the candles in one puff.

The silence is making me uneasy—it's as if people think Thomas is trying to defuse a bomb instead of blow out some candles on an overpriced cake that probably won't even taste good.

The silence stretches out as Thomas exhales, moving his head to catch every single flame. A door opens. Doors open and close all the time, and people barely even notice. No one apart from Thomas noticed my entrance a couple of minutes ago. *Everyone* notices this entrance. Heads turn, and I swear there are even a couple of gasps.

It's my sister, of course. Choosing the worst possible time to arrive—or the best, depending on your point of view.

She's wearing the red dress.

Laurel looks like a movie star who took a wrong turn on her way to the red carpet. Red shoes, a little black clutch that I recognize as Mom's. Her hair flows over her shoulders, shiny and glossy. Flawless makeup.

Laurel stops in the doorway. People stare.

Someone—I don't know who, but Dawn would be my first guess—starts clapping. A couple more people follow suit, and then the whole room is filled with applause. Martha's clapping, too—*Traitor.* The last people to join in are Mrs. Bolt and Thomas. At least he has the sense to look at me in bafflement before he puts his hands together.

Laurel looks as confused as I feel. Why are these people *clapping* for her? It's not *her* birthday. She spots me and hurries over, head down, a shy smile on her face. A couple of people pat her back as she passes them; she doesn't flinch.

"Hi! Sorry I'm late . . . and sorry about that. . . . I don't know why they . . ." She turns to Thomas. "Anyway! Happy birthday! I'm not interrupting anything, am I?"

Thomas gestures to the blown-out candles, tendrils of smoke wisping upward. "Not at all. Would you like some cake?"

I stand back as Thomas introduces Laurel to his mother. Mrs. Bolt smiles warmly at my sister. It's weird. You'd think she wouldn't want her here, if she'd been so worried about Thomas's "interest" in Laurel's story. But it seems the lure of my sister is irresistible to her, too.

Laurel asks me to hold her bag while she helps Thomas cut the cake. Surely that should be my job?

Some people are still staring, but most of them have returned to the serious business of drinking. Laurel seems perfectly at ease, despite the fact that she's seriously overdressed. Mrs. Bolt compliments her on the dress (of course) and asks her where it's from. Laurel says she can't remember, which is an odd lie for her to tell.

Laurel and Thomas hand out little plates, each with a slice of book cake and a tiny fork. The napkins have books on them, too. Clearly the one thing Mrs. Bolt knows about her son is that he likes to read.

Martha appears next to me. "So . . . your sister looks . . ." Martha does this weird grimace, making it look as if the bottom left side of her mouth has been caught by a fishhook. I look at her expectantly, waiting for the end of the sentence. If Martha says the wrong thing, this will be a very short conversation. "Kind of ridiculous."

I burst out laughing, narrowly avoiding spraying my

drink in Martha's face. "Come on," she says. "Have you tried the chicken satay skewers? I've had seven."

There's one satay skewer left, and I manage to nab it just as someone else is reaching for the platter. I'm wondering whether to tell Martha about Thomas. She might tell me to break up with him. And I'm not sure how I'd feel if she told me to do that. Maybe I'd be better off telling her tomorrow. I need to figure out how *I* want to handle the situation first. I don't want to do anything I'll regret.

My plan for the rest of the evening emerges before I've put the satay skewer in one of the little jam jars that have been placed on the table for that express purpose. Mrs. Bolt really has thought of everything. Military precision, I guess. The plan: try to get drunk enough not to care that my boyfriend may or may not only be going out with me because of my "famous" sister. Forget all about it, just for a couple more hours. Try to spend as little time as possible with the aforementioned boyfriend and sister, because spending time in their presence will make the not-caring somewhat difficult, and the forgetting even harder.

After about twenty minutes, Thomas and Laurel make their way over to us with two plates of cake. Thomas hands one of the plates to Martha and she thanks him. Laurel tries to hand me a plate, but I say I'm not hungry.

"But you have to have some birthday cake! Isn't it bad luck if you don't?" Laurel waves the plate under my nose.

"No. It's really not."

"It's really good, you know," says Thomas.

"I said I'm not hungry." I at least make an effort to keep the edge out of my voice.

Thomas kisses me on the cheek and says he'll save me some for later. "You might need it to soak up some of that alcohol," he says with a laugh. "You'd better go easy on the booze. . . . I think my mom's getting suspicious."

Martha comes to the rescue, wading into the awkward silence. "Laurel! That dress is so . . ." *Tacky.* I want her to say *tacky.* Or *over-the-top.* Or even *inappropriate.* But Martha doesn't even get the chance to finish her sentence because Laurel says, "Thanks!"

One of Thomas's uncles interrupts this little scene with a request for a second slice of cake. "Duty calls," Thomas says apologetically. "Laurel, if you want to stay with Faith, I can take care of this." But then the uncle sticks out his hand to her and says, "Laurel Logan, it is *such* a pleasure to meet you." She turns away to talk to him. No wonder it's taking the two of them so long to distribute the cake—everyone wants the chance to talk to Laurel. She didn't need to dress up like that to get people to notice her; all she had to do was step through the door.

I sit in a corner with Martha and drink. We pour the wine into empty Coke cans in case Thomas's mom happens to come over. I drink so much that Martha tells me it might be a good idea to slow down a bit. "But we're supposed to be *celebrating!*" There's no hint of a smile on my face when I say this.

Martha asks me what's up. "Is it Laurel?"

I clink my can against Martha's, so hard that some wine sloshes onto the table.

"Do you want to talk about it?"

"No," I say, adding "Thanks" as an afterthought.

Martha shrugs; she knows better than to push it.

"Mind if I join you ladies?" Martha and I look up to see a guy a couple of years older than us, shaved head, stubbled jaw. He's wearing a tight T-shirt with a scooped neckline, as if he has cleavage to show off. He looks, in short, like someone Martha and I would never talk to (and also, coincidentally, like someone who would never talk to us).

I gesture to the spare seat next to me. "Go ahead." I ignore the glare that Martha's sure to be giving me and turn to face the guy. "Are you a cousin, then?"

"I *am* a cousin, as it happens. Most people are, aren't they?" He smiles. He thinks he's being charming and amusing. "I'm Steve. It's a pleasure to meet you." I will let him sit next to me and try his best to be charming and amusing, because I need the distraction. The more I look at him, the more distracting he becomes. I just wish he'd stop talking.

CHAPTER
44

Martha is not happy, especially when she discovers that Steve is essentially a gate-crasher. He was downstairs watching the game and came upstairs "to take a piss." Martha wrinkles her nose in disgust at that little nugget of information. "The bathrooms are *down*stairs. Obviously."

Steve laughs. "Well, I know that *now*, don't I?"

"So hadn't you better go, then? We wouldn't want you having an accident, would we?" Normally Martha's snideness would make me laugh, but now it just seems rude.

"Thank you for your concern about the state of my bladder. I appreciate it, I really do. But I went for a piss and came back up here, so we're all good. The game was dull anyway. I'd much rather spend my time talking to beautiful ladies." The way he says *ladies* is almost too much for me. *Laydeeez.* "So whose party is this, anyway?"

"Her *boy*friend's," Martha supplies helpfully.

"Boyfriend, eh? Fair enough. Which one is he, then, this boyfriend of yours? If I had a girlfriend like you, I wouldn't leave you alone for a *second*. You never know who's going to swoop in, do you?"

"I'm perfectly capable of looking after myself, thank you very much. I don't need him to protect me." I sound prim and awful, but Steve doesn't seem to care.

He lifts his head and gives me a look—*the* look, you might call it—and says, "I'd swoop in on you any day of the week, and twice on Sunday!"

"What does that even *mean*?" Martha's had enough now. I'm glad, because I'd quite like her to go away. "I'm going to the bathroom." It's as if she read my mind. "Will you be okay?" she asks me as she stands.

"Of course she will!" Steve says, patting my knee. "I'll take care of her." I don't look at him to check, but I'm willing to bet he accompanies this with a wink. Martha's facial expression seems to suggest as much anyway.

I learn a lot about Steve in the next few minutes. He's twenty-one years old, studying tourism at the local college. He's the youngest of three brothers. He likes drinking, clubbing, and girls, mostly. He asks me what clubs I go to and seems disappointed when I say "None." He says we should go clubbing together sometime—"As friends . . . I wouldn't want to step on anyone's toes!"—and asks for my number.

I surprise myself by giving it to him. That's probably when I realize I am drunk. Completely wasted, not just halfway there. "So can I call you, then? Your boyfriend won't mind?" His hand is on my thigh. His hand is heavier than Thomas's. Meatier, somehow.

"Am I supposed to believe that you'd care if he *did* mind?"

"You got me there." Steve laughs. I like his laugh; it's genuine. Real.

I know I should tell him to move his hand, especially when I catch Dawn staring at me. But I don't. I tell myself that if he moves his hand higher up, *then* I'll say something. It's perfectly okay to touch someone's leg—it's friendly. Reassuring. It doesn't have to be sexual, does it? Anyway, it's not as if I'm touching *him*. I'm just sitting here, minding my own business, drinking more than is good for me.

"Seriously, though, which one is he? No, wait, let me guess . . . Is it *that* guy?"

"No."

"That one? The one with the nose?"

"Well, you're getting closer. My boyfriend does indeed have a nose."

Steve makes several more guesses, and I say no each time. He even makes me stand and crane my neck to see guys on the other side of the room. At least that solves the hand-on-leg problem.

"You're messing with me, aren't you? You don't have a boyfriend, do you? Your friend just said that to try to get rid of me." We sit down, and he moves his chair even closer to mine.

Steve is talking, but I'm not listening. I'm looking around the room. But I'm not looking for Thomas; I'm looking for the flash of red. I'm looking for the telltale crowd of adoring fans, but I don't see it. I spy Martha, back with the kids from school. She's obviously decided to leave me to make my own mistakes. I thought friends were supposed to stop you from doing things you'll regret, instead of running off at the first hint of trouble.

"So what do you say? You up for it?" Steve whispers, and I realize he's sitting so close he's practically on my lap.

"Up for what?" As if it's not completely obvious.

"Getting out of here . . . You can come back to my place."

I laugh, and at first Steve laughs along with me, but after a couple of seconds he realizes my laugh isn't the flirtatious, conspiratorial one he was expecting. It is not a nice sort of laugh at all. I stand, a little unsteadily this time. "There is no way I would ever, *ever* do that. I mean . . . *ever.*" His face is a picture.

I walk away without another word, without bumping into anyone (although there are a couple of near misses). I say hi to Dawn as I pass by, and she pretends not to hear me.

I feel a little bit sick. Whether that's down to the alcohol or having acted completely out of character, I can't say. I should probably go to the bathroom in case I really do need to throw up. But there's something I have to do first.

Thomas is nowhere to be seen. My sister is nowhere to be seen. I stopped believing in coincidences a long time ago.

It's funny, really. When you read about these things or see them on TV, it's always this huge shock. This big, dramatic reveal to end the chapter or just before the credits roll. The girl or the woman—it's hardly ever a man—never seems to *know*. It's like Dad's always saying about those boring old war movies he loves so much: as soon as a character says something like *I'm getting married next month* or *My wife is having a baby—due any day now,* you know they're dead meat. So I suppose in this case it would be something like *My boyfriend and I are sooooo happy together* or *Tonight I realized I really do love him after all.*

Dead meat. Except I'm not dying. But when I see them together, my heart certainly feels like a lump of dead meat nestled inside my rib cage.

I knew. As I checked downstairs and outside and in the bathroom, I *knew*. When I finally went to open that door—the one marked PRIVATE—I knew what I would find on the other side. I didn't need to see them together; it would only make things harder for me. But I wanted them to know that I knew.

There are chairs stacked up haphazardly against the walls. A strip light on the ceiling bathes the room in a sickly yellow glow. She is standing with her back to the door. He is standing, too. He has one hand on her back. I can't see what her hands are doing, which is just as well, I suppose.

Thomas looks over Laurel's shoulder and sees me standing there. "Wait! It's not . . ." I stare at him. He doesn't finish his sentence, thank god. *It's not what you think.* One of the oldest clichés in the book.

Laurel turns around, and the expression on her face isn't what I expect. It's not shock or embarrassment or shame or even surprise. It's impossible to read, notable only for its nothingness. She doesn't say a word.

Thomas moves away from Laurel, like he's afraid she might lunge at him again. Because that's what must have happened. There is no question in my mind about who is more to blame here. Of course, there's still enough blame to go around for Thomas to have his fair share. But this was her fault; she *made* this happen. "Faith, I can explain! Can we talk about this? Please?" Thomas begs.

"No. We can't."

"What are you saying?"

"I'm saying that I never want to talk to you again." I'm amazed that I'm not crying. I am made of steel and ice.

"Faith, *please!* Don't do this. You're making a mistake. We were just . . ." His words trail off into nothing. Thomas takes a couple of steps toward me, and I step back. His eyes are pleading, but I am made of steel and ice.

"I mean it. Don't call me, don't come over to the house, don't talk to me at school. We're finished." Just like that. My first relationship, over. Steel. Ice.

Thomas looks pissed off. He actually has the nerve to be annoyed at me. "You're making a big mistake."

"The only mistake I made was going out with you in the first place. You know full well I wouldn't have gone anywhere near you if I'd known you were only interested in finding out more about my sister."

That shocks them both; I almost smile. "What are you talking about?" he says.

"I had a nice little chat with your aunt earlier. She told me all about it. Your 'true crime' phase or whatever. Who do you think you are? Sherlock Fucking Holmes?"

"What is she talking about?" Laurel asks Thomas, but he just shakes his head.

"Oh, did he forget to mention it to you as well? So it turns out that Thomas here got a little bit *too* interested in your story. Read all the books, watched all the TV shows. Probably had a fucking scrapbook for all I know."

"Is this true?" Her expression is still unreadable, her voice almost bored.

Thomas is squirming now. "It's not as bad as it sounds . . . honestly."

I laugh. "And this"—I gesture with my hand—"is not as bad as it looks, I suppose? You two deserve each other. Really. I hope you'll be very happy together."

I open the door to leave, but close it again because there's something else I have to say. I look at Laurel, still red-carpet fresh, out of place in this dingy little storage room. I know I shouldn't say this. I know it's wrong, even after everything she's done. But I want to see her flinch. I want to see her feel *something*.

She stares at me, waiting. And I think maybe she knows what's coming. I clear my throat, which has chosen this exact moment to close up, as if it's trying to stop me from saying what I'm about to say.

I take one last look at Thomas before my gaze alights on her.

"I wish you'd never come back."

CHAPTER 45

She doesn't flinch. There's no hint of pain in her eyes. The first reaction is a slight tightening around the jaw. And maybe I'm imagining it—I must be, surely—because it almost looks like she nods.

"Faith!" Thomas is horrified.

I ignore him and address her. "I think it would be best if you stay at Mom's tonight. I'm sure Thomas will make sure you get home safely."

"What will I tell her? She'll know something's wrong," says Laurel.

"I don't care what you tell her. You could tell her you threw yourself at my boyfriend. . . ." The tears arrive now, seconds before I was going to make my escape. "Or . . . or just make something up. You're good at that." I spit out these last words, hoping the venom in my voice will distract them from the tears spilling down my cheeks.

Thomas wants to put his arms around me. He wants to comfort me, I can tell. This must not happen. I must stay strong. "You know something, Thomas?" There's hope in his face. He thinks that as long as I'm still here, talking, there's a chance things will be okay. He's wrong. I look at Laurel, who opens her mouth to speak (to apologize?). I get there first. "You don't know how lucky you are—being an only child. Having siblings isn't all it's cracked up to be." A thought strikes me—a terrible thought, but no worse than what I've already said. One last shot at hurting her the way she's hurt me.

"Then again," I say, swiping at the tears on my face, "it's not as if you're my real sister anyway. Not by *blood*. If Mom and Dad had known how much pain you'd cause, I bet they never would have adopted you."

I don't wait to see her reaction—or his. I leave the room and head back to the party. I manage to get my coat and bag without bumping into Martha or Steve, then I leave. I walk to Dad and Michel's place even though it takes nearly an hour. Martha texts to ask where I am. I tell her I'm not feeling very well—a lie that also happens to be the truth. She's annoyed at me for bailing without saying anything, but I tell her I puked and that mollifies her somewhat.

Dad's already in bed when I arrive. Michel is on the sofa, reading. Tonks is curled up next to him. I tell Michel the same lie I told Martha.

"Too much to drink?"

I nod and head to the kitchen to grab a glass of water.

"Where's your sister?" Michel follows me and leans against the counter, Tonks winding her way around his legs.

"She decided to stay at Mom's."

"Why?"

"How should I know? I'm not her keeper." Sullen, childish.

"Okay, okay. Sorry I asked!" He's wearing old tracksuit bottoms and a France rugby shirt. His feet are bare. His face is kind, attentive, worried. "Do you want to talk about it?"

I gulp down the water. God, I'm tempted to tell him everything. Every little thing I've been feeling and every not-so-little thing she's done. Michel wouldn't blame me for what I said to her. He would understand where those words came from—that dark, bitter place inside me. The place I'm usually so careful to keep hidden from the world.

I know I would feel better talking to him. And that he might make me see that there's a way for Thomas and me to work through this. To get past the fact that he kissed my sister, and the fact that he lied to me all this time about not really knowing about her story. And Michel would put Laurel and me in a room together and force us to talk. Maybe she would explain why she did what she did. And perhaps I would understand, and we would hug and agree to forget all about it, because sisters shouldn't let a boy come between them. Of course I would have to apologize, too. I'd have to say that I didn't mean those things I said. That I *am* glad she came home. That the fact that we're not actually related by blood means nothing to me. She's my sister—always has been, always will be.

I look at Michel, and the temptation to break down is so strong that I can barely stand it. I close my eyes, down the rest of the water, then say, "There's nothing to talk about. Thanks, though. And if you could forget to tell Dad about the barfing, I'd really appreciate it."

"Your secret's safe with me, *ma chérie.*"

"You're a poet and don't even know it."

His eyebrows knit in confusion, and I even manage to crack a small smile. It feels normal, doing this. Michel and me staying up late after Dad's gone to bed, talking about anything and everything. That's how things used to be— *before*. Before Laurel. And with that thought, the moment— the tiny crumb of comfort of talking to Michel—is swept away.

I hug him good-night, and if he notices that I hold on a little too tight and for a little too long, he doesn't say anything. I leave him in the kitchen, crouching down to pick up Tonks. "You sleep well, yes? You'll feel better in the morning."

I'm pretty sure he's wrong about that.

CHAPTER 46

I sleep surprisingly well and wake up at six-thirty. I'm not too hungover, which is pretty miraculous under the circumstances. There's a text from Martha waiting on my phone. It takes me a while to decipher it (autocorrect gone wild, drunken fingers)—the gist is that she might have kissed that guy Steve. It's so like Martha to say she *might* have done something that she blatantly *has* done. It's *unlike* Martha to kiss a random guy, particularly one like Steve. I'm not sure how I feel about this.

Thomas has left three voice mails; I delete them without listening.

There are no messages of any kind from Laurel. I don't know what to make of that. Is she sorry? Is she upset about what happened? Then that niggling question: is she even at home? When I close my eyes, it's all too easy to picture the two of them together, in the back of his van. Thomas wouldn't do that to me; I'm almost sure of that. But I can't say the same about her.

Has Laurel been after him the whole time? Was that why she spied on us having sex? It doesn't seem to add up, especially not when you consider everything that happened to her. For the first time, I consider the idea that maybe I got it wrong—that it wasn't what it looked like. After all, what had I seen, really? The two of them standing close together, his hand on her back. The angle had meant that I couldn't actually see if their mouths were touching. He could have been checking to see if she had something in her eye. They could have been whispering, exchanging secrets so sensitive they had to leave the party to find somewhere more private, and, even then, they needed to be whispered in case there were any recording devices in the immediate vicinity.

There are possibilities *other* than kissing. That's what I try to tell myself as I shower and dress and put on the bare minimum of makeup. I add a couple more ideas to the list: a huge zit had suddenly erupted on Thomas's nose and Laurel was helping him apply some concealer so it wouldn't show up in the photos; Thomas had lost his voice from trying to shout above the music upstairs so Laurel had to stand really close in order to hear his hoarse whispers. They're beyond flimsy, though, these possibilities of mine. They are the preposterous imaginings of someone who doesn't want to accept the truth.

I rush to leave the apartment before Michel and Dad get up. I leave a note on the kitchen counter. It's much easier to lie on paper than in person. Having said that, the lie I do tell is more than a little lame: a school project, spending the day in the library.

I wander the streets, but my feet start to hurt, so I actually do go to the library in the end. It calms me, walking among the shelves, picking up books and putting them down again. Then I accidentally end up in the poetry section, which makes me think of Thomas and spoils things a bit.

My legs take me up the stairs and past seven rows of shelves to the part of the library I know the best. Over the years, I've spent a lot of time here, reading as fast as I can, worrying that Mom will realize I'm not in the children's library downstairs. She never caught me, though, not once.

The three books are all there, present and correct. I thought someone might have borrowed them, what with all the press recently. But these days people can get all the information they need on the Internet, can't they? And these books are out of date now; the story they tell is incomplete.

Little Girl, Lost. Schmaltzy, over-the-top, written by a tabloid journalist who'd never even bothered to speak to my parents.

TAKEN! The REAL story of Laurel Logan. Another tabloid journalist, this one convinced that Laurel had been sold into slavery or prostitution. He spent months traveling around Europe trying to find her, and made bold claims that he'd arrived at some brothel in Eastern Europe mere *hours* after Laurel had been moved by "gangland bosses" who knew that he was "hot on their heels." (The police had followed up, of course. Lies, all lies.)

And then there's Jeanette Hayes. The book that my mother wouldn't allow in the house. She wouldn't have been happy about me reading any of these books, but if she'd caught me reading the Hayes one, she'd have gone apeshit. Mom always said that Hayes had some kind of vendetta against us. She refused to even say her name. In our house, Jeanette Hayes has always been known as "that woman."

I hate her for what she did to our family. I've been *conditioned* to hate her. I mean, Mom always *tried* not to talk about things like that when I was in the room, but she failed often and badly. Maybe that's not quite fair; as a child, I developed a habit of listening at doors before I entered rooms and after I left them. I heard many, many things that weren't meant for my ears, but I never felt guilty about it. I saw it as my right.

I sit down on the floor and cross my legs. The Jeanette Hayes book isn't as worn as the others; it's a new, updated edition that I haven't seen before. I check the date and see that it was published last year. I must have read the old version of the book four or five times. I would mark my place by folding over the corner of the page and continue where I left off the next time I was in the library. Mom and I didn't come to the library every week, so it took me a long time to finish reading it. Back then, I was looking for clues—reasons why this woman hated my family. I couldn't understand why she didn't care about Laurel, why she was the lone voice of dissent when everyone else was saying that everything possible must be done to find my sister.

Hayes argued that kids went missing every day, that there was no good reason for the police and the media to focus on "Little Laurel Logan" when there were all these other kids being ignored. The word that kept cropping up was *injustice*. She seemed to be saying that just because Laurel was white and blond and pretty and middle class, no one should care. But it wasn't Laurel's fault that the media latched on to her story. Why should she be punished just because people were more interested in her than the other missing children Hayes talked about?

I read the introduction once again. I know the words so well I could almost recite them by heart. And the strangest thing is that today I can almost see what Hayes was getting at. It wasn't fair. Of course it wasn't. Every missing child should be a priority. Who knows how many of these kids could have been found if even a tenth of the money and resources that were invested in the search for Laurel had been spent looking for them? It's a horrible, horrible thing to think about. That's why Jeanette Hayes got so much flack for it, I suppose. The hate mail and the death threats were because people didn't *want* to think about it. They didn't want to see the truth of it—the awful truth that they skipped over a one-paragraph news story about a missing black kid from a run-down neighborhood in Boston without even blinking. They would keep sipping their coffee or tea or orange juice without taking even a second to worry about the fate of that child. And if, by some miracle, they *did* think about it, they would assume that the kid had run away or been snatched by their deadbeat dad (because even in a tiny paragraph, the journalist had somehow managed to find space to mention that the kid had three siblings, all with different fathers).

It's despicable. And I'm despicable for not realizing that sooner. Even though I pored over Hayes's book for hours and hours, I often skim-read the parts about the other missing children. I didn't care about them. I only cared about Laurel. But at least I have an excuse—two excuses really: I was young, and Laurel was my *sister*. Still, I never thought to check the Internet to see what became of any of the other kids. For all I know, half of them are back with their families now. For all I know, some of them are dead.

I slam the book shut. I can't read any more. The thing I'm trying really hard not to think about is whether my little Jeanette Hayes epiphany is because this is the first time I've read her words since Laurel came home (possible), or whether it's because I'm reading them *today*. If I'd looked at the book a few days after Laurel came home, I'd probably still be calling Jeanette Hayes "that woman" and hating her, because that was what's expected in our family. Which leaves me with an uncomfortable explanation for my change of heart. I agree with Hayes now, this morning, today, that too much attention was paid to "Little Laurel Logan," because now, this morning, today, I hate Not-So-Little Laurel Logan. And even though I said those words in anger last night—not even believing them myself—I realize now that they were true.

I *do* wish she'd never come home.

CHAPTER
47

I should talk to Laurel. I know that's the sensible thing to do. We have to fix this, if not for our sake, then for Mom and Dad's. The two of us have to find a way to live together, even though she's exactly the opposite of the kind of person I want to live with.

With Thomas, it's easy. I can cut him out of my life like a malignant tumor. Of course I'll still see him at school, but I can tune him out, pretend his existence means nothing to me until it means nothing to me. Martha will be on my side—no question about that. Soon he will be nothing more than one of the "Others," as Martha used to call everyone at school who wasn't us. Thomas will cease to be Us and will become Them.

Laurel is family, though, and family's different. *Blood is thicker than water.* Even though we're not *actually* related by blood. I can't cut her out; all I can do is learn to live with her, try to minimize the damage she does.

I text her: **We should talk.**

I keep reading Jeanette Hayes's book while I wait for a reply. This time I read some of the stories about the other kids. Each one represents a family destroyed. A family like mine, but different. We are the lucky ones. Our missing jigsaw piece was found and returned to us. Who knows what these families are still going through?

Half an hour later, there's still no reply from Laurel, but I'm not giving up that easily. Perhaps she's scared to talk to me, worried I'll tell Mom and Dad. She has no way of knowing that's the last thing I'd do—that it would be excruciatingly embarrassing to admit that my sister stole my boyfriend. (*Has* she, though? Has she stolen him? Is he gone for good? There's no way of knowing unless I talk to him.)

I send another text: **We'll be OK, you know.**

I nearly didn't hit send on that one, because I doubt it's the truth. And if *I'm* doubting it, then Laurel probably is too.

I read more stories, more families torn apart, more parents bitter that their little boy or girl was considered less important than my sister. I wonder what it was like for Hayes, actually sitting down with these people, witnessing their grief firsthand.

My phone buzzes with a text. Finally. But it's not from Laurel. It's from Kirsty Fairlie: **Hey. Am in town. Feel like a coffee? Flying out tomorrow.**

We've been texting a bit since we all had lunch together. The Fairlies have been doing the rounds, looking at universities and staying with various relatives. I type a reply: **Can't today, I'm sick. Sorry!**

I'm about to send the message when I change my mind. I can't just stay here all day, can I? Plus I'm starving. And

Kirsty is nice, if a little loud. It might take my mind off things. So I text her back and we arrange to meet in a coffee shop that's about twenty minutes away from the library. I put the Hayes book back on the shelf, ignoring the temptation to shove it in my bag. Then I rearrange the shelf so that the book is standing in front of the others, with the cover facing out. Other people should read this book; it's important.

Kirsty's already there, devouring a slice of chocolate cake. I order the same and ask for a slice of carrot cake, too. Kirsty gives me a look as if to say *Greedy bitch!* and I mutter something about having forgotten to have lunch. Then she orders some carrot cake, too, and says, "Well, I had my lunch, but it was revolting."

We talk about our plans for college, a subject that we didn't get around to at lunch, because that was all *Laurel this* and *Laurel that*. It turns out that there are a couple of the same universities on our lists. She asks which one is my top choice, and I say, "Whichever is farthest away." It doesn't come out quite right, though; I'd meant it to sound like a joke, like something anyone might say when they're talking about escaping from their family. But from the way Kirsty is looking at me, I can tell she caught the bitterness in my voice. I try to make light of it and say something about not wanting Mom to turn up on my doorstep every weekend, but Kirsty leans toward me, looking concerned. Her hair brushes over the top of her cake, but I don't say anything. "Are you okay? You seem a little . . . I don't know."

A sip of my drink buys time. A second sip buys more. "I'm

fine. Just tired. Late night." Two-word sentences, stripped bare of emotion.

"Are you sure?" God, she's as bad as Michel. I hate people being nice to me when I'm trying not to cry. Hate it.

This time, the "I'm fine" dies on my lips and is swiftly replaced by "Not really." And the desire to talk is just too overwhelming. It's like when I talked to Kay, but better because I know nothing is being recorded.

I don't tell Kirsty everything, of course. Just the high(low)lights. I don't tell her about Laurel walking in on me and Thomas having sex, because nobody needs to hear that. I do tell her about the book deal and how I'm only doing it for Laurel's sake and how does she repay me? By kissing my boyfriend.

"Holy shit!" Kirsty says, sitting back in her chair. "That is fucked *up*." And I swear I could kiss her right now. It's such a relief to be talking to someone who isn't Laurel or Thomas or even Martha, and to have her say exactly what I've been thinking: it *is* fucked up. "What did you do to them?" Her eyes are wide, and her expression is sort of gleeful, but I don't really mind.

"What do you mean?"

"Well, I can tell you something for nothing . . . if it had been my sister and my boyfriend, I'd have given *her* a good slap and kicked *him* in the nads. At the very least, there would have been a drink chucked in someone's face."

"Um . . . I didn't really *do* anything. Just . . . you know . . . said some stuff."

Kirsty's disappointed. "Like what?"

I'm too embarrassed to say. "Just . . . *stuff*."

"Aw, girl, you didn't *cry*, did you?"

I nod.

She shakes her head sadly. "Ah well, can't be helped. No use crying over spilled tears. You dumped him on the spot, though, right? Tell me you did *that,* at least?"

I nod again. Someone seems to have pressed my mute button.

"Thank fuck for that. *Bastard.*"

I clear my throat. "I'm more angry with her than him." It feels shameful to admit this, as if it's a betrayal of my sex.

"I don't blame you. He's just some guy, right? Like, I'm sure you love—loved, past tense, thank you very much— him and everything, but he's just a guy. She's your *sister.* Nothing should come between you two. Blood is—"

"Don't say it. Please, don't say it."

Kirsty sits back, shoves some more cake in her mouth. I'm grateful for the pause in her ferocity, however brief it might be. It turns out to be very brief, because she starts talking again before she's swallowed her second bite of her second slice of cake. "I can't believe it. I mean, you'd have thought . . ."

"Thought what?"

She looks down, carving off a mountainous slice of cake with her fork. "Nothing . . . It's just . . . I dunno. You'd have thought getting with a guy would be the last thing on her mind, after all that . . . y'know."

I nod again. Kirsty might be a little over the top, but she definitely talks sense. She narrows her eyes, thinking hard. "Unless she just wanted to . . . I don't know, *experiment* or something? Like to see if it was okay, kissing a guy who wasn't going to torture her and rape her or whatever?" She winces, reaches out to touch my hand. "Sorry, that was . . . Sorry."

I turn that thought over in my mind. *An experiment*. I suppose if you were going to conduct such an experiment, Thomas would be a good option. And for Laurel, the only option. She doesn't know any other boys our age. Boys *my* age, actually. Thomas is nineteen months younger than Laurel.

It's an interesting theory; the more I think about it, the more I like it. If Laurel just wanted to kiss a boy to see whether she could do it without freaking out or having flashbacks or something, it would still be wrong. I mean, you can't just go around kissing other people's boyfriends like that. But at least it wouldn't be *as* wrong. I realize I'm desperate to find a way for this to be okay. I don't *want* to hate my sister. I would love to have a decent reason to not hate her.

"Maybe that's it. . . ." I take another bite of cake, and for the first time, it doesn't feel like it wants to lodge itself in my esophagus.

"Of course, she could just be a massive slut," she says with a sly grin.

"Kirsty!" I have to act shocked—I can't *not*.

"Sorry! I forgot you're not supposed to say anything bad about people like her. *Victims*. It must be pretty cool, actually. She gets a free pass to be a total dick for the rest of her life, doesn't she?"

I know I should say something to defend my sister. Kirsty is practically a stranger to me; there should be no question

about where my loyalty lies. But it's so nice to talk to someone who doesn't think Laurel is a fucking saint for a change.
It's a breath of fresh air in the fetid stink that my life has
become.

"Anyway, at least your sister has half a brain—even if she
was schooled by a psycho rapist. Bryony is as dumb as a
brick. You should hear some of the stuff she comes out with
sometimes. You know she used to think baked beans were
made of pasta? And for a whole year when we were kids, I
managed to convince her that unicorns were real—not that
it took a lot of convincing."

I laugh, but admit that I used to get confused between
dragons and dinosaurs when I was little. "Do you think
we'd have been friends if your family hadn't moved?" As
soon as the question is out of my mouth, I regret it. It's an
odd, needy sort of question. A pointless one, too. What-ifs
are the worst.

Kirsty looks at the wall above my head. She takes her
time, really thinking about it. "Yes. I think we would . . .
and then *I* could have kicked your boyfriend in the nads for
you last night." Her smile is rapidly replaced by a frown.
"But it would have been weird for Bryony, I think. We'd
have had to let her hang out with us because *her* friend would
be . . . gone. God, it's freaky even thinking about it."

"Did Bryony say anything about that lunch? I thought
things between them were a little . . . weird."

Kirsty shrugs. "It's not exactly a normal situation, is it? I
think Bry was just freaked out. I suppose she was a bit quiet
for a couple of days afterward—withdrawn, you know? I just
enjoyed the peace—made a nice change. Oh man, you're

gonna love this . . . it's priceless! You know, she actually asked me if I thought Laurel might have been brainwashed! As if that's a thing that actually happens in real life and not just in shitty movies." She laughs. "Honestly I find it hard to believe we're related sometimes. I think she must have been dropped on her head right after she was born. Slipped right out of the nurse's hands like a greased eel."

"*Brainwashed?* Why would she say that?"

Kirsty's eyes bug out, and she makes a Scooby-Doo noise. "I dunno. . . . Well, she said something about Laurel not seeming to remember stuff. Like, things they did together when they were little, you know? Playing with dolls and stuff. Apparently they had this secret language? That must have been Laurel's doing, because English is more than enough for Bry to cope with. So anyway, Bry started talking to your sister in this bullshit made-up language, and your sister just looked at her like she was a fucking nutcase. So of course that *must* mean she was brainwashed."

Something niggles at the back of my brain, like a raised hand at the back of the classroom trying to attract attention. But Kirsty is so full-on that the hand has to be ignored. "I didn't know anything about a secret language."

Kirsty laughs. "Um . . . why would you? It was secret. That's kind of the whole point! Poor Bry was so disappointed, though, you know? It was almost like Laurel didn't remember her at *all*. And Bry prides herself on being memorable. I mean, she is, I guess, but for all the wrong reasons. I set her straight, though. Laurel's been through a lot of shit, you know? Shit we can't even begin to imagine. So it kind of makes sense that there's stuff she doesn't remember . . .

from before. There's only so much a person's brain can deal with, right?"

The hand at the back of the classroom appears again, but I can't think straight. "I think I have to go now."

Kirsty looks taken aback. "Er . . . okay. Is it something I said?"

"No, not at all. I just . . . there's somewhere I have to be. I forgot."

I can tell she's pissed off even though she tries to hide it. "Listen, thanks so much for meeting up with me. I feel a lot better about everything."

She looks at me like *Really?*

We agree to stay in touch. I say that it would be cool if we ended up at the same university, and I actually mean it. I thank her again, then rush out the door, leaving a half-drank cup of coffee, a whole slice of carrot cake, and a slightly baffled Australian girl.

CHAPTER
48

I close the front door behind me as quietly as possible, and I listen. Nothing. Maybe Mom and Laurel have taken the opportunity to go on another one of their little mother-daughter outings. Mom probably didn't even question why Laurel came back here last night instead of staying with me at Dad's. I bet she wishes it were like this every weekend. Just the two of them.

The plan isn't really a plan as such. It's more a vague idea of a rough sketch of a half-remembered dream of a plan. Something isn't right—that much is obvious. I need to look in her room.

I creep up the stairs. Somehow it doesn't really feel like my home anymore. I don't seem to belong here quite like I used to.

Laurel's door is closed, and I don't think anything of it at first, because she's been keeping it closed recently.

I open the door.

The closet is open, clothes strewn on the bed and floor. A

huge backpack—an old one of Dad's—lies on the bed. Unless Laurel is hiding under the bed, she's not here.

I hurry toward my room. My hand is on the door handle (my door is closed, too—why didn't I notice that before?) when the door opens from the inside and Laurel is standing there in front of me.

"Hi!" she says. Too loud. Forced. "I thought you were—"

"What are you doing in my room?" I ask as she tries to squeeze past me.

"I was just looking for . . . something." She couldn't look more suspicious if she tried.

"What's that behind your back?"

"Nothing. I . . . Nothing."

"Show me."

For a second, I think she might try to barge past me, but we both know that I could take her in a fight.

"Listen, it's not what you think."

"*Show* me."

She holds out her hand. Five twenty-dollar bills, six tens, three fives, and a few singles. I only know this because it's exactly how much money there was in the little tin next to my alarm clock.

"Give me that!" I reach for it, but she puts her hand behind her back again.

"I need it."

"Need it for what?"

She looks scared. Why is she scared of me? "I can't . . . Look, I have to go. She'll be back soon. You have to let me go." Then she does barge past me, and I don't stop her. I just follow her back into her room and watch as she stuffs the money into the side pocket of the backpack and starts shoving clothes inside.

"What's going on? Is this because of last night?" I take a deep breath and prepare to be the bigger person. "You don't have to worry about it. I'm not going to tell Mom and Dad." She keeps on packing, but I know she's listening. "Thomas wasn't right for me anyway. We'd have broken up sometime . . . You just helped it happen sooner rather than later. Hell, I should probably *thank* you!"

She stops for a moment. She's holding the red dress, the fabric all scrunched up between her clenched fists. She throws it back in the closet. "I'm sorry," she says. And I know she's not apologizing about her treatment of the dress.

"It's okay." I touch her arm and her shoulders slump. "You don't have to run off, you know. People make mistakes." I look around the room. "Do you want me to help you sort this out before Mom gets back? Where is she, anyway?"

"I asked her to get me some cough medicine from the drugstore. I needed to get her out of the house." Laurel sounds tired, numb. That makes two of us.

I'm wondering whether I should hug her—whether I can bear to hug her after what she did to me—when she takes a deep breath and starts packing again. "Laurel! Stop! What are you doing? I told you, everything's going to be fine!"

She's shaking her head and muttering under her breath. "*I'm not* . . . I'm not . . ." She starts to cry softly.

I grab her shoulders and turn her to face me. "Laurel! Please! You have to stop this. It's insane."

She looks into my eyes, and I look into hers. I see something there, and I'm not even sure what it is, but it stops me dead.

She opens her mouth to speak, and I know what she's going to say. I finally pay attention to the hand at the back of the classroom. "You're not . . ."

"I'm not Laurel."

CHAPTER
49

She's not. I know she's not. I've no idea how it's possible that I know this, but I do. Have I always known, on some level? Or was it a gradual thing? An accumulation of tiny things that don't add up to my sister.

She's not Laurel.

I'm gripping her shoulders so tightly that she has to wrench herself out of my grasp. She cowers away from me, as if she's expecting me to hit her. The tears are really flowing now, and these sobs are coming out of her—great big gasping sobs like there's not enough air in all the world for her to be able to catch her breath. "I'm sorry I'm so sorry I didn't mean to I mean I did but I'm sorry." Her hands are balled into fists, and she seems smaller than she did a minute ago—a little girl, lost.

She's not Laurel. I look at her and wonder how I ever could have believed she was my sister.

Relief. That's what I feel first, I think. It's hard to pinpoint each feeling, though. There are so many and they're so noisy, and they're all bumping into one another because so many of them are contradictory. But I am glad this girl is not my sister.

Then it hits me. If this girl is not Laurel, then Laurel is still missing. The nightmare of the past thirteen years continues. It's bad enough knowing the real Laurel is still out there somewhere—alive or dead—and no one's been looking for her because we thought she was home. But the thing that is unimaginable to me is that someone's going to have to tell my parents. It will have to be me. This will shatter them into a thousand tiny pieces, and I don't think anyone or anything will be able to put them back together again.

A stranger is in front of me, staring at me like I'm a land mine she's just stepped on. We're both frozen, each of us waiting for the other to say something.

"Who are you?"

She shakes her head. "It doesn't matter, does it? I'm not her."

My sister is still out there, and nobody knows except me. And this girl, whoever she is. I wait. Her eyes keep darting between the backpack and the clock by the bed. She keeps clasping and unclasping her hands. For the first time, I feel fear. I don't know what this girl is capable of. I know nothing about her, except that somehow—how?—she managed to fool us all. What if this Not-Laurel girl wants to hurt me? She could have a weapon in that backpack, for all I know. But I suppose I can't really believe that, or I would be running down the stairs and out the front door right now.

I take my phone out of my jeans pocket and hold it in front of me. "Tell me who you are or I'm phoning Mom right now." *My mom,* I should have said. She's mine, not hers.

"Don't do that! Please. I'm begging you." Her pale face is blotchy from crying.

I touch the screen, bring up my contacts. Scroll down to find Mom.

"Sadie. My name is Sadie, okay? Now, please, put the phone away!" I should call Mom, get her to come home right away and deal with this madness. But I can't do it to her, not yet. I need to find out the truth first.

Sadie. It's quite a pretty name, familiar somehow. A phone chimes with an incoming text, and I know it's not mine because I keep mine on silent. The girl flinches and starts rummaging underneath the clothes on the bed until she finds her phone. "Shit. *Shit.* I have to go. Now. Mom's on her way back." My eyes bore holes straight into her brain. "Your mom, I mean."

"You're not going anywhere."

"I have to! You don't understand!"

The land mine finally explodes. "You're right. I *don't* understand. How the hell am I supposed to understand some stranger coming into our family and pretending to be my long-lost sister? Pretending to have been *abused*! What kind of person even does that? Is it about the money? Is that it? Or the fame? Did you like being on television, telling all those lies? Were you laughing at us? Was this funny to you?" By the end of this little speech, the girl is backed up against the open closet, and I am shouting in her face. One more step and she'll be inside the closet. I could shut her in there, find something to wedge the door closed, and wait until Mom gets back.

The girl is breathing hard; I am, too. The seconds are ticking away.

"Do you really want to know the truth?" the girl asks quietly.

I nod.

"Then come with me."

"Are you out of your mind?! I'm not going anywhere with you!"

I nearly add that she could be some psycho killer for all I know, but she seems to read my mind because she says, "I'm not going to hurt you."

I shake my head, but I step back and she moves past me to finish packing her bag.

I stand in silence as she buckles the top, then checks to see if she's forgotten anything. The bag doesn't look heavy; clearly she wants to travel light. She puts on her jacket, then shoulders the backpack.

I want to know the truth. I need to. But this is madness.

She sees me wavering, this girl called Sadie. "You'd better decide right now, because I'm going—with or without you."

"What about Mom? If she comes back to find you gone, she'll freak out. Probably call the police in two seconds flat."

She comes up with a plan. She'll leave a note for Mom, saying that she's decided to stay at Dad's tonight. I'll text Dad and tell him I'll be home late. Dad will never know that "Laurel" is supposed to be at his place, and Mom won't know that she never turned up there. Until it's too late.

"I don't think this is a good idea," I say, making one last attempt at being sensible.

Not-Laurel/Sadie stands in front of me, too close. *Family*

close. "I'll make you a deal. If you come with me right now, I'll do whatever you say. After. If you still want me to come back with you, I'll do it. I swear." She's careful to maintain eye contact as I examine her face looking for the truth. I would probably believe her if I didn't already know that this girl is the best liar I've ever met. But it almost doesn't matter if she's telling the truth or not. If she's lying, I'll deal with the fallout afterward. My need to know the truth—why she would do something like this, go to such extreme lengths to steal my sister's identity—outweighs everything else.

"Okay, let's go."

CHAPTER
50

We're ready in five minutes. While she was writing the note to Mom, I briefly wondered whether I should take a knife from the kitchen. Just in case, you know. But the thought of actually using it—actually stabbing it into someone's flesh, even if that someone was trying to hurt me—was so absurd that I dismissed it immediately.

Sadie pauses before closing the front door. She looks at the hallway and stairs with such intensity that I wouldn't be surprised to see the wallpaper start to melt. There's nothing much to see: shoes in a neat little row against the wall, a shopping bag and a couple of coats hanging from pegs by the door, a pile of envelopes on the bottom step. I watch as she gulps hard and clenches her jaw. I know what it's like, trying to swallow your feelings so they won't overwhelm you.

We turn right at the end of the road and wait at the bus stop. "So this is where you've been disappearing to?"

She looks like she's about to disagree, to tell another lie, but I think we both realize the time for lying has passed. "Just once."

"Are you going to tell me where we're going?"

"It's better if I show you."

The bus pulls up and we get on, and Sadie hurries to the back with her head down, clearly worried that someone will recognize her. Unlikely, though—she's got her hair hidden under a black beanie and she's not wearing any makeup. She looks like a normal girl today. One you wouldn't even notice unless she did something to attract your attention. The only person to look up at us as we walk down the aisle is a boy around our age, but it's the uninterested, unfocused gaze of someone whose mind is elsewhere. He's busy talking on the phone. "Dude, awwww, dude! You would not believe what happened last night with Fat Jim! Duuuuude . . . for real, man, I'm not even joking!"

Sadie breathes a sigh of relief when we reach the second-to-last row. She sits next to the window and puts the backpack on her lap; I'm tempted to sit across the aisle, but that would risk someone else getting on and sitting next to Sadie.

It feels wrong sitting so close to her, our thighs touching. I've sat this close to her loads of times over the past couple of months, but we were sisters then.

I can't even begin to imagine where we're going, but that doesn't stop me from trying. A high-rise apartment in one of those rundown housing projects? One of those buildings where there is an elevator but it stinks of piss and is always broken. I've never been to a place like that before, but I've seen them on TV. I can picture the two of us walking down a corridor and standing in front of a door and the door opening and a woman standing there. I look from this woman to the girl standing next to me and back again, and I can't believe I ever thought the girl was my sister.

The woman—the mother, the real mother—was probably in on it. Maybe it was even her idea. She was flicking through the newspaper one day and noticed that Sadie looked a bit like the age-progressed photos of that missing girl—the one there was all that fuss about. Money—that was the motive, surely. But you'd have to be mad to think you could get away with something like this. It would only be a matter of time before someone from Sadie's real life recognized her and phoned the police. It suddenly dawns on me that *this* is why Sadie kicked up such a fuss about the DNA test. The game would have been well and truly up as soon as the results came in. Looking back, it seems ridiculous that none of us were suspicious about that. We were so desperate to believe that Laurel had come home to us that logic and common sense were forgotten.

I stare out of the window. My sister is still out there somewhere. She needs me and I am off on some wild-goose chase with this unstable girl. For all I know, Laurel's time could be running out and I am wasting it. All this time, the police haven't been looking for her, thinking the case was all tied up neatly with a ribbon. So maybe an extra couple of hours won't make a difference, but I've read enough about these cases to know that they can be—and often are—crucial.

I won't give up on you. I will find you. I will. I say the words over and over in my head.

It's strange. It's never occurred to me before that the search for my sister was something I could be involved in. It was always something for other people to do, and if I was lucky, I might overhear something about it. I must have heard the phrase *The police are doing everything they can* a thousand times during the course of my childhood. I was a kid; there was nothing I could do to help. But I'm not a kid anymore. There *must* be something I can do now. I'm not stupid enough to think that anything I could do would be a match for the teams of detectives who have worked on Laurel's case over the years. But maybe I could give some interviews, go on TV and do an appeal. Something. I could visit the countries that have had the strongest leads in the past. *Talk* to people.

Someone, somewhere, knows where Laurel is. It's just a matter of finding that someone—and getting through to them. It's time I stopped being so passive.

"You should text your dad."

She remembered this time that he's my father, not hers. I text him. Movies with Martha is my cover story. He texts back right away, asking me to pick up some of those Cookie Dough Bites at the concession stand. He's addicted to those things.

"Are we almost there?" I don't turn to look at her when I speak, so I feel rather than see the shrug of her shoulders.

"Where are we going?" I know she's not going to answer. There's a stillness to her now. I can't seem to stop fidgeting and looking around, but she is a statue next to me. If there were even the remotest chance she would tell me, I would ask what she's thinking.

• • •

The journey is interminable. One of those bus routes that stops at every little back-end-of-beyond place you can think of. The bus is almost empty by the time Sadie reaches across to press the stop button. I look out the window for clues, still half expecting to see the imaginary high-rise building where Sadie's imaginary mother is waiting for us. But all I can see are trees. I have no idea where we are. I probably should have paid more attention.

We stand on the road and wait until the bus has turned the corner. There's a short row of houses on the other side of the street. They look like they don't belong here, because here seems to be the middle of nowhere.

Sadie starts walking away from the houses, in the direction the bus came from. I have no choice but to follow. I stay a step or two behind so I can keep an eye on her. It will be getting dark before too long.

A couple of cars pass as we walk. Sadie keeps her head down, but I look at the drivers, half hoping that one of them will stop and ask if everything's okay. But why would they? We are just two girls out for a late-afternoon stroll in the sunshine. They have no reason to notice us in the first place, let alone stop and talk to us.

After about half an hour, we come to a patch of woods. At first glance, it looks exactly the same as every other patch of woods we've passed. It's the countryside—it all looks the same to me. Then I notice that there's a track running into this particular stretch of woods. There's a gate, with a sign that reads KEEP OUT. It's hidden; you wouldn't even notice it if you were driving past.

"What is this place?" My voice sounds too loud out here, without people and sirens and traffic. The only sounds I can hear are our feet on the road and the occasional tweeting of birds.

Sadie turns to look at me, as if she's expecting some kind of reaction to the sight in front of us. There's something not right here. Something not right with her.

"We're here."

CHAPTER
51

Instead of opening the gate, Sadie walks around it. It's not attached to a fence or a wall or anything. It can stop vehicles, but not us. She walks off down the track, but I hesitate. We are literally in the middle of nowhere. Anything could happen; I could scream for help and no one would hear. My parents could be about to lose another daughter.

I've come this far, though. I might as well see this through. Plus I'm not exactly wild about the idea of being left out here on my own. I edge my way around the side of the gate, trying to avoid stepping in the muddy ditch.

The track curves gently through the woods. It's gloomy in here, the treetops tightly knit overhead. I think of Little Red Riding Hood, and suddenly I can't remember the end of that story. Did she escape? Did she kill the wolf with her bare hands? Or did she curl up in a corner and wait for him to eat her up?

Finally there's a house in front of us. I'm not sure what kind of place I was expecting to find, but it definitely wasn't this. The house is ugly and gray and squat, with a flat roof and peeling paint around the windows. It's best for everyone that it's hidden in the woods, a house this ugly. That's when I realize I was half expecting something from a fairy tale. A little white cottage with a thatched roof with smoke puffing out of the chimney. This place looks more like a military installation than a home.

The weirdest thing is the yard, which *does* look like something out of a fairy tale. There's even a white picket fence around it. There's an ornamental rock garden and ceramic pots of herbs, and ivy climbing up the wall next to the front door. It's as if this ugly building has landed here in a tornado, crushing the little old lady's house that belongs here to smithereens. If I look closely, I might see a pair of old-lady shoes peeking out where the wall meets the ground.

On closer inspection, the yard looks a bit neglected. Weeds are starting to take over. The little square patch of grass is overgrown; it clearly hasn't seen a lawn mower in a long time.

Sadie watches me as I take it all in. "What is this place?" I ask for the second time.

"Home." She laughs, but it sounds all wrong.

She doesn't knock on the door or ring the doorbell (not that I can see a doorbell). She doesn't take out a key, either. She just puts her hand on the doorknob and turns. She walks in, leaving the door open behind her.

The first thing that hits me is the smell. It seems to coat the inside of my nose and throat. It's thick and cloying and deeply unpleasant. I stop worrying about someone else being here, because this house is empty. You can just feel it. I leave the door open in the vague hope that some air will start to circulate.

The inside of the house doesn't match the outside, just like the outside doesn't match the yard. A dusky-pink carpet runs through all the rooms, with various hideous rugs placed on it at regular intervals. Green patterned wallpaper. There is a lot of furniture, some of it antique, some of it from the seventies by the looks of it. Every surface has ornaments on it—little crystal animals or jugs in the shape of squat little men or dainty little teacups and saucers. I spy an ancient-looking TV in a corner.

There's a hulking bookcase opposite the front door. The books are an odd mixture of true crime and romance, black spines stark among the pinks and peaches and purples. The bottom shelves are filled with textbooks and reference books.

None of the rooms have doors, not even the bedroom or the bathroom. It doesn't even look like the doors have been removed—the house must have been built this way to someone's (a *weird* someone's) specifications. I peek into the bathroom—more dusky-pink carpet. Pink toilet, sink, and bath, too. Lots of bottles and jars lining the windowsill. Old-lady beauty products to match the old-lady decor.

The bedroom has an enormous bed with a flowery bedspread and too many pillows and cushions. In the corner there's a much smaller bed—almost small enough to be a child's. Next to this bed, there are three bottles of pills and a leather-bound Bible. Instead of decent bed linens, there's a pancake-flat pillow and a filthy sleeping bag—a discarded cocoon. On the floor next to the bed lies a laptop, its once shiny casing smeared with fingerprints.

The bigger bed has been made neatly, all the corners tucked in. On the bedside table there is a cup. The cup has something dark green and mottled and foul in it. There's a framed photograph of an old woman and a younger man. She's sitting ramrod straight in a comfy chair. She is smiling (or grimacing—it's hard to tell) and her cheeks are rosy with too much blush. A bright blue handbag sits on the floor to her left. The man kneels on her right. He is small and pale, with big, round eyes. There's something nocturnal about him. His face is bland, almost but not quite good-looking. He isn't smiling.

"What are you doing?" Sadie has crept up behind me, scaring the life out of me. Her voice is dull, toneless, her facial expression hard to read.

"I was just . . . looking around." I indicate the photo on the bedside table. "Do they . . . ? This place is so . . ."

"Weird?"

I nod. "And what is that smell? It smells like . . ." I have no idea what it smells like. Nothing good, that's all I know.

She turns around, and at first I think she's ignoring my questions, but then it's clear that I'm expected to follow her. She heads into the living room and stands in front of the overstuffed sofa.

My view is obscured at first; the smell is stronger than ever. I cough, trying to clear it from my throat. Sadie steps aside, and that's when I see it.

The stain is big. The size of a pillow or a medium-sized dog or a sweater. It's remarkably even around the edges, as if someone has carefully poured a pot of paint onto the carpet.

The stain is dark. Black? It could be oil or treacle or bal-samic vinegar.

But it's none of those things. It's blood.

Some things you just *know*, without having to be told. It doesn't stop me asking, though. "What . . . ? Whose . . . ? That's blood. Isn't it? What happened here?"

Sadie is staring at the stain with a strange, almost dreamy look on her face. "Smith."

CHAPTER
52

I don't understand. I take a step backward, knocking the backs of my calves on the sofa. I feel dizzy all of a sudden. The stench of blood is thicker and heavier, and I feel like it's suffocating me. I want to sit down, but I can't sit down here. Not in this place.

"I don't . . . But you made that stuff up. About Smith and the basement and . . ."

I follow her gaze to a door in the hallway. I didn't notice it before. The only door in the house, apart from the one we came in. There's nothing particularly noteworthy about this door, but Sadie is staring at it with a look so intense that it burns. I walk over to the door, a little unsteadily. My legs feel like they belong to someone else.

The door has a lock with a key in it. It's a Yale lock, big and sturdy. I turn the key and open the door. I look back at Sadie, still rooted to the spot next to the stain on the carpet. She nods at me.

I think I'm starting to understand.

In front of me there are stairs leading down. The stairs are rough concrete. There is a bare lightbulb overhead with a cord hanging next to the door. At the bottom of the cord there is a doll's head. The cord is tied around her hair. The doll's eyes are closed, as if she's sleeping. Or dead. I don't want to touch the head, so I grab the cord just above the doll and pull. The light comes on, illuminating the rest of the stairs.

I want Sadie to come with me, but something tells me I can't ask her.

I count the stairs. Seventeen. One for each year of my life.

At the bottom of the stairs, there is another door, identical to the first. Another lock with another key. I unlock this door and push it. Darkness beyond.

I fumble around on the wall inside, searching for a light switch. I could use the light from my phone, but I'm too scared to go inside unless I can see every corner. You never know what could be lying in wait in the darkness. I look around me and realize there's a light switch at the bottom of the stairs, outside the door, almost too high for me to reach. There is no good reason to have a light switch that high up. I manage to flick it with the very tips of my fingers.

I step into the room. I know this place.

The cot against the opposite wall. The small stainless-steel sink with a red bucket next to it. The bookshelf—again, almost too high for me to reach—with different-colored folders lined up neatly. Labels on the spines with neat black writing. *Math. English. Science.*

There's a rickety chair and a Formica-topped table against

the left-hand wall. On the table sits an ancient desktop computer. The keyboard in front of it is missing three of its keys.

There's a pile of what look like old clothes and blankets
in one corner.

Then I look up. Above the door, there is a tiny video
camera, pointing at the cot.

This is not a room. It's a cell.

CHAPTER
53

The walls seem to close in on me. I've been standing here less than a minute, and the door is wide open behind me. If someone was to lock me in here and turn out the light, how long would it be before I lost my mind?

I turn and go back up the stairs as quickly as I can, not bothering to turn out the lights or close the doors. The front door is open. She's sitting on the steps. I sit down next to her.

"How long?" I ask, staring at a patch of pink heather clinging to a rock.

"Fifteen years."

"You killed him." Not quite a question, not quite a statement.

She nods.

"And then . . . ?"

"I had nowhere to go."

So she came to us. She needed a family. We fit the bill.

I can't get my head around it. It's too much, too crazy. It

doesn't make sense. . . . There's so much that doesn't make sense.

"I'm sorry," she says, before I can even manage to form a coherent thought.

What is she expecting me to say? That's it's all okay and I forgive her for what she's done to us? Because it's not okay and I do not forgive her. She tricked us all. Lied to us.

"So all that stuff about Smith . . . the things he did . . ."

"All true."

I wait. The sky is red. If I concentrate hard enough on the pretty garden in front of me, maybe the house of horrors behind me will cease to exist.

Sadie starts to talk. Slowly, haltingly at first. Then faster and faster, as if she's racing to get the words out before darkness falls.

She is twenty-three years old now. She was eight years old when she was taken. It happened in a mall, lots of people around. She can't remember much about her life before. "There were men," she says. "Bad men."

I ask about her family. Her *real* family. She tracked them down. It was the first thing she did when she escaped. Her mother is dead. Overdose.

"What about your dad?" I ask.

"Don't have a dad," she says.

I ask about Smith. "Is he the one in the picture?"

She nods.

"So you lied to the police about what he looked like?"

She nods again. "I couldn't have them finding out who he really was."

I think about this for a moment. If she had accurately described Smith, there would have been a good chance someone out there would have recognized him. Even if he did live like a recluse, someone would surely have been able to identify him. Then the police would have come here. Found the bloodstain on the carpet. "Where is he? . . . Did you bury him?"

"Back there." She gestures with her head, nodding toward a path leading around the side of the house.

I try to picture her dragging his body through the house and out the front door. The head, thunking on the steps we're sitting on. She must have wrapped the body in a sheet or something. There were no signs of blood on the carpet other than the stain next to the sofa.

I want to ask how she did it. What it was like to kill a man. Was it quick?

It's as if she reads my mind. "I only hit him once. I didn't mean to. I just wanted to knock him out. Give myself a chance to run. His back was turned. He was crying. I think he expected me to comfort him. I picked up the iron without thinking. It was just sitting there next to the fireplace. I'd never even noticed it before. It belonged to his mother, I think. Probably an antique." She pauses and a ghost of a smile plays across her lips. "Caved in his skull. Didn't know my own strength."

What do you say to someone who is essentially confessing to a murder? But does this even count as murder? I don't think it's self-defense. Still, it's hard to imagine a jury convicting her, after everything she's been through.

I ask her if she ever tried to escape before. "A couple of times," she tells me. "Mostly in the first year or two."

"And after that?"

Sadie shrugs. "I stopped trying. I got used to it. Got used to *him*. He took care of me." She sees the horrified look on my face. "I know how fucked up it sounds. You don't need to tell me."

"I'm sorry."

"No one can ever understand what it was like. No one except . . . me."

Something isn't quite adding up. Lots of things, in fact. "Why didn't you just go to the police? After you . . . after he was dead."

"I didn't know *what* to do. I was alone. For the first time in my whole life, there was no one telling me what to do. I ate when I wanted and slept when I wanted and went on the computer and walked in the woods. It was . . . peaceful. It was only when the food started to run out that I realized I couldn't stay."

This is the part that doesn't make any sense. The missing piece of the puzzle. Everything else I can sort of understand—or at least try. But how did she come up with the idea to pretend to be my sister? I wait for her to explain, but she says nothing.

It's almost completely dark now. I'm not looking forward to walking back to the main road. "I can call Dad, you know. He could come and get us." I stop and think for a second. Yes. This could work. "We can explain everything. I know it won't be easy, and of course they'll be upset. . . ." Understatement of the century, but I keep going. "But they'll . . . I think they'll understand. In time. And I'm sure we can find someone—a family member or whatever—to take care of you. You must have grandparents or aunts or something. And they will have been looking for you, just like we've been looking for Laurel. Just think what it will be like, when you turn up after all these years." I know exactly what it will be like. A miracle. And for them, the miracle will actually be real.

"Faith," she says, but I carry on gabbling about how everything will be okay and people should really know that this Smith guy is dead. Right now the police are wasting valuable resources looking for a guy who doesn't even exist when they should be looking for my sister. I keep talking, hoping that something I say will get through to her. I know I could just call Dad anyway—I don't need her permission—but suddenly it seems important that Sadie is okay with it.

"*Faith!* Stop! Just . . . stop." Sadie gets up and starts pacing. Gravel crunches underneath her feet. She brings her hands up to her face and mutters something. When she moves her hands, there are tears in her eyes. She's biting her lip so hard that it's started to bleed.

I stand and put my hand on her shoulder, trying to reassure her. But she flinches at my touch. She backs away from me. "I need to . . . I didn't want to . . . There's something you need to see. I'm sorry."

I follow Sadie around the side of the house. Her shoulders are hunched, and she's sobbing. I don't know what to say to her. I don't know what's going on here.

There's no backyard. The trees are so close that the branches brush against the windows. I have to get my phone out and use the screen to light my way. Sadie doesn't seem to have any problem seeing where she's going, though. She's used to the dark.

We walk past a mound of earth, about six foot long. She doesn't stop. She doesn't look down as we pass. She doesn't say anything at all to give me an idea of what is underneath that mound. She doesn't have to. I wonder what the body looks like. Decaying flesh, sunken eyeballs. Worms and insects.

Finally, Sadie stops in a small clearing. The moonlight shines overhead. It might be a nice spot for a picnic, in the daytime.

"I'm sorry," she says again. Why does she keep saying that?

Then I see. I *see.*

Another mound of earth, about the same size as the one we passed. Someone has placed lots of tiny stones around it, forming a border. A crooked wooden cross sticks up from the earth. There's something leaning against the cross. I move closer to see what it is.

A teddy bear, missing one arm.

I stare at the mound of earth.

I fall to my knees in front of my sister's grave.

CHAPTER
54

ONE MONTH LATER

My sister has been dead for just over four months. I have been mourning her for one month. Apart from Sadie, I am the only person in the world who knows that Laurel Logan is dead. I intend to keep it that way.

These are the facts as Sadie told them to me that night. I have no way of knowing if she lied to me about any of it. I have no choice but to trust her version of events. Well, there *is* a choice. But the idea of telling my parents, calling the police, and sending them to that awful house is too horrific to contemplate. I keep picturing my parents standing over that shallow grave, knowing their little girl is in there. The body—my *sister's* body—would have to be dug up. Examined and tested and touched by strangers. No.

No.

I have to trust what Sadie told me. I *have* to. And any

questions I might want to ask must remain unanswered: she's gone.

Sadie was the first girl the monster took. She was not the last. Something drove him to take my sister. Another little girl, younger this time.

Sadie hated my sister. She was jealous of her. Little girls like attention—that's what she told me. Sadie used to pinch Laurel and pull her hair. Once, after about six months together, Sadie pushed Laurel into a wall. Laurel lost a tooth. Smith punished Sadie; she didn't say how.

My sister didn't hate Sadie. She clung to her whenever she got the chance. *"Will you be my new sister?"* she asked as the two of them lay in the darkness. My sister slept on the cot, Sadie now relegated to the floor.

Every night, Laurel talked about her family. She talked for hours and hours, in between fits of tears. At first, Sadie stuck her fingers in her ears and told Laurel to be quiet. But eventually she came to like Laurel's stories. She looked forward to them. She didn't have any stories of her own; most of *her* memories were unhappy ones.

Sadie built up a picture in her head—of me and Mom and Dad and our home. Laurel told her about a night-light called Egg, about playing in the sandbox with her little sister. She said that Sadie could borrow Barnaby the Bear if she ever felt like she needed a hug.

They lived together for thirteen years, spending almost every minute of every day together. Except for the times when the monster took Laurel upstairs.

I asked Sadie why he kept her around, once he had Laurel. "Why didn't he just kill me? That's what you're really asking, isn't it?" Sadie said. "I don't know. I think . . . I think he was sort of lonely." It scared me when she said that; it almost sounded like she felt sorry for him.

Eventually, Sadie stopped hating Laurel. Time and Laurel's goodness wore her down. Laurel let Sadie sleep next to her on the cot, the two girls often falling asleep in each other's arms.

Laurel never gave up hope. She knew we would be looking for her. When the monster told her that we didn't care about her, that she had a *new* family now, she shook her head, mouth clamped stubbornly shut. She knew we loved her. That comforts me, when I'm lying awake in bed at night, wondering whether I've done the right thing. Her belief in us was unshakeable, right to the end.

I asked Sadie what Laurel was like. "She had a good heart," she said simply. I pressed her for more details. "There was . . . It was like she had a light inside her. Something pure and good that I never had." The age-progressed photos didn't do her justice. Sadie said the two of them looked similar, at first glance. Laurel was more fragile, though. She was weaker than Sadie. She got sick a lot. And of course she never saw a doctor.

They were happy sometimes. When the monster left them alone. He would leave them alone for twenty-four hours or more on a regular basis. On those days, they would be hungry, but they never minded that. They were safe, at least.

They made up stories together. They pretended they were princesses, locked up in the dungeon by an evil ogre. Laurel made up a story about Sadie coming to live with our family. She said they would share a room, like sisters. That was Sadie's favorite story.

I asked about the scar on Sadie's cheek—the one that matched the scab that Laurel had when she was taken. She didn't want to tell me at first, but eventually I got it out of her. Laurel had been sick for over a month—headaches and vomiting. Smith was getting frustrated, so he took Sadie upstairs. He cut her hair and dressed her up in my sister's clothes. But that wasn't good enough: he wanted his Laurel substitute to look exactly like her. He cut her cheek with a kitchen knife and said, *"There, that's better."* She didn't say what happened next.

Things changed as the years passed. Sadie told me that the sexual abuse stopped when Laurel reached puberty. By that point, the monster hadn't abused Sadie for years—not sexually, at least. Both girls were convinced that he would bring home another little girl one day, but he never did. Sadie could never quite decide if she was relieved about that.

I forced myself to ask more questions I wasn't sure I wanted to hear the answers to. I asked if Laurel had been scared. I asked if she remembered us—remembered *me*—after all those years away from us. I asked how she died.

The answers:

Sometimes. She never got used to the darkness.

She never forgot us. Never stopped talking about us.

The last question was the only one Sadie couldn't answer. I didn't believe her at first; I was sure she was lying to protect me. She insisted she was telling the truth. "One morning she just didn't wake up," she said, eyes pleading, begging me to believe her.

I couldn't accept it. "People don't just die," I said. But of course they do. People die every day. Old people and middle-aged people and young people and babies. And who knows what kind of health problems Laurel might have had, living the way she did? Maybe if she'd had access to proper medical care she would still be alive, but it's pointless to think that way.

My sister was an hour away from home when she died. She'd been an hour away from us for thirteen years, and we'd had no idea.

The monster was inconsolable. He kept on saying, *"I loved her,"* over and over again, clutching my sister's body in his arms. He blamed Sadie. He shook her and shouted at her to tell him what she'd done. She cowered in the corner under her filthy blankets. She didn't cry. She was in shock.

Smith made Sadie dig the hole to bury my sister. She was the one who arranged the smooth little pebbles around the mound of earth. She found the sticks to make the cross. Smith wanted to bury Barnaby the Bear with Laurel, but Sadie begged him to let her keep the bear. He wouldn't listen. He said Laurel needed Barnaby *"to help her sleep well."* But he left Sadie alone to fill in the grave. He left her out there all by herself, to shovel soil on top of my sister's body. Sadie took the bear from the grave and hid him under some leaves.

It's strange, that I forgot all about Barnaby. That should have been the first thing I thought of when Sadie told me she wasn't Laurel. I should have realized there had to be a connection between the two of them, but I didn't. Maybe my brain didn't want me to realize there *was* a connection. Maybe it was desperate for me to believe that my sister was still out there somewhere, waiting for us to find her.

Sadie killed the monster three days after Laurel died. "I should have done it sooner. We could have got away," she said. I told her she needed to stop thinking like that. I told her I didn't blame her. I said the words *I forgive you* repeatedly, until she listened.

The plan emerged in my mind almost fully formed, minutes after seeing my sister's grave. It sprang from one thought: that I never, ever wanted my parents to feel what I was feeling. They would never recover.

It was getting late. The last bus back to town was in less than an hour. It wasn't easy to persuade Sadie to come back with me. She wanted to stay there, figure out her next move. "I'm not leaving you here," I said. "That is not an option." I told her the plan. We would get the bus home. I'd tell Dad that I'd invited Laurel to the movies at the last minute and she'd decided it'd be easier to stay at his place rather than going back to Mom's.

Sadie backed away from me, and I was scared she was going to bolt into the woods. I wouldn't let that happen, though. I would chase her down and drag her back with me, if that was what it took. But it didn't come to that. I talked her into it, made her see sense. I managed to make her understand that she didn't stand a chance without my help.

We didn't say a word to each other on the bus back to Dad's house.

• • •

It took us four days. We could have used more time, but the police were coming to do the DNA test on Thursday. She had to be gone by then. I pretended to be sick and stayed home from school. Mom didn't even question it, especially once Sadie/Laurel agreed to stay home and look after me. Mom was going to be busy all week—she was planning some big charity dinner or something.

Money wasn't a problem. Sadie had her share from the book deal, and I had a decent amount in my savings. I withdrew that and gave it to her. She didn't want to take my money, not at first. But I knew she'd need every penny she could get. She wouldn't be able to go abroad, which made things more difficult.

That left two problems. Problem one: the fact that she was one of the most recognizable people in the country. Problem two: my parents would want to look for her. Obviously.

The first problem was solved easily enough. At least I assume it was solved, because I've been checking the Internet every day since she left, half expecting to see that someone's spotted her. A pair of scissors and some brown hair dye in the dead of night. But even with short brown hair, she was still too easy to recognize. She let me shave her head. The effect was startling. She looked like a skinny, beautiful boy.

The issue of my parents was trickier. They'd only just got their daughter back. Were they really going to just sit back and accept losing her again?

I wrote the letter, and Sadie copied it in her own

handwriting, under strict instructions not to change a single word. It was vital that the letter did its job. Sadie kept asking me if I thought it would work. "Of course it will work," I said, even though I couldn't possibly know. It took me two hours to get it right, to strike the right balance. It was horrible, writing that letter. I just had to keep telling myself that I was doing the right thing—that I was doing this to protect them.

I said good-bye to Sadie just before five o'clock in the morning the Wednesday after Thomas's party. We were in my bedroom and she'd just done a final check of her backpack. We'd gone over it again and again, making sure she had everything she needed. There was one last thing I wanted to give her.

"What's this?" It was wrapped in a T-shirt of mine that I knew she loved. "Egg!" The penguin night-light. The one Laurel had talked about so much that Sadie had been able to describe it down to the tiniest detail. "I can't take this. Or this," she said, holding out both the night-light and the T-shirt.

"I want you to have them." She shook her head, but I was ready for that. "Mom would expect Laurel to take the night-light with her. So you might as well take it so I don't have to chuck it in the trash. Besides . . . I think Laurel would want you to have it."

Sadie gave me this look, like she knew exactly what I was playing at, but she nodded and wrapped the penguin in the T-shirt and managed to fit him in a side pocket of the backpack. "Thank you," she whispered. And it seemed like she wasn't really thanking me for the night-light or the T-shirt. It was a *bigger* thank-you than that, weightier somehow.

"Right," she said. "I'd better get going."

"Okay. Okay," I said, and I suddenly felt panicky. There was no way this plan was ever going to work, so why were we even trying? It was madness. What if we'd forgotten something? "Are you sure you've got everything? And the map? You know where you're going? We can go through it again if you like. We've got plenty of time before Mom gets up."

Sadie put a hand on my arm. "It's okay. I know what I'm doing. Everything will be fine."

There were so many questions I hadn't thought to ask about Laurel, and this was my last chance. But if I started down that path, I'd probably never stop. The more Sadie told me, the more I wanted to know. I would *never* know enough about my sister, about how she lived. And how she died.

There was one question I could ask, though. Something I needed to know before she left. A selfish question. Silly, really, given everything that's happened since. But I asked it anyway as Sadie was shouldering the backpack, testing the weight. "Why did you kiss Thomas?"

Sadie stopped and stared at the wall for a second, as if the answer might be written there. But then she looked at me. "I needed you to hate me." I clearly had no idea what she was talking about, so she elaborated. "I knew I needed to leave before the police came over. But I couldn't make myself actually do it. I . . . I like it here. A lot. I thought it would be easier if you pushed me away. I was right." She smiled ruefully. "You should probably know that he didn't kiss me back."

I thought about that for a second. It made a weird sort of sense. But there was something bothering me, like a pebble in my shoe. "How did you know I was going to walk in and see you two?"

She gave me this strange look, like she knew I'd caught her. "Okay, maybe there were two reasons. I wanted to see what it felt like. With someone . . . someone who wasn't Smith."

There was nothing I could say to that. Not one single thing.

I'm not sure who initiated the hug. Maybe me, maybe her. Or maybe we both had the same idea at the same time. It didn't feel strange to be hugging her. It didn't feel like hugging a stranger. And when it came down to it, I really didn't want to let go. She was the first to pull away.

"I'm sorry. About everything. I never meant to hurt anyone. I hope you know that." There were tears in her eyes. In mine, too.

I nodded. "You . . . you take care, okay?"

"I will."

She walked over to the door, then turned. We looked at each other in silence for a moment or two. If everything went according to plan, I would never see her again. She smiled sadly, and it made me wish for things I could never explain, even to myself. She spoke softly. "You know something? I liked being your sister, even for a little while."

She closed the door behind her. I listened for her footsteps on the stairs, but I heard nothing. I went over to the window and watched her walk down the street. She didn't look back.

"I liked being your sister, too," I whispered.

CHAPTER
55

If saying good-bye to Sadie was hard, watching my mom read the letter was worse. I thought she would never stop crying.

"Did you know about this?" she said, holding my shoulders and shaking me. I didn't break.

"No, I swear. I had no idea." Mom phoned Dad, and he arrived within twenty minutes, face still creased from sleep. He didn't cry. He was too stunned, I think.

I watched as they read the letter again, heads close together. I had to remember to ask to read it myself. I wasn't supposed to know every word by heart.

Dear Mom, Dad, and Faith,

I have to go away for a while. I'm sorry. I know this won't be easy for you to understand, but I need you to know that it's the right thing for me. It's what I want. I need some time to find out who I am and what I want to do with my life. I need to be alone. I'm sorry I can't explain it better than that.

*Please don't blame yourselves. Coming home to you
was better than I could have ever dreamed. You are the
best family in the world. I am so lucky to have you in
my life.*

*I'm excited about the future. About going to new
places and making new friends. Meeting people who have
never heard of Laurel Logan. A fresh start. I want to
see if I can stand on my own two feet. I'm sure you can
understand that.*

*Please, PLEASE don't come looking for me. I beg
you. I need to do this, and I need to do it without your
help.*

*I'm not sure how long I'll be gone. But I will come
back to you, one day. I love you all.*

Laurel

Reading it again, over the shoulder of my sobbing mother
and frozen father, it didn't seem good enough. Not even
close. I should have said more, really laid it on thick. It was
too short, too stilted.

I'm not sure my acting was up to much. I didn't even
manage to cry.

"How could she do this to us? I don't understand." Mom
fell into Dad's arms. He murmured words of comfort. I took
the letter, stared at it just for something to do.

Mom pulled away. "I can't lose her again, John. I . . . I
just can't. We need to phone the police. She can't have gone
far. Let me find that . . . Where's that number again?" She
opened the kitchen drawer where all the takeout menus and
random scraps of paper are stored.

"Stop," said Dad, but Mom didn't listen, so he had to

go over and close the drawer and take her hands in his. "*Stop.* We have to . . ." He swallowed hard. "I don't like it any more than you do, but we have to let her do this. She's nineteen, Olivia. She's an *adult*. This isn't about us. It's about what's best for Laurel."

"And you think what's best for her is being out there all by herself?" Mom shouted. Her face was red and wet with tears that she didn't even bother to wipe away. "Anything could happen!"

"You mean something worse than what's already happened?" Dad said quietly.

That's what did it, I think. She didn't come around to the idea right away, but she at least started to listen. I put the kettle on, trying to ignore the mug with Laurel's name on it when I opened the cupboard.

We sat around the kitchen table, talking things through. Mom had the idea of calling Laurel and begging her to come home. Dad didn't object. Mom was the only one who was surprised when we heard the phone ringing upstairs.

Three hours later, my parents had both agreed to abide by Laurel's wishes. "We owe it to her," said Dad. "She'll come back when she's ready. And we'll be here waiting, ready to welcome her back with open arms. That's all we can do." He didn't sound convincing—or convinced—but it was a start.

I was the first one to mention the press. Sadie and I had talked about it. Even if Mom and Dad decided not to look for her, the media would be all over it in a matter of days. There would be no escape. So we decided that it would be best to preempt the problem. Release a statement saying Laurel was abroad, maybe seeking long-term treatment for some medical problem or other. And that's exactly what we did.

The story died down much quicker than I'd expected. Without her here, there were no photos to accompany the articles. People aren't as interested when there aren't any pictures. Yesterday I did my usual trawl of the Internet, looking for any mentions of Laurel Logan. For the first time, there was nothing. Not even a single random conspiracy-theory blog post. I sat back and smiled. We'd done it.

Things haven't been easy, especially with Mom. She barely left the house for the first couple of weeks. She's been letting the phone ring, saying she doesn't want to speak to anyone. The book editor, Zara, has left seven messages for her already. Who knows what's going to happen with the book deal. Perhaps we'll have to pay the money back, or maybe they'll still want to publish the book, even though "Laurel" is gone.

Mom kept on asking me what she did wrong; she still doesn't really accept my answer of "nothing." I think she'll be okay, though, in time. She's going out for drinks with her friend Sita tonight. That's got to be a good sign, right?

Dad seems to be coping better. He's really busy at work; he says it helps keep his mind off things.

We had dinner together on Sunday—Mom, Dad, Michel, and me. It was Mom's idea. She thinks we should do it every week. I think she's hoping that doing lots of family things together will make Laurel come home sooner, as if she'll somehow *know,* wherever she is.

Dad and Michel came over early. Dad read the papers, while Mom fussed around in the kitchen, worrying that she hadn't bought a big enough piece of beef. Michel insisted on peeling the potatoes. "You go and put your feet up, Olivia," he said. Mom smiled and thanked him, and both the smile and the thanks were genuine—for the first time ever, I think. I was about to go and sit down, too, but Michel asked me to stick around and keep him company.

I hadn't been alone with him since she left. I've been avoiding Martha, too, as best I can. The urge to talk—to tell someone the truth—has been so strong at times that it's almost overwhelmed me.

I see Thomas at school. I spied him sitting in the courtyard with Martha the other day. He hasn't tried to speak to me, not even once. I thought he might have tried harder to fight for our relationship, but it seems like he's given up. I can't help thinking it's a bit odd, especially if Sadie told the truth about him doing nothing wrong. The weird thing is, I don't miss him. Not even a little bit. We should never have even been together in the first place; it feels right, being alone.

"So how are you doing? It's been a crazy couple of months, *hein*?" said Michel, rinsing the potatoes under the tap.

"I'm okay." Keep it simple. First rule of lying.

"Really? You don't look okay. You look like you haven't slept in a month."

I laughed and elbowed him. "Jeez, thanks, Michel! You know you should never, ever tell a girl she looks tired, don't you?"

Michel didn't laugh. He didn't even look at me. He just started peeling the potatoes. I stood next to him, ready to cut them into perfect-sized chunks. After a while, he spoke, so quietly I had to lean in to hear him. "There's something I want you to know. I hope you know it already, but I'm going to say it anyway. There are some things in life that are too big to deal with on your own. You might think you can cope by yourself, but a thing like that can . . . eat away at you. It can poison you. A burden like that, it's too heavy for one person. So if there's ever anything you wanted to talk to me about—*anything*—you need to know that I'm here. You can trust me."

I listened and watched his profile as he concentrated on the potatoes. What was he talking about? He couldn't possibly know. Sadie and I had been so careful. "Um . . . thanks. Everything's fine, though. Really."

Then he turned to me. His eyes locked on mine. He started talking in a faux-casual voice as if this was a perfectly normal conversation after all. "Did you know that cuckoos don't have nests of their own?" I shook my head, thinking he had well and truly lost the plot. "They lay their eggs in another bird's nest and then leave. The other bird has no idea, because the eggs are camouflaged to look the same as *its* eggs. So it ends up caring for the cuckoo's eggs along with its own. The poor bird is none the wiser, even after the eggs hatch."

My heart was slamming in my chest, my mouth bone dry. He knew. Somehow, he *knew*. I looked toward the door; it was still shut. "What are you . . . I don't understand. What are you saying?"

Michel shrugged in that impossible French way of his. "Nothing. I'm saying nothing. It's just interesting, that's all. Some people, they think that this makes the cuckoo evil."

"What do you think?"

Another Gallic shrug. "Me? I think it's a survivor. What's that phrase? *La fin justifie les moyens*. The end . . ."

"Justifies the means," I finished the sentence for him.

So Michel knows the truth—part of it at least. There's no way he could possibly know what really happened to Laurel; maybe he suspects that she died years ago. I should probably be panicking that he might say something to Dad, but I'm not. I think if he were going to do that, he would have done it already. Maybe he has his reasons for staying quiet, just like I do.

I've slept better since that night, which surely can't be a coincidence. Maybe Michel was right about sharing the burden. Still, I have no intention of ever actually talking to him about it. Because he must never be allowed to know the whole story.

I made a promise, one that I intend to keep for the rest of my life.

The phone rang this morning, just as I was leaving the house. A flash of hot panic when I heard Mom say, "Hi, Natalie." I slammed the front door shut so Mom would think I'd left. I stayed in the hall. I needed to hear this. Why was Sergeant Dawkins calling Mom? Maybe there had been another sighting of "Smith"; there have been a lot of those recently. I bet there's some poor guy out there who looks *exactly* like the description Sadie gave the police. I just hope he doesn't get arrested.

I crept closer to the living room door. "Any news?" There was a pause as Mom listened. "But there must be something! Someone must have seen her, surely! She can't have just disappeared off the face of the planet."

I closed my eyes and leaned against the wall. Took a deep breath. I should have known. It was too good to be true that she would just accept Laurel disappearing again. That she wouldn't try to find her. *Fuck.*

I get on a bus going in the opposite direction from school. I spend the whole trip hoping and praying that Sadie is better at hiding than the police are at seeking.

I walk down the country lanes in the rain. I forgot to bring an umbrella.

Barnaby the Bear is sodden. I pick him up and hold him close.

I kneel on the ground next to the grave, and I talk. I thought it might feel silly, doing this, but it feels like the most natural thing in the world. I tell Laurel about Mom and Dad and Michel. I only talk about the good things, the happy things—the things I would want someone to tell me if I'd been away from my family for years and years.

I tell her I'm sorry. I tell her we did everything we could to find her. I tell her we never gave up hope.

I tell her I'm not sure I've done the right thing. I ask her what she would have done in my position, and I actually stop and listen as if I'm expecting an answer.

I tell her I'm proud of her, for being so brave all those years when she must have been so very, very scared. I'm proud of her for befriending Sadie, for being there for her when no one else was.

I tell her that I love her.

There's nothing left to say after that. I'll be back—in a week or a month. Whenever the urge to tell someone gets too much for me, I'll come here and talk to my sister. She's the only one who understands. That's one thing I'm absolutely sure about. Some people might find it hard to accept why I've done what I've done. They might think it's unforgivable, that my parents deserve to know what happened to Laurel.

But my sister and I know the truth.

We know that sometimes you have to do whatever it takes to protect your family.

Imagine you're playing in the sandbox in the front yard on a warm summer's day. You're showing your little sister how to build a sand castle. Your mom is inside, in the kitchen, perhaps. You can hear your dad mowing the lawn in the backyard. A man stops to talk to you. He seems nice. He looks up and down the street, then opens the gate and walks toward you. The man takes your sister by the hand; he says he's taking her to get an ice cream. What do you do? You tuck your teddy bear under your arm, then push your sister away—so hard it makes her cry. You say, "No! *I* want an ice cream! Faith can stay here." And you walk away with the man, quickly. You don't look back.

You do whatever it takes.

Excerpt from *The Forgotten Children*, by Jeanette Hayes
(New and Updated Edition, 2015)

Sarah Braithwaite, known to her family as Sadie, was last seen on 7 April 2001. The police were convinced she was snatched by her father, notorious local criminal Eddie Gibbons. Sarah's mother, Gail, never believed that version of events. Sadie's disappearance was only reported to the police after a week. For seven whole days and nights, no one was aware that anything was amiss. It was only when a neighbor visited, finding Gail Braithwaite unconscious in a pool of her own vomit, that the alarm was finally raised.

Gail Braithwaite was unable to help the police with their inquiries. A drug-and-alcohol addict for many years, she was not a credible witness. The police investigation into the disappearance of Sarah Braithwaite was closed within a month; the investigation into Laurel Logan's disappearance is still ongoing, twelve long years after she went missing. The fact that the two little girls lived less than an hour away from each other only serves to highlight this terrible contrast.

UPDATE: I visit Gail again, thirteen years after Sadie's disappearance, ten years after I last saw her. The town of Blaxford may have changed little since my last visit, but the woman who greets me at the door could not look more different from the one I interviewed all those years ago. Today, she may look slightly older than her forty-three years, but Gail Braithwaite is healthy and, to some extent, happy.

"Sober for eight years," she says. "I want Sadie to be proud of me when she comes home. I want her to see that I've changed. Things are different now."

"I think about her every day, you know. She's the first thing I think about when I wake up in the morning and the last thing I think about before I go to sleep at night."

As we're talking, a little face peeks out from behind a door. "This is Selina," Gail says proudly. The little girl is shy at first, but before long she's sitting on her mother's knee, bouncing up and down and pretending to ride a horse. Looking at mother and daughter playing together, you'd never guess at the terrible tragedy that tore Gail's life apart all those years ago.

Selina's resemblance to Sadie is striking, and I say so. Before Gail can say anything, the little girl pipes up. "Sadie! Sadie! Sadie!"

Gail smiles sadly. "We talk about Sadie a lot. I think it's important that Selina knows all about her big sister. So that she's not confused when Sadie comes home to us."

Selina's face shines with hope as she looks up, unaware of the living hell her mother has endured. "Sadie come home?"

Tears glisten in Gail's eyes as she looks at the photo of her missing daughter, in pride of place in the middle of the mantelpiece. "One day, sweetheart. Maybe one day."

ACKNOWLEDGMENTS

Sincerest thanks to Allison Helleghers, Julia Churchill,
Emily Easton, Samantha Gentry, Roisin Heycock,
Ray Shappell, Trish Parcell, Alison Kolani, Talya Baker,
Glenn Tavennec, the Sisterhood, UKYA bloggers,
Mari Hannah, Gillian Robertson, Sarah Stewart,
Lauren James, Cate James, Ciara Daly,
Robert Clarke, and Caro Clarke.

ABOUT THE AUTHOR

CAT CLARKE is a full-time writer, and one of the UK's leading YA authors. She was previously an editor at Scholastic UK, where she worked on some of the UK's biggest nonfiction bestsellers. Cat has always been fascinated by the media coverage surrounding missing children—it was this idea that inspired her to write *The Lost and the Found*. She lives in Edinburgh, Scotland. You can find out more about Cat on her website catclarke.com, or follow her on Twitter at @cat_clarke.